RT IN BLUE

Portrait in Blue

Lucinda Chester

HEADLINE
Liaison

First published in 1996
by HEADLINE BOOK PUBLISHING

A HEADLINE LIAISON paperback

10 9 8 7 6 5 4 3 2 1

ISBN 0 7472 5283 1

Typeset by CBS, Felixstowe, Suffolk

Printed and bound in Great Britain by
Cox & Wyman Ltd, Reading, Berks

HEADLINE BOOK PUBLISHING
A division of Hodder Headline PLC
338 Euston Road
London NW1 3BH

For JRS
Guroc says hello

One

Jake was just about to leave the bookshop when he heard a voice which sent his pulse rocketing – very English, a little on the deep side, and extremely sexy. It was difficult to say what intrigued him more: the voice, or what she was asking for. *Wicked Victorians*, an anthology of Victorian erotica which had been published in the early seventies, and had been out of print ever since.

On impulse – and knowing that he ought to have been several stops away from Holland Park at least half an hour ago, not browsing at his leisure in a second-hand bookshop – Jake turned back, pretending that he'd just spotted something interesting on the shelves. He took a book down at random, and turned slightly so that he had a clear view of the information desk.

What he saw took his breath away. She was, quite simply, one of the most striking women he had ever seen. She wasn't particularly tall – about five foot four, he guessed – and she wasn't particularly thin, but there was something about her which hit him straight in the solar plexus. Whoever she was, he wanted to know more about her. A lot more.

The man on the information desk flicked through a

computerised list, then shook his head; the woman smiled ruefully, shrugged, and left the shop. Jake quickly replaced his book and followed her out of the door. He had no idea what he was going to say to her, but that was a minor detail. The important thing was that he should speak to her.

Luck was obviously on his side, he thought with a mixture of amusement and relief, as she walked into the *patisserie* two doors down. It was the perfect opportunity. He too went into the *patisserie*, and sat at a table a few feet from hers. He ordered a cup of black coffee, and sat pretending to be absorbed in his own thoughts, while surreptitiously watching her.

She looked a bit like a student, dressed in black leggings, a black T-shirt and Kicker boots, teamed with a loose denim shirt worn open, like a jacket, with the sleeves rolled halfway up to her elbows. She wore no jewellery apart from a large and slightly mannish watch. Her hair was mousy, with red and gold streaks when she tossed her head back or pushed her fringe out of her eyes and her hair caught the light; it was parted on one side and was slightly wavy, as if she were growing out a perm.

Her skin was pale, though her tip-tilted nose was slightly sun-burned, as though she'd been reading outdoors while wearing sunglasses, and had been so wrapped up in her book that she hadn't noticed the strength of the sun. Her mouth was generous; if pushed, he would have described it as a perfect cupid's bow. She had a full lower lip – he would have liked to draw his tongue along it, taste the softness of her skin.

She appeared to be writing notes in a small leather Filofax, and the handbag at her feet reminded him more of a briefcase

2

than anything else. Perhaps she wasn't a student, then. Maybe she was a businesswoman on her day off – a lawyer or an accountant, something professional to go with the briefcase. Though her hair didn't quite match that sort of image, and besides, why would a lawyer or an accountant want a book of Victorian erotica? It was too specialist for everyday reading.

There was only one way to find out. And he had to do it now, before she finished her coffee and walked out of the *patisserie* – and his life. He drained his coffee in one gulp, and smiled wryly at himself when the cup clattered on the saucer. He was so nervous that his hands were shaking, which he knew was ridiculous. He'd never had a problem talking to women. Plenty of housewives had thrown themselves at him when he'd been doing some minor building work for them, and he'd never been short of girlfriends in the past. They'd been attracted by his dark-haired good looks, the muscles which were the result of his job, and the sensitivity which, he'd been told, was betrayed by his dark eyes.

Here goes, Jake thought, and walked over to her table.

'Excuse me,' he said quietly.

She looked up, her eyes a sharp and analytical blue. 'Yes?'

'I – er—' Oh, for Christ's sake, Matthews, he thought, stop acting like some stupid love-lorn schoolboy. Talk to her. 'I wondered if you'd like another cup of coffee. With me, that is.'

Her face was still quizzical, as if wondering what someone who was so obviously a workman, dressed in the almost regulation jeans, checked shirt and heavy boots, was doing in an upmarket *patisserie* like this. Then she smiled, and

3

Jake found himself struggling with an instant erection. Her smile, quite simply, was breathtaking, and her voice sent another thrill down his spine.

'Thank you. That'd be nice.'

For the first time, he smiled back at her. 'I'm Jake Matthews,' he said, extending his hand.

'Debra Rowley,' she said, taking it.

'How do you like your coffee, Debra?'

'Dark and strong.' The impish smile added the rest of the cliché for her: *like my men.*

He grinned. 'Coming up.' He strode over to the counter, feeling like he ought to be whistling, and was faintly amused at himself for wanting to preen. He ordered two more coffees, then returned to her table.

'Are you a student?' he asked.

'Close,' she said. 'I lecture on Victorian studies, and I'm researching a book.'

'So that's why you wanted the erotica,' he said, without thinking – and stopped, horrified at what he'd just blurted out.

Her eyes narrowed. 'You were in the bookshop?'

He sighed. 'I suppose I might as well come clean. I was just about to leave the shop, when I heard you ask for a book of Victorian erotica. I wondered why you wanted it, which is why I followed you in here.'

'Well, now you know.'

'Mm.' Jake felt embarrassed, unsure what to say next. After all, he'd virtually stalked her. No doubt she was thinking that he was some kind of maniac, who'd seem nice on the surface and then start a terror campaign when she refused to get involved with him.

The waiter brought their coffees over, dispelling the awkwardness.

'Thank you for this,' she said, sipping the steaming dark liquid. Her eyes met his over the rim of the cup. 'So what were you looking for, then?'

'Nothing much. I suppose I just can't pass a second-hand bookshop.' Not that he was going to tell her why. It would have sounded like whining – especially in the circumstances.

'Right.' She tipped her head slightly to one side.

He grinned. 'I know. What the hell does someone who looks like a navvy want with books?'

She flushed. 'I didn't mean to be a snob.'

'Let's just say I have a book habit.' His lips twitched. 'And I suppose I am a navvy, more or less. I work for my brother, as a builder.'

'Right.' Debra still looked faintly embarrassed.

'And as for what I'm doing in Holland Park. I'm doing some work a few stops down the line, in Ealing. I remembered that there was a bookshop here, and I just fancied spending my lunch-hour indulging myself.' Hankering after what might have been: it was a habit which Jake had tried to break, without success. He knew that he should be grateful that he even had a job, not whining that it wasn't the one he'd originally wanted.

'Lunch-hour?' Debra queried, her eyebrows raised slightly. It was getting on for three o'clock.

Jake glanced at his watch, and smiled disarmingly. 'Which finished a long time ago, but what the hell? I'll work late, to make up for it.'

'Right.' She sipped her coffee.

'So what's your book about?'

'Victorian sexuality. The difference between the way women are portrayed in most of the novels of the period, and the way they're portrayed in pornography.'

'An interesting choice of subject.'

She grinned. 'My mother always said I had a mucky mind.' There was a slight hint of a Northern accent when she quoted her mother; Jake, who'd spent all his life in the South, wasn't sure if it was Yorkshire or Lancashire. What he did know, from having Northern friends, was that they were touchy about it if you guessed wrong; he decided not to comment, and simply returned her grin.

'And that's what you're working on, this afternoon?'

She nodded. 'I've no lectures or tutorials on Wednesdays. So I can get on with what I really want to do.'

Jake's eyes widened. For a moment, she'd sounded as disillusioned as he'd once been. 'So you don't like your job, then?'

'Oh, I do.' She smiled wryly. 'Once the freshers have settled in and stopped thinking that they're something special, that is. But once I start working on a research project or a book, I suppose I resent spending time on anything else.'

'Cue for Jake Matthews to bugger off back to work and let you get on with it?'

She shook her head. 'I wasn't intending to be rude.'

'Neither was I.' He sighed. 'I suppose I'd better get back to work, or Adam – that's my brother – will moan at me all afternoon.' He drained his coffee. 'Though I'd like to see you again. If you're not too busy, that is.'

Something in his smile made her agree. 'Why don't you come over for dinner tonight? If you're not too busy, that is.'

The teasing note as she echoed his own diffident words amused him. 'I'd love to. Where, and what time?'

'Eight o'clock.' She gave him her address.

He whistled. 'Are you sure you're a lecturer? Or are you a rich heiress, on the quiet?'

'Living in Holland Park, you mean? It's actually little more than a bedsit, and it's an attic conversion.'

'A penthouse flat. Even swisher,' he teased.

She grinned. 'You can eat your words, when you see it.' A sudden thought struck her. 'Oh – are you vegetarian?'

'What a question to ask a jobbing builder.' He grinned. 'Though my taste-buds can cope with more than just extra-strong lager, chicken vindaloo and chips.'

'I'm glad to hear it.'

He took her hand, squeezing it briefly. 'I'll see you tonight, then.'

'Have a nice afternoon.'

'You, too. Hope the book goes well.'

'Thanks.'

After he'd left, Debra stayed in the *patisserie* for a while, finishing her coffee; then she stretched, picked up her bag, and headed for home.

She still couldn't quite believe what had just happened. A man she'd never met before had approached her table, asked if he could buy her a coffee – and she'd invited him back for dinner. It was completely out of character for her. Since she'd split up with Marcus she'd buried herself in her work and steered well clear of dinner invitations from friends with match-making tendencies. She certainly hadn't made the first move herself, even if she'd found a new acquaintance attractive.

Though there was something about Jake Matthews that intrigued her. She guessed that he was about the same age as she was – late twenties, early thirties – but he wasn't like the builders she'd come across at home, full of dirty jokes and leering at anything in a skirt. She knew that she was being an intellectual snob, but very few manual labourers, in her experience, were interested in second-hand books. And the way he'd neatly side-stepped her own attempts at questioning him . . . There was more to Jake than met the eye – more than just the good-looking man with dark sensitive eyes and a sensual smile.

'Debra Rowley, you snobby bitch,' she said softly. 'After a bit of rough, are we? Who do you think you are – Lady Chatterley on the lookout for her Mellors?' All the same, Jake was attractive. Her libido had switched into overdrive as soon as he'd spoken to her. Had he been one of the academic types she worked with – the sort who relied on sweeping you off your feet with their cleverness, which rapidly turned to sulking and acid wit if you didn't succumb – she would have given him the brush-off.

But he wasn't a bit like them. Quite apart from the way he dressed, and the fact that his body was powerfully built and muscular from physical work, he had an innate sensuality which attracted her instantly. His hair was a little on the long side, brushed back at the sides and parted on one side with a tousled fringe. His mouth was generous and inviting, and there were two grooves running down to the corners of his mouth, as if he laughed a lot. His nose was very slightly misshapen, as if he'd had a clash with someone on a rugby pitch, and there was a cleft in his chin which gave him the look of a lovable rogue.

She couldn't help wondering what he would look like naked. Or what his cock would be like. At a guess, she'd say it would be big and powerful, like the rest of him. And yet he wouldn't be rough with her: something in his eyes made her think that he'd be a considerate lover, making sure that she had as much pleasure as he did . . .

Even so, she was taking a risk, inviting him back to dinner. They barely knew each other, and he'd already admitted that he'd followed her into the *patisserie* from the bookshop. Who was to say that he wouldn't turn out to be a knife-wielding maniac who'd hold her hostage?

She shook her head, laughing at her fears. She was being ridiculous. More likely, he'd come over with a bottle of cheap wine, they'd have a good meal, and – she admitted it to herself with a shiver of delighted anticipation – they'd probably end up in bed together . . .

Debra was pleasantly surprised when the buzzer rang, and she answered the door. Jake was leaning against the door-jamb, and her eyes widened. Wearing a well-cut pair of dark trousers and a blue-and-green patterned silk shirt – a far cry from the slightly grubby denims and checked brushed cotton shirt he'd worn earlier – he looked absolutely stunning. A pulse began to beat between her legs: this evening, she thought, was beginning to look very promising indeed.

She, too, had changed, into a bright yellow silk shirt and a pair of tapered navy trousers. As was her usual habit when at home, she was barefoot, and she had to tip her head back slightly to meet his eyes.

He smiled at her, and handed her a bottle of wine. 'I forgot to ask if you'd prefer red or white. This goes with most things, though.'

She unwrapped the tissue paper to discover a New Zealand Chardonnay; her eyes widened in a mixture of pleasure and surprise.

'Expecting Liebfraumilch, were you?' he asked, a teasing glint in his eyes.

'Um.' She coughed, embarrassed that he'd read her thoughts so easily. 'This looks very nice. Thank you.'

Jake smiled, amused, as he followed her into the flat. She obviously had him pegged as a stereotypical navvy, despite his gentle warning that he wasn't just a lager-and-vindaloo man.

She quickly regained her composure. 'Would you like a guided tour of the penthouse?'

'Thanks. That'd be nice.'

She smiled. 'This is the sitting room.'

Jake loved it. Plain white walls, stained floorboards covered with Turkish rugs, and heavy curtains. There was a futon at one end of the room – obviously it was her bed, as well as acting as a sofa during the daytime – and there were three Pre-Raphaelite prints on the walls, framed in perspex. A small table next to the futon housed a computer, and one wall was almost completely covered with bookcases; Jake itched to skim the shelves, but held himself back. Not until she'd invited him – or at least had left him on his own in the room.

A small bistro-style green aluminium table stood at the other end of the room, flanked by four chairs, also in green aluminium, with green cushion pads tied onto them. Next to the table was a miniature stereo, which was currently playing a Mozart piano concerto. Debra was obviously a past master at living in small spaces, he thought.

'This is the bathroom.'

Again, it was white, with black and white chequered tiles. The harshness of the colour scheme was softened by a cascade of plants in one corner, and a brass candelabrum on the windowsill.

'And finally, the kitchen.'

Again, the walls of the tiny galley-style room were white; the cupboards were pine, the worktops were a soft stone colour, matching the flooring, and the floor-length window overlooked the park opposite the house.

Jake sniffed. 'Something smells nice.'

'Tarragon chicken. With new potatoes, french beans and carrots – I hope you like them?'

'Yes, I do, thanks.' His lips twitched. 'Dare I ask if the chicken's home-made, or an M&S job?'

'M&S.' She flushed. 'I could have made it myself, but I wanted to work on the book.'

He smiled, taking her hand. 'Sorry, Debra. I didn't mean to tease. I'm sure that whatever you cooked would be lovely.'

She ignored the comment. 'Still convinced that I live in an heiress's pad, are you?'

He laughed. 'No. Though I do like it.'

'Mm, it's a nice flat, but I could do with a bit more space. I'm actually looking for somewhere of my own, but I don't think that it'll be in Holland Park, somehow.'

'Unless you get an incredible advance from your publisher. Or suddenly become the department's professor, on a huge salary . . .'

She grinned. 'I wish!' She glanced at her watch. 'Anyway, dinner's just about ready.'

'Anything I can do?'

She nodded, opening a drawer and handing him a corkscrew. 'Sort the wine out, and sit down.' He uncorked the wine, then took it through to the sitting room. Debra followed a couple of minutes later, carrying two plates.

'Crostini,' he said, his eyes glittering with pleasure as she put them on the table. 'I adore these.'

Debra was careful to mask her initial surprise. She'd already underestimated him about the wine, and she didn't want to make things worse. 'You like blue cheese, then?'

'Yes. Dolcelatte, blue Brie, Roquefort . . . When I lived at home my brothers were always rummaging through the fridge, and as soon as they came across my cheese, they threw it out, saying that as it was obviously mouldy, it had gone off!' He gave a small sigh of pleasure, and bit into the toasted bread. 'Mm. This is wonderful, Debra.'

'Thanks. And this, at least, is home-made.'

They chatted lightly during the meal and Jake discovered that Debra was twenty-nine, three years younger than himself, and had worked as a lecturer and research student in London since finishing her degree course. The Northern accent he'd picked up was indeed Yorkshire – her parents lived in a village in the middle of the Dales – and although she loved going there for weekends, she was happier living in London.

Debra learned that Jake was the youngest of three boys – not an only child, like herself – and most of his family lived in London. He had a rented one-bedroomed flat in Walthamstow, because he liked having his own space, but he saw quite a lot of his family. Like her, he enjoyed good films; he also played the guitar badly, and liked Victorian art.

She was touched that he insisted on helping her to wash up; when they'd finished in the kitchen, they returned to the sitting room. Debra sprawled on the futon while Jake chose some music; he'd intended to pick some slushy pop music, but he couldn't resist the lure of Rachmaninov's third piano concerto.

As Debra recognised the first few bars, she frowned slightly. The choice was out of character: she knew that she was being an intellectual snob, but builders just weren't into classical music – or if they were, it was usually the well-known pieces used as part of film scores or played often on the radio. Not for the first time, she wondered what the truth was about Jake. Thinking of the way he'd skipped over his education, when she'd asked where he went to school, she had a feeling that he was hiding something from her.

'This is one of my favourite pieces of music,' he said, coming to join her on the futon.

'Mine, too.' She paused. 'Where did you hear it, first?'

'I don't know. It was a long time ago.' He shrugged. 'School, probably. How about you?'

She shook her head. 'I don't know. A record, the radio – or maybe my mother played it. She's a music teacher.'

'Right.' Jake topped up their glasses; as he handed her

13

glass to her, his fingers brushed against hers. It felt like an electric shock, and he almost dropped the glass. Her pupils had expanded: obviously she had felt it, too.

Unable to help himself, he traced her lower lip with his forefinger. 'Debra.'

She placed her glass on the floor, and faced him. 'So, what now?'

'I think,' he said, 'that I'd better go. I don't want to outstay my welcome.'

'Who says you're doing that?' Her eyes had darkened almost to navy.

'But if I stay,' he said softly, 'I'll end up making love to you.'

She tipped her head to one side. 'That's not a problem for me.'

Jake swallowed hard. 'So, what now?' He echoed her earlier question.

'I believe,' she said, a hint of mischief in her eyes, 'that you just announced your intention of making love to me.' She took the glass of wine from his hand, putting it next to hers on the floor. 'So unless you're a dab hand with a futon, I suggest you go and close the curtains.'

With a shiver of anticipation, Jake stood up and walked over to the window, drawing the curtains; then he switched on the uplighter at the far end of the room. By the time he'd rejoined Debra, the futon had turned from a sofa to a bed.

'Oh, Debra,' he said softly, cupping her face and drawing it closer to his. Her skin felt soft and smooth under his fingertips, and he itched to touch more of her.

He kissed her lightly, his lips barely touching hers. She

slid her hands round his neck, pulling him closer and tangling her fingers in his hair. Her mouth opened invitingly under his, and he slid his tongue along her lower lip; impatiently, she kissed him back, her tongue flickering against his.

Automatically, his hands cupped her waist. He inched up the edge of her silk shirt, sliding his hands under the material and splaying his palms against her back. He eased one leg between hers; through the thin stuff of her trousers, he could feel the heat of her quim.

He tore his mouth from hers. 'Debra?'

'Mm?'

'Are you absolutely sure about this?' he asked softly. 'If you want me to stop, tell me now.'

In answer, she smiled, and pulled his shirt out of the waistband of his trousers. 'Oh, I'm sure,' she said, her voice husky. She undid the buttons slowly, and stroked his chest, delighting in the feel of the crisp hair under her fingertips. Her hands moved over his midriff, and then she undid the button of his trousers.

He was breathing harder, anticipation making his cock so hard that it almost hurt. 'Debra . . .' A sudden need to touch and taste her made him move her hands gently away from the fly of his trousers. He unbuttoned her shirt as slowly as she'd unbuttoned his, his pupils dilating as he pushed the material from her shoulders.

She was wearing a white lace bra, and the dark, erect nipples were clearly visible through the thin material. Jake couldn't resist drawing one finger down her cleavage; immediately, Debra took a sharp intake of breath, tipping her head back and offering her throat to him.

He kissed the curve of her throat, licking the hollows of her collarbone. As his lips moved downwards, he undid the clasp of her bra, freeing her breasts and rubbing his face against them to take in her perfume. He took one nipple between his lips, flicking at the peak of hard flesh with his tongue, and then drawing on it until Debra gasped, pushing her fingers into his hair.

He dropped to his knees before her, easing her trousers down to the floor. She stepped out of the garment, kicking it to one side. Jake noticed with pleasure that she wore knickers to match her bra, sheer and delicate white lace. He slid one hand between her thighs, cupping her mons veneris; the heat of her quim pulsed against his fingers.

Gently, he hooked his fingers into the sides of her knickers. pulling them down to her ankles. She stepped out of them, and he rubbed his face against her thighs. The musky scent of her arousal made him long to taste her; when she shifted slightly, widening her stance, he breathed a silent prayer of thanks, then slowly kissed his way up the smooth flesh of her inner thighs.

Debra gasped as she felt his breath fanning against her quim, and her fingers dug into his shoulders when he drew his tongue along the satiny furrow, parting her labia. He took his time, exploring her intimate topography in a way that made her shiver; then, at last, he reached her clitoris, teasing the hard bud of flesh from its hood with rapid flicks of his tongue.

He continued to caress her until she cried out, her sex-flesh suddenly quivering madly against his mouth. He smiled against her quim, tasting the sweet juices of her orgasm.

When she'd stopped shaking, he got to his feet, taking her into his arms. 'Okay?'

'Very okay.' Her voice had deepened with arousal, and her pupils had expanded so that her sharp blue eyes were almost black.

'Good.' He kissed her lightly on the mouth. 'Now, where were you, before I distracted you?'

She smiled. 'Here, I think.' She unzipped his trousers, and eased the material over his hips. His cock was visible through his underpants, long and thick; she couldn't resist curling her fingers round it, and rubbing it experimentally.

'Nice as it is, I prefer skin to skin,' he said softly, removing her hand and pushing his underpants down. He finished undressing swiftly, then took her hand. 'And now?'

'Come to bed, Jake.'

'I thought you'd never ask,' he teased.

'Well.' She sank down onto the bed, pulling him down with her.

He lay on his side next to her, tracing the curve of her body with the flat of his hand. 'Beautiful,' he pronounced, cupping one breast and dropping a kiss on its rosy tip.

She smiled. 'It's sweet of you, but I don't think so. I'm too short, and not skinny enough to be fashionable.'

'I prefer curves to ironing boards,' Jake mused.

'Oh, yes?'

His eyes danced. 'Would you like me to prove it?'

Debra grinned. 'At last, the penny drops . . .'

He laughed, and pushed one thigh between hers. 'Oh, Debra. You feel so good. All warm and soft and sweet . . .' He kissed his way down her body, licking her breasts and her abdomen before testing her arousal; her quim was still heated, her labia dark and puffy, and he smiled in satisfaction. He knelt between her thighs, positioning his cock at her entrance, and slowly pushed deep inside her.

Debra gave a small sigh of pleasure, wrapping her legs around his waist. As he began to thrust, she drew her hands down his back, feeling the interplay of muscles under his skin. She pushed hard against him as he slid into her, and flexed her internal muscles as he withdrew.

Jake groaned softly, and she felt his balls lift and tighten against her. As he came, she felt the familiar warm glow of orgasm fizzing through her veins, and suddenly explode in her solar plexus.

They lay locked together for a while; then Jake withdrew, turning onto his side and pulling her into his arms. Neither of them felt the need to talk; just lying together was enough.

Eventually, Jake moved. 'I could make love to you all night,' he said softly, 'but we've both got to go to work in the morning.'

She stroked the hair from his forehead. 'You don't have to go home tonight.'

'Yes, I do.' He kissed her lightly. 'But first . . .'

She drew one hand along his thigh, her nails lightly grazing his skin. 'Oh yes?'

He chuckled. 'Actually, I didn't mean that. I was going to ask you to come over to my place for dinner, tomorrow night.'

'I'd like that,' Debra said.

'Good.' He kissed her lingeringly. 'Same time?'

'That's fine by me.'

'I'll see you tomorrow, then.' He kissed her again, and moved lithely out of bed.

Debra watched him dress, a smile on her face. 'Are you sure I can't tempt you to stay?' she asked, folding her arms under her breasts and pouting at him.

He leaned over to kiss her breasts, then her mouth. 'Tomorrow,' he said firmly, his eyes dancing.

'Tomorrow, then.'

He stroked her face. 'I'll see myself out. Don't get up.' Unable to help himself, he bent to kiss her again, then stood up with an effort. 'Hasta mañana.'

Debra grinned. 'Hasta la vista, baby!' she said, doing a passable impression of Schwarzenegger.

He grinned back. 'I think I'd rather make love to you than to Arnie . . .'

Two

Jake opened the door, and smiled as he saw Debra. 'Punctual. I like that.'

'In a woman?' Her face tightened slightly at the suspected chauvinist streak.

'In a *person*. I wasn't being gender-specific.'

Debra was mollified – and intrigued, at the same time. Yet again, the phrases he'd used just didn't fit her image of a jobbing builder.

'Anyway, come in.' Jake, who had been about to say how nice she looked, decided not to risk commenting on her clothes. 'Drink, first, or a guided tour?'

'Guided tour,' Debra said promptly.

'Okay. This is the sitting room.'

It was painted cream, with pale carpets; there were a couple of perspex-framed prints on the walls, a television in one corner, and a small hi-fi in the other. A large sofa dominated the room, and the alcoves either side of the mantelpiece were crammed with bookshelves. A small table stood against one wall, with two chairs; Debra noticed that the table was laid properly, with a table-cloth and an unlit candle.

'The bathroom,' Jake said, shepherding her to the next room before she had a chance to ask him about the books.

It was simple, with an avocado-coloured bath, black and white chequered flooring, and pale walls down to dado-rail height; below the dado rail, the walls were panelled in pine, as were the ceiling and the side of the bath.

'It's a bit fake-sauna for my taste,' he said, 'but I can live with it.' He ushered her into the next room. 'The kitchen.' It was small, with white units and a grey marl work-surface. 'My mother says that it's too small, but it does the job,' he said with a shrug.

He nodded at the final door. 'My bedroom.'

'Aren't you going to show it to me?' Debra asked, surprised.

He grinned. 'Not before dinner. It's a casserole, so it won't spoil, but I'd rather eat, first.' He pulled her into his arms, kissing her lightly. 'So, would you like a drink?'

'Please.' She handed him a wrapped bottle. 'For you, before I forget.'

He removed the tissue paper and looked at the label. 'Sancerre. Very nice.' He smiled at her. 'Thank you.'

'You didn't say if it was red or white, tonight,' she reminded him.

'Red, actually – so how about we save this for another night?'

'Sure of yourself, aren't you?' she teased.

He grinned. 'It's called being persistent. If you'd said no, I'd have started a campaign of flowers and chocolates, delivered to your flat and your office. And if that didn't work, I'd have stood outside your house and serenaded you with my guitar.'

'I thought you said that you played badly?'

'Exactly. So you'd have had to agree to see me again, to shut me up – or else you'd have had a lot of explaining to do to your neighbours . . .'

She laughed, and followed him into the kitchen.

'Would you prefer wine, or a G and T?' he asked politely.

'Wine, please. I can't mix my drinks,' she told him.

'Actually, neither can I.' He poured two glasses of wine, handed one to her, and lifted his glass in a toast. 'To us, and a pleasant evening,' he said.

Debra echoed the toast, and they walked back into the sitting room.

'Dinner will be about another twenty minutes,' he said. 'Baked mushrooms in cream to start, then beef in red wine, jacket potatoes and snow peas. And ice-cream for pud, because I'm lazy.'

'Sounds gorgeous to me,' Debra said. 'Actually, it smells gorgeous.'

'Garlic,' he said. 'And fresh herbs.'

'Don't tell me you garden, as well?'

Jake was tempted to say, "Just call me Mellors"; he only just managed to bite it back. 'In a packet from the supermarket, actually,' he said. 'Anyway, come and sit down.'

Debra curled up on the sofa next to him. 'Is that what I think it is?' she asked, peering at the picture on the chimney-breast.

'*The Hyacinth Girl*, by Henry Walter Buchan,' he said. 'I've always liked it.'

'Me too. It's one of my favourites, though I've never managed to find a print anywhere.'

He smiled. 'It's a very cheap reproduction – a bit too orangey, really, if you've seen the real thing in Birmingham – but it took me a hell of a long time to get my hands on it. I got it from the gallery's shop, in case you were wondering. I rang them up and asked them if they just happened to do a print of the Buchan. They did, so I gave them my credit card number, and they posted it off to me.'

'I didn't think of that,' Debra said ruefully. 'I've only ever popped into the Tate, asking them if they could get hold of it, and they've always said no. The nearest I've got to seeing it is when they had an exhibition, and they had one of the pencil studies of it. It was just her face, but the hairs went up on my arms when I saw it.'

'So Victorian art's your favourite, too, then?'

She nodded. 'Pre-Raphaelite, really – and especially Buchan. Though it seems you can only ever find prints of Waterhouse, Rossetti and Millais. Everyone ignores Buchan.'

'That's because he's minor,' Jake reminded her. 'Though still well-known enough for the originals to be unaffordable.'

Yet again, Debra felt that there was more to Jake than met the eye. Pre-Raphaelite art had become popular, she knew, with posters available in all the chain store art shops, but minor artists like Buchan weren't particularly well known. How had Jake come across him?

She took a sip of wine, and gave him a sidelong look. 'Jake?'

'Mm?'

'Your second-hand bookshop habit.'

'What about it?'

'I have a similar one. Whenever I see bookshelves in someone's house, I can't help being nosy. Do you mind if I have a browse?'

Jake sighed inwardly. Still, she would have found out, sooner or later. It might as well be now, as any other time. 'Be my guest,' he said lightly.

'Thanks.' She was quiet as she glanced along the shelves; then turned thoughtfully to him. 'So are you trying to tell me that your second-hand book habit includes the complete works of Plato, Aristotle, Sophocles, and some classical poets I've never even heard of?'

'Some people just happen to like that sort of thing,' he said amiably.

'Jake, what's going on? You tell me you're a builder, but you don't talk or act like one.'

'That's stereotyping me – not to mention being snobbish.'

She frowned. 'Don't side-step the question.'

He sighed. 'All right. If you must know, I did a classics degree.'

Debra's suspicions deepened. 'Where?'

'Does it matter?'

'Yes.'

He coughed. 'Cambridge.'

'Cambridge.' She took one of the books down at random; sure enough, it had *Jake Matthews, Queens* written inside the front cover. There was a small book-plate underneath his name, which said that he'd won some sort of college prize. Her lips twitched. 'First class with honours, was it?'

'Mm.' He avoided her eyes.

'I see.' She paused. 'So we're talking about a first-class

classics graduate from Cambridge. How come you're a builder, now?'

'It was a choice of either sitting on the dole and sponging off everyone else, or going to work with my brothers. So I joined Adam and Joe in the family firm.' He sighed. 'Oh, well. You might as well know the whole sordid story. I wanted to be a lecturer – like you, but in a different field, obviously. Anyway, there were three research students, all going for the same post. I didn't get it.'

'That's not sordid,' Debra said.

'Believe me, it was. There was a lot of political back-biting beforehand, and I really couldn't handle it. It just seemed so bloody *pointless*.' Jake spread his hands. 'I found out afterwards that the bloke who got the job had been sleeping with the head of department.'

'Ouch.'

He nodded. 'Exactly. Anyway, it disillusioned me. I suppose it was a bit naïve of me to think that academics were more high-minded than businessmen, and you'd get a job on what you knew rather than who you knew or who you were screwing.'

'That's a bit cynical.'

'But true.' Jake shrugged. 'Anyway, I decided to do something else for a living. I didn't want to be a journalist or an accountant, or a dealer in the city. Then Adam suggested I joined the family firm. Maths isn't my strong point, so being their finance man was out: so he offered to teach me the trade.' His lips twitched. 'He had a point. Building houses is a bit more solid than building castles in the air. They don't come crashing down over your head, either.'

'So that's why you have a book habit.' She came to sit beside him, taking his hand. 'I'm surprised you didn't run a mile when I told you what I did.'

'Well, you know the problem with most men. Their genitals rule their brains,' he quipped wryly.

Debra grinned. 'Oh yes?' She put her glass down on the floor, and took his from him. 'Is that all the time, or just part of the time?'

'That depends on whether you like burned food.'

Debra gave him a sultry look. 'I've had an idea.'

'Oh, yes?'

'Mm. We have dinner, then take the ice-cream to bed. That way, we get the best of both worlds.'

'I knew you were a genius, the first time I set eyes on you.'

'And I knew that there was something different about you . . .' She kissed him lingeringly.

'You,' he admonished, stroking her face, 'are an intellectual snob. Just because someone doesn't have paper qualifications, it doesn't mean that they're stupid. Joe and Adam are bright, but neither of them was interested in school. They've no qualifications to speak of, but they'd run rings around an academic when it came to negotiating a business deal.'

She bit her lip. 'Sorry. I suppose it's the ivory tower effect – being an academic means you're cut off from the real world, a bit.'

'Well, now's your chance to do a Rapunzel.'

She frowned, not following him, and he grinned.

'Let your hair down and escape from the tower. Or let someone else in.'

She rolled her eyes. 'All I can say is that Rapunzel must have had a steel skull.'

'To withstand the force of someone heavy hanging on the end of it?'

'And to cope with it being piled up on top of her head, if she had hair that many feet long.' Debra was thoughtful. 'You know, she must have been an ancient crone, for it to be sixty feet long, or whatever. Besides, hair has a natural length, so it would probably have broken off after it reached her feet. Not to mention all the split ends, since she'd never had it cut. And if she washed it, it would have taken *days* to dry . . .'

Jake laughed. 'Lucky it's just a fairy story!'

She laughed back. 'Which I, in true academic fashion, have just wrecked.'

'That, too.'

She traced his lower lip with her forefinger. 'You said that Joe and Adam weren't interested in school. How come you were?'

'I don't know. Maybe it's because I was the baby of the family. When Adam was born, Mum had to cope with Joe in the "terrible twos" as well as with a squalling infant. When I was born, Joe had just gone up to senior school, and Adam was at middle school, so she had more time with me.' He smiled wryly. 'Though they've almost always called me "Professor", even when I was a kid. Maybe it was just something that was in me.'

'Why classics?'

He glanced at his watch. 'Dinner, first. Then I'll tell you. Do you want to put some music on, while I bring in the mushrooms?'

'Okay.' While Jake went into the kitchen, Debra looked through the CDs.

Jake came in, carrying two plates, and smiled approvingly at her choice. 'Paul Weller. I love this album.'

'Me, too. Good for late-night listening.'

He gave her a sidelong look. 'Was that an announcement of your intention to stay the night?'

'Think about it. If Rapunzel's hair was that long, it must have got caught on the bedstead, meaning that she had to stay in bed with her prince, all night . . .'

He laughed. 'Lucky I bought a new toothbrush, yesterday, and haven't opened it yet!'

He poured them both another glass of wine; Debra took a forkful of mushrooms, and sighed in bliss. 'This is gorgeous. Where did you learn to cook?'

'My mother. She likes experimenting, and it's rubbed off on me.' His lips twitched. 'Or maybe I discovered that the way to a woman's bed is through her stomach.'

'I'll tell you, over ice-cream,' Debra promised. 'Anyway, you were going to tell me what started you off on classics.'

'It was a school trip. I must have been about six. Anyway, we went to Colchester museum, and learned all about Boudicca's rebellion and the burning of Camulodunum – present-day Colchester. Anyway, it set me wondering about the Romans. They did good things as well as bad.'

Debra's lips twitched. 'See Monty Python, for details of what the Romans have ever done for us!'

He laughed. 'Mm. I loved that film, too. Anyway, one of my primary school teachers was pretty enlightened. As soon as she'd sussed that Mum had taught me to read before I went to school, and I was bored with the school's reading system, she said I could read what I liked while the others were working through it. She lent me books about the Greek mythological heroes – bastardised Homer, I guess – and Mum indulged me a lot. She used to take me to the British Museum on Sunday afternoons to see the mummies and the Elgin marbles.

'I thought about being an archaeologist, for a while – when I was really small, I dug up Dad's allotment to try and find buried Roman treasure, and he was furious because I'd ruined his potato crop – but then I got hooked on Roman poetry. Anyway, I decided to read classics, and maybe teach afterwards.' He smiled wryly. 'It just didn't work out quite the way I planned. Luckily Adam and Joe were okay about it. They taught me everything I know about building, gave me a job, and didn't lecture me about wasting my time in books. I work hard and don't give myself airs and graces just because I've been to Cambridge, so everyone else accepts me, as well.'

'Right.' She had a sudden thought. 'Your long lunch-break, yesterday . . . were they annoyed about it?'

Jake grinned. 'At first, yes. Then I explained that a young lady was involved.'

'Oh yes?'

'Before you start thinking it, they didn't way "woarrgh, she's a goer, get in there my son and give her one",' he said drily. 'And I didn't tell them that I'd heard you asking for Victorian porn, either. I just said that I saw you in the street and decided that I wanted to know you better. They're both itching to marry me off so that I can carry on the Matthews

30

dynasty, so they were okay about it.'

'Aren't they married, then?'

'Yes, and they have an average of two-point-five kids between them. Joe and Allie have two boys, and Adam and Lyn have two girls and a boy. They forgive me a lot, for being the perfect babysitter.'

'Oh yes?'

He nodded. 'Uncle Jacob tells brilliant stories about monsters and horses with wings, and can keep his nephews and nieces quiet for hours on a Sunday afternoon.'

'Jacob? That's your full name?'

'Mm. Dad likes Biblical names. No one's ever actually called me that, though – like no one ever calls Joe "Joseph". And if they could think up a decent short version of Adam, they'd all use that.'

'Right.' Debra smiled at him, and finished her mushrooms. 'That,' she said, 'was gorgeous.'

'Glad you liked it.' He cleared the plates away, and returned a few minutes later with the main course.

Debra tasted the casserole, and shook her head. 'Damn. A man who can cook better than I can.'

'I'm older,' he pointed out, 'So I've had more practice. Besides, I bet your Yorkshire pud's better than mine.'

'It had better be,' she retorted laughing.

'I can feel a competition coming on . . .' He blew her a kiss. 'Anyway, you were going to tell me why you specialised in Victorian studies.'

'Well, my parents are both teachers. Mum teaches the piano, and Dad's head of English at the local grammar school. I was brought up on Shakespeare and poetry – and we lived in Brontë country, so you couldn't exactly miss *Jane Eyre* and *Wuthering Heights*. Anyway, it was always assumed that I'd be a teacher. I was good at English, and liked it, so I went to UCL. The nineteenth century course was my favourite, and I had a chance to do an MA. I decided I'd rather do that than a post-grad teaching course. I suppose I was in the right place at the right time when a job came up.'

'So why are you writing a book about Victorian erotica?'

She grinned. 'I told you yesterday, I have a mucky mind. And it makes a change from writing about the place of the industrial revolution and social realism in the Victorian novel.'

'True.' He paused. 'Isn't all the erotic stuff just whipping and spanking, though?'

'The English vice, you mean?' She wrinkled her nose. 'There's quite a lot of it in the later stuff, but it isn't all about the birch and the cane. And it does show exactly what the social realist novelists left out – if you read something like Walter's *My Secret Life* and then Dickens' description of dockyard pubs, it's really amazing how Dickens managed to get the tone of the people, but kept out all the smut.' She pulled a face. 'And now I'll shut up. I can get very boring on the subject.'

Jake's dark eyes were lively. 'I don't know about that. I'd rather like you to bore the pants off me.'

She laughed. 'Oh, really?'

'Mm.' He gave her a sultry look. 'Or maybe just take them off me, then ravish me.'

'Ravish you, eh?' She looked thoughtful. 'You can do a lot with a tub of ice-cream . . .'

'In that case . . .' He took their plates into the kitchen,

returning with a tub of vanilla ice-cream and a spoon. 'Come into the garden, Maud.'

'Would that be the paradise garden?' she teased.

'Or even the perfumed one.'

She laughed. 'Don't tell me that *that* was part of your degree.'

He grinned. 'Not quite – though I have read it.' He slid his free hand under her hair to stroke the nape of her neck, and kissed her lightly on the lips, before leading her to the bedroom.

He put the carton of ice-cream on top of the pine bedside cabinet, and switched on the small lamp before closing the curtains. He pushed the duvet back, and looked at her, his head tipped slightly to one side. 'And now for the re-enactment of the ravishing of Paris.'

'Hm?'

'Like the seduction of Helen – but from his point of view,' Jake supplied with a grin. 'And you just promised to ravish me, did you not?'

'Actually, I didn't. It was your suggestion. But,' she gave him a wicked grin, 'I'm always willing to consider new ideas.'

She undid the button of his jeans, then slowly unzipped them. Deliberately, she brushed the backs of her fingers against his hardening cock as she pushed the faded denim over his hips. Jake swallowed hard and closed his eyes as a vision of her flashed into his mind: Debra kneeling before him, her fingers curled round his cock and a smile on her face as she bent her head . . .

He opened his eyes again as she tugged at his T-shirt; he

lifted his arms, letting her pull it over his head, and stepped out of his jeans. Debra coughed, and he removed his socks, grinning. 'I know. The most unerotic sight in the world – a near-naked man in socks!'

'Definitely.' She tipped her head slightly to one side. 'Even Michelangelo's *David* would look gross in little knitted bootees.'

'Which means that the rest of us have no chance.'

'I dunno about that.' She hooked her thumbs into the sides of his underpants, drawing them down; he stepped out of the garment, so that he was standing naked before her.

Nice, she thought, as she surveyed him. Very nice. The physical nature of his work had given him broad shoulders and firm muscles; his stomach was flat, not flabby from drinking too much beer and eating junk food, and his thighs promised staying power. And then there was his cock, rising thick and hard from the dark hair at his groin; it made her feel wet just to look at him, let alone remembering how well he'd used it, the previous night.

'Turn round,' she said softly.

The back view, she thought, was perfect. Firm buttocks and broad shoulders tapering to a narrow waist. She smiled as he turned round and adopted a pose.

'All I need is the collar,' he said.

'Hm?'

'Slave collar. You know, for young men bought on the market to pleasure lusty Roman women. According to popular myth, that is.'

'And are you going to enlighten me?'

'I was rather hoping,' he said with a grin, 'to do something else to you. Or, rather, since you're the ravisher, for *you* to do something to *me*!'

'Hint taken.' She was about to walk over to him when he shook his head. 'What?'

'You're fully dressed. Which makes me feel like a cheap tart.'

She chuckled. 'Now, "cheap" isn't a description that I'd apply to a man who buys decent ice-cream.' She'd already noted the label – Jake obviously liked very rich and very expensive vanilla ice-cream.

'Ice-cream which will be melted, by the time you get round to ravishing me. Aren't you supposed to be ripping your clothes off, and then bonking me senseless?'

In answer, she grinned, and stripped exceedingly slowly. First her silk shirt, then her ankle-length pleated skirt, and her silk and lace half-slip. Jake's eyes widened as he took in the fact that she was wearing a white lacy teddy, and navy hold-up lace-topped stockings.

'Well, you're certainly dressed for seduction,' he said admiringly.

She laughed. 'Well, I don't dress like this for lectures, believe me!'

'If you did, and your male students had any idea what you were wearing, they wouldn't pay any attention to what you were saying. They'd just see you undressing for them, and wonder what it would be like to peel the clothes from your body and lick you all over.'

Debra raised an eyebrow. 'Is that what you thought about your lecturers, then?'

He shook his head. 'Apart from the fact that they all

seemed too old, none of them could even begin to compare with you.' Unable to resist, he drew his finger along the lace across her breasts. 'God, Debra, you're lovely.'

She blushed then. 'Do you mind? I'm the one supposed to be ravishing you.'

'Be my guest.'

'Now. Where was I?'

'I think,' he said, his voice husky, 'you were undressing.'

'So I was.' She pushed down the shoulder-straps of the teddy over her shoulders, shaking her hair back, and then peeled the stretch lace downwards until it rested just below her breasts. She cupped her breasts in both hands, lifting them up and together to deepen her cleavage; her nipples were erect, and her thumbs brushed across them, sending a frisson of pleasure through her.

Jake swallowed hard, itching to push her hands away and caress her breasts himself, maybe stooping to suckle one nipple while his thumb and forefinger aroused its twin, but he forced himself to stay where he was. Debra was setting the pace.

She noticed that a droplet of clear fluid was resting at the tip of his cock, and smiled to herself. Jake was as aroused as she was, wanting her desperately. This was going to be good, she promised herself. Slowly, she brought her hands back to the teddy, and peeled it downwards. She wriggled her hips, and finally stepped out of the material. Then she turned round and rolled her stockings downward, giving him a view of her quim which made him shiver.

'You,' he said huskily as she turned back to face him, 'are a wicked little tease.'

She gave him an impish grin. 'That's not all.' She took his hand, and drawing him towards the bed, reached up to kiss him. Again, Jake let her set the pace, only kissing her properly when she nibbled at his lower lip and pushed her tongue into his mouth.

She pushed him back onto the bed, and knelt on the mattress between his thighs. 'Prepare for a ravishing,' she informed him, her face lit with a mixture of arousal and mischief.

'Yes, my lady,' he quipped.

As she bent her head and he realised what she had in mind, his hands came up to grip the struts of the pine headboard. He closed his eyes, tipping his head back into the feather pillows and groaning softly as she cupped his balls gently in one hand, ringing the shaft of his cock with her other hand, and slowly easing her mouth over its swollen tip.

She traced the outline with the tip of her tongue, making it into a hard point and flicking it across the sensitive groove at the base of his glans; Jake cried out, his grip on the rail tightening. Then she began to work along the shaft, sucking and nibbling and licking, while her other hand caressed his balls. A few minutes of this treatment had Jake almost sobbing as he came, his semen thick and salty as it filled her mouth.

Smiling, Debra sat up. 'Okay for a first attempt?'

His eyes were slightly unfocused. 'Very okay,' he said, stroking her hair. 'Thank you. That was fantastic.'

She shifted up beside him, and bent over to rub the tip of her nose against his. 'Glad you enjoyed it. And at least it's taken your mind off the fact that your ice-cream's melting.'

'That's true.' He kissed her lightly. 'So we'd better eat it, before you finish ravishing me.'

'Finish?'

He gave her a hammed-up sexy pout. 'Oh yes. Let's go all the way . . .'

She laughed, and he sat up, taking the lid off the ice-cream and offering her the first spoonful. She ate it with relish; he fed himself a spoonful, then held the next spoonful for her, drawing it away from her so that she leaned forward and he could see her breasts swinging free.

'Lecher,' she complained when he did it a second time.

'Your breasts are adorable. I can't help wanting to look at them!'

'Hm.' She ignored the comment, and ate another spoonful of ice-cream.

Eventually, Jake sighed. 'Last one, I'm afraid,' he said, feeding her a spoonful.

'I could eat that stuff all night,' she said regretfully.

He put the spoon back in the carton. 'I can think of other things I'd like to eat all night.'

Her face flamed. 'Jake!'

He nibbled her earlobe. 'Sorry. That was a bit crude. Mind you, you knew exactly what I was talking about . . .'

'Mm.'

'Make love to me, Debra,' he urged, his voice low and sultry. He stroked her shoulders. 'Please.'

It was a request, not a demand, and she responded to the tone of his voice by shifting slightly to kiss him. He lay back against the pillows, bringing her down with him so that she was lying half on top of him.

She shifted to straddle him, tipping her head down slightly so that the ends of her hair brushed his face. His cock was already hard, and she lowered herself so that her quim rested along its length.

Jake swallowed hard. 'Oh God, Debra. Don't tease me.'

'Tease you?' She blew him a kiss, and shimmied slightly so that her breasts swung from side to side.

'Cruel hussy,' he mouthed, pulling a dejected face.

She grinned. 'You old ham.'

He lifted her slightly, and she slid her hand between them, curling her fingers round his cock and guiding its tip to her entrance. Then she lowered herself slowly onto him.

Jake gasped. 'That's good. You feel like warm wet velvet.'

'Oh really?'

'Mm.' He stroked the soft swell of her buttocks. 'I love the way you feel and smell and taste.' He lifted his upper body so that he could nuzzle her breasts, licking her skin and then breathing on the hard tips of her nipples.

She shivered, and began to move over him, her hips tracing small circles over his. She lifted up from until he was at the point of slipping out of her, then pushed back down hard until her pubis ground against him.

Jake gave small moans of pleasure as she flexed her internal muscles round his cock. As she rode him, she felt her own climax nearing: the familiar sensation of warmth rolling through her veins, from the soles of her feet up to her quim, then radiating out in every nerve as her muscles contracted hard round him. She cried out as she came, and dimly heard Jake's answering cry as the rippling of her quim round his cock pushed him to his own orgasm.

He wrapped his arms round her, holding her close; she rubbed her cheek against his. 'Mm. I enjoyed that.'

'You're not the only one,' He nuzzled her earlobe. 'I could get used to this.'

'If you scoff ice-cream like that every night, you'll be incredibly fat within the next six months,' she said, deliberately misinterpreting his words.

'Mm, I suppose so.' He shifted so that she was lying next to him, her head cradled on his chest.

'You know, Jake, you're really lucky.'

'How do you mean?'

'All this space.' She waved her hand at the room. 'Whereas I have to sleep in my living room.'

'Walthamstow isn't exactly Holland Park, is it? I mean, those beautiful houses . . .'

'What about William Morris?' she retorted.

'Okay, so there's a lot of Arts and Crafts stuff around here. Even so, if I had the chance to live in Holland Park instead of here, I know which I'd choose.'

'Mm.' She stretched. 'It's about time I got round to buying my own place, though. I'm heading for thirty, and house prices are never going to be this affordable again.'

'What sort of place are you looking for?'

'I don't know, really. Probably a crumbling Victorian terrace in need of doing up, so I can have it the way I want it, right from the start.'

He stroked her hair. 'Well, if you find somewhere and you want a professional opinion of it before you start spending money on surveyors, I'd be happy to offer my services. Or Joe's – he's good at spotting things.'

'Thanks.' She kissed him lightly. 'I might just take you up on that.'

'And in the meantime—' he slid one hand along her thigh '—if you were serious about spending the night with me . . .'

Three

'You look pleased with yourself, Deb.' Judith Sellers leaned against the doorframe. 'What's his name, then?'

Debra looked up from the computer screen, where she was working on the first draft of her book. 'Hello, Jude. I don't know what you're talking about.'

'Yes, you do.' Judith came into the small room which acted as Debra's office, and sat down on the comfortable chair next to her desk. 'And before you claim that your book's going well, work doesn't put *that* kind of smile on your face, even with the subject you're working on. Or shadows under your eyes, as though you're not getting enough sleep – for all the right kind of reasons, that is.'

Debra laughed. 'Okay, okay. I give in.'

'Then *tell* me.' Judith rolled her eyes. 'I want to know everything.'

'His name's Jake, I met him in a bookshop, and he's a builder.'

'A builder?' Judith was surprised. 'I wouldn't have thought you'd have that much in common.'

'Don't be such a snob. We have.'

'Tell me more,' Judith invited.

'Do you want a coffee?'

'Yes, but stop trying to avoid the subject.'

Debra grinned, and poured them both a mug of coffee from the filter machine on her desk. 'I've run out of milk, so you'll have to drink it black. And it's a bit stewed.'

'It's caffeine, so who cares?' Judith retorted. 'Anyway, your builder.'

Debra smiled. 'He's got a First in Classics – from Cambridge.'

Judith's eyes widened. 'You're kidding!'

'No, honest. It took me a while to get it out of him.'

'It doesn't add up, Deb. Why would someone like that be a builder, and not a professor or a research fellow or something?'

'Because he was disillusioned with the academic rat-race.'

Judith took a swig of coffee. 'He's got a point, there. It *is* a rat-race. You never know which of the research students fancies your job and is secretly trying to ease you out, or if Mac's decided that you're difficult and he'd rather take on the next bimbo who thinks she knows everything about Shakespeare and is willing to suck his cock to prove it.'

Debra frowned at her best friend's unexpected tirade. 'What's happened, Jude?'

'Oh, nothing much.' Judith waved her hand dismissively. 'Just one of the usual departmental storms in a tea-cup. It'll blow over by tomorrow – I just get a bit sick of it while it's happening, that's all. Bloody office politics! Anyway, you were telling me about Jake. Looks?'

'Twelve out of ten, definitely.' Debra moistened her lower

lip with the tip of her tongue. 'About six foot, dark hair, dark eyes, all his own teeth, muscles in all the right places. No flab, and the sexiest smile you've ever seen.'

'A good cock, and knows how to use it?'

Debra smiled. 'Trust you to ask that, Jude!'

'Well?'

She grinned. 'Yes. Absolutely. Twenty out of ten, on that score.'

'Some women have all the luck,' Judith sighed theatrically, raking a hand through her short red hair. 'I dunno. I never get picked up by gorgeous men in bookshops. And if I decide to make the first move on a man at a party, he turns out to be either a closet gay who just wants to tell me his life story and howl on my shoulder, or the most arrogant bastard under the sun.'

'You didn't sleep with Marcus, so you haven't picked up the most arrogant bastard,' Debra reminded her. 'Just one of them.'

'True.' Debra's ex-lover had slept with half his students and most of his department while he was living with Debra — and he'd had the gall to try it on with a couple of her friends before she had realised what was going on and thrown him out. 'So when are we going to meet this new man of yours, then?'

'Soon. I'll get round to organising a dinner party, or something. I might get him to cook, actually.'

Judith groaned. 'No. Not only does she find a man who's intelligent, good-looking and can shag like a donkey, she finds one who can cook as well!'

Debra spread her hands. 'Well, it makes up for three years

of Marcus.' Marcus, whose sole concession to cooking was to make a peanut butter sandwich, and in the process manage to dirty three knives and leave a trail of peanut butter over the worktops – not to mention a pile of crumbs on the floor. Marcus, who was fond of arranging dinner parties – and happy to let Debra do all the cooking, as well as all the clearing up, the next morning. Marcus, who was also allergic to the iron, the vacuum cleaner and the washing machine.

'Well, it's nice to see you looking so happy,' Judith said. 'How's the book coming on?'

'Okay. Though I haven't done that much on it, for the past couple of weeks.' Mainly because she'd spent all her free time making love with Jake; she stretched luxuriously at the thought, her smile betraying what was on her mind and making Judith feel a twinge of envy. 'The house hunting's looking good, though. Liv says she's found me the perfect place, and I'm going to have a look at it, tonight.'

Judith frowned. 'I don't know why you want to leave your flat, Deb. It's gorgeous.'

'I know it is, and I love Holland Park – but I need more space. And I'm tired of spending dead money on rent.'

'Fair enough. Well, if you want a second opinion on it, let me know. I love spending other people's money.'

'Thanks. Though I was going to take Jake with me – in a professional capacity, of course. He might spot things I miss.'

Judith stared at her friend. 'You're not thinking about buying a place with him, are you?'

'No – don't be stupid! I've only known him for a couple of weeks.' Two very intense weeks, where they'd spent every possible moment together. A smile curved her lips at the thought, and Judith was surprised by the sheer sensuality which crossed her friend's face.

She drained her coffee. 'Well, I'd better let you get back to work. See you later. And I want to be the first one to meet him.'

'You will be,' Debra promised.

To Jake's surprise – and pleasure – Debra was waiting at the entrance to the tube station at Ealing. He kissed her lingeringly. 'Hello! I wasn't expecting to see you tonight. I thought you said that you were busy?'

'I am – but it's something that you can do with me, if you like.' She laughed at the lustful expression on his face. 'And no, I didn't mean sex.'

'Pity.'

'Later,' she promised. 'First, you need a bath.'

He sniffed. 'Mm, I do smell a bit high. That's the downside of doing what I do for a living – sweat.' He gave her a sidelong look. 'Though some people find it sexy.'

She grimaced. 'Not me, I'm afraid.'

'No. Me neither.' He smiled at her. 'Well, I haven't got a change of clothes with me, so the bath will have to be at my place. Unless whatever you had in mind meant that I didn't have to wear any clothes?'

'You,' she laughed, 'are an incorrigible sex fiend.'

'And that is entirely *your* fault, Ms Rowley.' He smiled at her. 'So what is it you have in mind?'

'Did I tell you that my friend Liv is an estate agent?'

'No. Why?'

Debra rattled a bunch of keys at him. 'She's found me a house. Anyway, I thought I might take you up on your offer of having a look at the place with me.'

'Fine.' He took her hand. 'So where is it?'

'Islington – and it's in my price range.' She squeezed his fingers. 'Liv says I'll really like it.'

'Hm.' Jake was thoughtful. 'I know a good pizza place in Islington. How do you fancy eating out, tonight, after we've had a look at the house?'

'Sounds good to me.'

He gave her a sidelong glance. 'And in return for me giving the house the once-over with my professional hat on . . .'

She laughed. 'Okay, the pizza's my shout.'

'Actually, I had something else in mind.' He bent his head so that his lips were just touching her ear. 'Like staying over at your place, tonight.' He licked her earlobe. 'Especially as you told me that tomorrow's your late morning . . .'

'And you told me,' she reminded him, 'that you're supposed to be working early every single day this week.'

'But your flat is nearer to where I'm working than mine is,' he retorted, 'so I won't have to get up quite as early as I would, normally.'

She laughed. 'Okay, okay, you've sold it to me.'

'Good.'

They went back to his flat. 'What time do we have to be at the house?' Jake asked as they reached his front door.

'Whenever we like. Though before it gets dark – it's empty, and there isn't any electricity at the moment.'

He frowned. 'Does it need a lot of work doing to it, then?'

'I won't know until I've seen it. Liv said it'll need rewiring, and a bit of decorating.'

'Right.' He ushered her inside. 'In that case, you have a choice. You can either make yourself a coffee while I have a bath, and we'll go in about half an hour – or we can open a bottle of wine, and you can wash my back for me.'

Debra grinned. 'Last time I washed your back, we both ended up looking like prunes for staying in the bath for too long! And I really do want to see the place tonight, Jake. I'm meeting Liv for lunch and giving her the keys back, tomorrow.'

He sighed. 'You're a hard woman. Go and make yourself a coffee, then.'

'Do you want one?'

He shook his head. 'I'm fine. See you in a minute.'

He left the bathroom door open, in case Debra decided to change her mind, but when she didn't appear, he scrubbed himself quickly, washed his hair, and emerged with a towel wrapped round his waist.

'No,' she said, laughing. 'We don't have enough time.'

'I didn't say anything,' he protested.

'I could read your face.'

He grinned, unabashed, and went to dress, reappearing a few minutes later in clean jeans and a white cotton shirt. 'Shall we take my car, or do you want to get the tube?' he asked.

She spread her hands. 'Well, if you're staying over at mine, we'd better get the tube.'

'Fine. I take it that you know where this place is?'

She fished in her handbag, and brought out a piece of paper. 'Directions.'

'Good.' He kissed her lightly; when her mouth opened under his, the kiss deepened, and he burrowed under the hem of her loose tunic-style shirt, stroking her midriff.

Laughing, she pushed him away. 'If you start that, we'll never get to Islington before it's dark.'

'You started it,' he reminded her, ruffling her hair. 'Okay, house it is.' He put his work clothes in a carrier bag, and they set off for Islington.

They found the house with little difficulty; Jake frowned as he saw the outside. 'It looks structurally sound, from here, but the windows are rotting, it needs complete redecorating, and it wouldn't surprise me if there was some damp underneath the window.'

'I know, but look at the mouldings.' There was a frieze of oak leaves above the windows, and embellishing the porch. 'And the path's original – all I'll have to do is lift up the slabs, level off the ground, and replace the slabs again.'

'Hm.' Jake wasn't convinced.

'And I've always liked sash windows.'

He squeezed her hand. 'Debra, wait until you've had a look inside. If it needs too much doing to it, it might not be worth buying. And it might not be mortgageable, either.'

'Says the builder.'

'Well, you did ask me to come with my professional hat on,' he reminded her.

She sighed. 'I know. Sorry. I've just got this gut feeling about the place. It's got wonderful vibes.'

She unlocked the front door, which creaked slightly as it opened.

'A bit of oil on the hinges will sort that,' Jake told her,

squinting at the door. 'The shape's true, so at least the front of the house is okay.'

Debra's eyes widened as she saw the banisters. 'Jake, look – there's a mermaid or something carved into it!'

'So there is,' He brushed away the dust.

She glanced up at the ceiling. One or two hairline cracks ran along it, but the mouldings and cornices were original. Jake gave her a sidelong look. She'd fallen in love with the house on sight: he hoped for her sake that there wasn't anything seriously wrong with it. If there was, it would be a hell of a job to argue her out of buying it.

'Come on. Let's have a look at the rest of it.' She opened the first door, into a good-sized sitting room. 'They've still got the original fireplace,' she said, delighted.

'Mm.' Jake gave a couple of experimental bounces on the floorboards, then lifted up the carpet at the corner, checking along the skirting board. 'The floor's okay,' he pronounced. 'No sign of woodworm or dry rot.'

'Good.' She wandered into the dining room, Jake following her. Again, there was the original fireplace, and original cornices and mouldings. A dado rail ran the length of the wall. 'I can just see it, now. The top half painted pale green, and the bottom half in Morris wallpaper.'

'Mm.' Jake was busy inspecting the floorboards. Three or four needed replacing, but it was basically sound.

The kitchen-cum-scullery was long and narrow; there were no units, merely a stone sink in one corner. 'A fitted kitchen, from scratch, won't be cheap – not if you want it a decent one.'

'I'll have a pine dresser and some open shelving instead,'

she told him. She peered under the carpet, and exclaimed in delight. 'Look – pamment flooring! Imagine if that was done up properly, polished back to its original state.'

'Hm.' He frowned. 'It's unusual to see so many original features, Debra. Most places done up in the sixties and seventies had them ripped out.'

'Liv said that an old lady had lived here for most of her life, and she hadn't changed anything. She'd only had a bathroom installed because one of her nieces insisted – and even then, she refused to have central heating put in, or anything like that. She died, a few months back, and the niece who inherited it is getting on a bit herself, and she can't afford to modernise it properly, so she's selling it.'

'You're lucky it hasn't been snapped up by a builder,' Jake told her. He wandered over to the door at the end, peering through the grimy windows. 'There's a decent garden, too. Overgrown, but you could have it cleared and start again. Maybe a courtyard garden, with lots of terracotta and stone troughs and pots – and a sun-dial.'

'Mm.' She took his hand, smiling to herself. He was beginning to sound as enthusiastic as she was about the place. 'Let's go upstairs.'

They walked up the stairs, which creaked loudly. 'Typical old house,' she said confidently. 'The stairs always squeak.'

Jake smiled as they reached the landing. 'You're going to buy it, aren't you?'

'There's just something about it,' she said. 'I don't know what it is. I know it needs complete redecorating, and probably rewiring; there's no central heating; the carpets are awful . . . It's going to take ages to get it how I want it. But I don't care

– there's something about this place.'

He was thoughtful. 'Mm. You're right. There *is* something.'

She smiled at him. 'I'm glad you can feel it, too.'

He spun her round to face him. 'It's actually making me feel very randy.'

'You're just over-sexed,' she teased.

'No, seriously. There's something about this place that makes me want to . . .' He gave up trying to explain, and kissed her.

'Jake! Not here,' she protested half-heartedly.

'No one's going to interrupt us. The front door isn't on the latch, and there isn't a friendly estate agent showing us round and diverting our attention away from the damp patch in the corner.'

He kissed her again, burrowing under her shirt and stroking her midriff; this time, Debra didn't push him away, but kissed him back. Taking heart, Jake eased his hands round to her back, unclasping her bra and letting her breasts spill into his hands.

Her nipples were already erect, he discovered, rubbing his thumbs over the sensitive peaks of flesh. Debra gasped, and he took advantage of her position to push one leg between hers. He could feel through the thin silk of her knickers that she was aroused; her quim felt like a furnace, and he knew that if he bunched her skirt up and replaced his thigh with his hand, insinuating his fingers into her knickers, her quim would be moist and ready for him. She was as aroused as he was.

Jake tore his mouth from hers. 'Debra?'

'Mm?' Her eyes were sightly unfocused, and her lower lip was full and red, making him itch to kiss her again.

'I want you,' he said softly.

'I know.' She slid her hand down to his groin, cradling his cock through his jeans.

'Then, if you don't mind . . .' He placed his hands over hers, encouraging her to undo the button of his jeans, then lower the zip.

'We really shouldn't be doing this,' Debra informed him.

He smiled, recognising the half-heartedness of her tone. 'Who's going to know about it?'

'True.' She tugged at his underpants so that they slid over his hips, revealing his erect cock; she drew her tongue along her lower lip and curled her fingers round the rigid shaft.

He lifted her, then, balancing her weight against the wall, and lifted the front of her skirt. He curved his fingers round the edge of her knickers, and pulled the gusset aside. He positioned his cock at her entrance, and pushed into her; in response, she wrapped her legs round his waist.

Jake began to thrust, very slowly moving into her, then withdrawing until he was almost out of her, before moving slowly back into her warm wet depths. Her arms were round his neck, and she caressed the nape of his neck, pushing her other hand into his hair. She drew his face towards hers, and began kissing him, hard.

It was enough to tip Jake over the edge; as he came, he felt her quim fluttering round him, contractions that began softly and then suddenly became hard, taking them both by surprise. He waited until her flesh had stopped quivering, then gently withdrew and set her on her feet again.

He kissed the tip of her nose. 'Sorry. I couldn't resist that.'

'So I gathered.' A smile on her face belied the dryness of her words.

'Well, it's a way of christening the house . . .'

'Who says I'm going to buy it?'

'Because you've obviously fallen for the place.' He took a handkerchief from his pocket, and cleaned her up before setting her clothes to rights. Pleased with the final effect, he smiled at her, and kissed her again. 'You're so beautiful, Debra.'

Debra, who'd only ever thought of herself as passable, on a good day, was surprised. She said nothing, though, not wanting to seem as though she was fishing. 'Come on. We haven't finished looking round.'

There turned out to be two large bedrooms, both with a fireplace and proper sash windows; at the back was a small and very ugly bathroom. Debra grimaced. 'Yuck.'

'The room's okay. It's just the layout,' Jake told her. 'If you don't mind sacrificing a shower, you could have an original Victorian bath. I know a place that resurfaces them.'

Debra grinned. 'You've fallen for it, too, haven't you?'

He coughed. 'I can see its potential. As a builder.'

'Tell me your gut reaction. Could you live here?'

He looked at her in surprise, his dark eyes gleaming with interest. 'Are you asking me to live with you, Debra?'

So much for telling Jude that she had no intention of living with Jake, Debra thought wryly. 'Well, we've only known each other for a couple of weeks,' she prevaricated.

His gaze was very intense. 'It's long enough.'

'To know someone?' Debra thought of Marcus again. If she was honest with herself, she'd known right from the outset that he was a bastard, and wouldn't be good for her. Whereas with Jake . . . she felt completely at ease with him. She liked his sense of humour; he was bright enough to keep her mind satisfied as well as her body; and she responded sexually to him more deeply than to any of her previous lovers. 'Mm.'

He stroked her face. 'The answer's yes. Though maybe we ought to sleep on it. If we still feel the same, tomorrow morning . . .' He kissed her lightly. 'Then we might as well go the whole hog and buy the place together, too.'

'Supposing we hate each other, in another month?'

He curled his fingers round hers, squeezing her hand. 'I don't think so. I'm not hiding a split personality from you – what you see is what you get. And I think you're the same.'

'Mm,' she agreed wryly.

'So how about we drop the subject and have dinner? Then maybe tomorrow – if we still want to move in together – you can persuade your friend to let us have the keys again, so we can come back and have another look at the house?'

She grinned. 'You're so sensible, Jake.'

'It's my age,' he quipped. 'Come on. I always think better after I've been fed.'

She gave him a sidelong look. 'Or after making love.'

He grinned. 'That, too.' He stooped to kiss the tip of her nose. 'Come on.'

The next morning, Jake woke with Debra curled in his arms. She was still sleeping soundly, so he decided not to wake her; he lay there, thinking. Living with Debra. The idea was appealing. Working together on the house, making it something special. As she'd said, the night before, they hadn't known each other long: but it was long enough for him to know what he wanted.

He lay there, watching her sleep, until her alarm suddenly shrilled. She opened her eyes, and smiled as soon as she saw him.

'Hello.'

'Hello.' He kissed her softly. 'How does breakfast in bed sound?'

'It depends who's making it.'

'Me.'

She smiled again. 'Then it sounds perfect.'

He kissed her again, and scrambled out of bed. One thing, he promised himself, if they lived together, he'd insist on a king-size proper bed. Futons were just a bit too close to the floor for comfort.

He made breakfast quickly, and came back to bed with a tray of coffee, cereals and toast. Debra was sitting upright, the duvet barely covering her breasts, her nose in a book.

He coughed. 'A bit early to start working, isn't it?'

'Before breakfast, you mean?' She slipped a bookmark in between the pages. 'I suppose so.'

'Breakfast is served, Madam.' He gave her a small bow, put the tray down beside the bed, and climbed back in beside her.

'Mm. Perfect,' she said, sipping her coffee. 'That's one thing about you – you make excellent coffee.'

'Only one thing?'

She grinned. 'Stop fishing, Jacob Matthews.'

He pulled a face at her, and took a mouthful of his own coffee. 'Debra – about last night . . .'

'The big decision, you mean?'

He nodded. 'We've slept on it. How do you feel, this morning?'

She shrugged. 'Well, we could talk about it and think about it for months. There's only one real way to find out if we can live together – and that's to do it.'

'Renting's one thing; we're talking about buying a wreck and doing it up. That's a hell of a commitment – something we can't walk out of in a week's time, if one or the other of us changes our mind.'

'True.' Debra ate a piece of toast. 'You said yesterday, we've been together for long enough to know. Unless you've got a Jekyll and Hyde personality, and you've hidden half of it from me very successfully, well, I'm game.'

He grinned. 'You mean, you haven't worked out that I'm a secret axe-murderer?'

She clicked her fingers, bringing her hand across her body as she did so in a hammed-up gesture of disappointment. 'Damn. And I had it figured that you were a poisoner.'

He stroked her face. 'That's settled, then. Though I think we need another look at the house – a proper look, this time. Maybe I could ask Joe to come along, too, in case one of us misses something?'

'Fine. I'd like to meet him. And Adam.'

'I'd better warn you, the family's pretty close. Once they meet you, and they decide they like you, there's no escape.

And you'll be put through the babysitter test,' he said, only half joking.

'Not to mention my mother's vetting procedure. A tramp across the moors, then a test to see whether you drink proper tea or Southern muck . . .'

Jake took the mug from her hand, setting it back on the tray. 'What if we fail the tests?'

'We cheat, on the other one's behalf.'

He grinned. 'Sneaky.'

'But it'll get us what we want.' She ran her hands over his chest. 'Anyway, I can't see you failing.'

'Or you.'

'So it's settled, then.' She shifted so that she was half-kneeling over him. 'I talked Liv into letting us have the keys, tonight. You ask your brother to come and look at it, and if we still like the house, we'll go for it.'

'What if there are problems?'

'Then we wait for another house.' She rubbed her nose against his, and lowered herself so that his erect cock lay full-length along her quim. His eyes darkened, and he moistened his lower lip; Debra immediately took advantage of his position and began kissing him.

'I'm going to be late for work,' he said, when she took her mouth from his.

'You can work through your lunch-hour, to make up for it.'

He grinned. 'Debra Rowley, you wanton—' The rest of his sentence was lost in a sigh of pleasure as she curled her fingers round his cock, bringing it to her entrance and pushing down hard so that he sank into her.

She sat up properly, then, leaning back slightly to deepen the angle of his penetration, she slowly lifted and lowered herself onto him. As her excitement grew, her pace quickened; Jake caressed her breasts, loving the way they swelled under his fingers, the nipples becoming hard at his touch.

At last, she gave a cry, and Jake felt her internal muscles contracting hard around his cock, pushing him into his own release. He wrapped his arms round her as she sank back onto him, burying her face in his shoulder. This, he thought, was a moment he wished could last forever . . .

'Debra, these are my brothers – Joe and Adam. Joe, Adam – this is Debra Rowley.'

'Nice to meet you,' Joe said, taking her hand and squeezing it.

Adam went one better, kissing her hand. 'Hello, Debra.'

She smiled broadly at them. They were older versions of Jake, though Joe was greying at the temples and Adam's build was stockier. But they had the same smile as Jake, the same dancing dark eyes. She had a feeling that she was going to like them.

'Nice to meet you, too.'

'Jake tells us you want to buy this place,' Joe said.

'Together, yes.' She nodded. 'Provided there aren't any major problems.'

'There's only one way to find out.'

'Right.' She took the keys from her handbag, and opened the front door. 'This is it, anyway.'

Adam smiled at her. 'Give us half an hour, and we'll tell you the verdict.'

'Over a pint,' she insisted.

Joe smiled approvingly at her. 'You're on.'

Debra was on tenterhooks as Jake's brothers looked round the house. 'Supposing they hate it?' she whispered fiercely to Jake.

'It's our choice, not theirs.'

'Or if there's something wrong with it?'

'Then we find another house.' He stroked her cheek with the backs of his fingers. 'Stop worrying. Come on, let's have another look round.'

They wandered round together, hand in hand. The more Debra saw of the house, the more she wanted it. It was the perfect house; all it needed was a bit of work doing to it.

Eventually, Joe and Adam met them by the front door.

'Well?' Debra asked.

Joe kept his face deadpan. 'I thought you said we were going to discuss it over a pint?'

Adam judged him. 'Don't tease her, Joe.'

'It needs a few things doing to it – the wiring needs completely redoing, the plumbing had better be checked over, and a few of the floorboards need replacing – but it's structurally sound. No damp, only a tiny bit of woodworm, and no dry rot,' Joe said.

Debra hugged him in delight. 'That's brilliant!' She hugged Adam, too, and Jake coughed loudly. 'What?' she asked.

'Don't I get a hug, too?'

In reply, she gave him a playful cuff.

'What was that for?'

'Being cheeky,' she retorted, taking his hand. 'Come on. We're celebrating!'

Four

Debra stripped off the last piece of paper, and surveyed her section of the wall. 'Well, it doesn't look too bad.'

Jake came over to inspect it. 'Not bad, but not good enough though.'

'Why?'

'We'll have to skim the walls, if you want the top half painted, otherwise every little imperfection in the walls will show up as a shadow on the paint.'

'Oh.' She looked disappointed. 'Will it take long?'

He laughed. 'Don't be so impatient! We agreed to do this properly, didn't we?'

'Mm.' She sighed. 'Oh, well. Next wall.'

'Not until you've finished taking all the little bits of paper off that one.' Jake pointed out the tiny strips which Debra hadn't removed. 'And I mean *all* of them, sweetheart . . .'

A wet sponge hit him squarely in the face, covering him with a mixture of ancient paste and water; he wiped the mess from his skin, and dipped his own sponge into the bucket. 'Right. This is war!'

Debra ran from the room, shrieking; Jake followed, waving the sponge threateningly at her and dripping water everywhere.

'So this is what you call work, is it?' a voice asked, amused.

Jake and Debra stopped dead in their tracks, and turned round to see a man and a woman in the hallway.

'Jude!' Debra went over to her friend, and hugged her. 'Excuse the mess. We're stripping all the old paper off the walls – including this impossible layer of varnished paper which Mr Fussy says has to come off, too.'

Judith grinned. 'Don't worry about the mess. I know you're renovating. I'm just being incredibly nosy – from what you told me, the other day, I couldn't wait to see it!' She turned to Jake. 'Hello, you must be Jake.' She went over to him, and kissed him. 'I'm Judith – though everyone calls me Jude – and this is David.'

'Pleased to meet you.' Jake warmed to her infectious smile and decided immediately that he liked her. He turned to the quiet man who'd been hanging back behind the effervescent Judith, and hadn't even spoken to Debra. 'Hello, David.'

David simply nodded in acknowledgement.

Jake gave up, and turned back to Judith. 'Would you both like a coffee?'

'Love one. White, with half a spoon of sugar for me, please; David drinks his black, no sugar.'

'Rightio. I'll go and put the kettle on.'

'Is it instant coffee?' David asked.

Jake was surprised at the question. Considering the state of the house, wasn't it obvious that they didn't have a filter or a cafetière? 'Well, yes.'

'Then I'll have mine white, please.'

'We haven't got a fridge installed here, yet, so it's only powdered milk,' Jake warned him, feeling a certain malicious delight at the other man's grimace.

'That's fine,' Judith said, giving David a warning scowl. 'Caffeine's caffeine.'

'Come through,' Jake said, smiling at her. 'Do you want a look round before or after your coffee?'

'Before,' Judith said immediately. 'I've been dying to have a nose, ever since Deb told me that you'd bought the place – but she kept putting me off.'

'Well, looks a bit of a mess at the moment,' Jake told her. 'But we're getting there.'

'When you're not chasing each other with wet sponges.' Judith gave him a warm smile. Debra had told her that Jake was good-looking, but she hadn't expected him to be quite so handsome. She could see immediately why Debra had been so taken with him – and why she'd decided to move in with him after knowing him for such a short time. Jake was one of those people you just felt comfortable with, straight away.

'Well, this is going to be the front room.' Jake couldn't resist hamming it up – and making his accent very East End – because he knew that it would annoy the other man. Jake couldn't bear snobbery, and he had a fair idea that David looked down on him as a 'mere builder'. If that was what the man wanted, Jake thought, that was exactly what he'd get. 'We were thinking about doing it in woodchip – it looks quite classy, you know, once you've slapped a bit of emulsion on it. Make it a nice peach or pink, then some brass fittings and a proper chandelier, and Bob's yer uncle.'

Debra gave him a look of pure amazement: then, suddenly realising what Jake was up to, had to turn a giggle into a cough. 'All the dust, you know. Makes me cough,' she said, flushing and trying hard to stifle another giggle.

'And we'll eat, here, though I think Debsie wants to put her books everywhere,' Jake added, showing them through to the dining room. 'Still, we could always put the ones she doesn't use in the loft. I mean, you don't read all your books all the time, do you, babes?'

Debra dug her nails into her palm. Considering that Jake, if anything, had more books than she did, arranged alphabetically by author and then chronologically by work.

'And this is the kitchen. It's a bit poky, but once we've put some nice lino down and got some of those oak-effect cupboards up, it'll do. We'll probably have a built-in microwave so we can just get dinner from Sainsbury's and heat it up, without having to bother about pots and pans.'

David's face was showing more and more disgust, and it was all Jake could do not to laugh. 'Well, I'll switch the kettle on, then,' he said brightly. 'It'll be boiled by the time you've seen upstairs.'

'I'll lead the way,' Debra said hastily. 'Come on, David.'

Judith lingered behind, putting a hand on Jake's arm. 'Jake. I'm sorry about David. He – um – used to have a bit of a thing about Debra, when she was with Marcus. I think he was rather hoping that when they split up, he'd have a chance, but she turned him down.'

'And he feels that a lowly builder's got no business with a lecturer,' Jake added.

Judith flushed. 'Something like that.'

were dragged along to, or on the tube – or in the British Museum, our sticky fingers pressed to the manuscript room cases.'

'Maybe.' She reached up to kiss him. 'Anyway, I'm glad we did.'

'Me, too.'

'What I'm trying to say is – I think I love you, Jake.'

He rubbed the tip of his nose against hers. 'We'll have to agree to differ, there.'

'How?'

He smiled at the slight sharpness in her voice. 'Because, Debra Rowley, I *know* that I love you.'

'Shouldn't you be saying that by moonlight?' she teased, secure again.

He grinned. 'If you really want me to walk over to the curtains and open them, exposing you to the curious gaze of anyone on the top deck of a passing bus, just so I can tell you that I love you by moonlight . . .'

She laughed back. 'Point taken.'

He drew her hand down to his stiffening cock. 'I thought you'd never offer . . .'

Jake stood back and surveyed the finished bathroom. 'What do you think?' he asked Debra.

She peered over his shoulder. 'In a word – perfect. And that goes for the decor, as well as the fact that you found us an original bath.'

'Glad you approve.'

She slid her arms round his waist. 'I think we ought to christen the bath.'

'No worries.' Jake shrugged. 'Actually, I owe *you* an apology, for playing up to him. But I can't bear snobs.'

'God knows how you survived more than three years at Cambridge, then.'

Jake's eyes widened in surprise. 'Debra told you about that?'

'Mm. Though I haven't said anything to David about it.'

'And if you hadn't known?'

Judith smiled. 'Deb's been happier since she met you than I've ever known her. I couldn't care less whether you're a hard-up bin man—'

'Refuse disposal expert, *please*!' Jake teased.

'—or a managing director of some huge conglomerate, earning a couple of hundred grand a year.' Judith finished, laughing with him. 'Deb's my best friend, and if you treat her well, then nothing else matters.'

To her surprise, Jake hugged her. 'Thanks. I think we're going to be friends.'

'And David?'

'All I can say is that he must be incredible in bed,' Jake said drily.

'How do you mean?'

'Well, he doesn't have the sort of personality that someone like you would go for.'

'Now who's being quick to judge?'

Jake bowed. 'Oliver Mellors, at your service, ma'am.'

Jude couldn't help laughing. 'Oh, really!'

'Well.' Jake rolled his eyes. 'I don't know what you see in him.'

'For your information, he's just a friend.'

Jake grinned. 'So he's *not* good in bed, then.' He tipped his head to one side. 'What's his subject?'

'History.'

'Which period?'

'Tudor and Stuart. Though he likes to think himself an expert on other eras.'

'Roman?' Jake asked hopefully.

'No.' Judith had a good idea of what he had in mind. 'Jake, don't be mean.'

'Only if provoked,' he promised. 'Go and see the rest of the house; I'll bring coffee and biscuits through.'

'Thanks.'

Jake finished making the drinks, only just resisting the temptation to add four spoonfuls of sugar to David's coffee, and met them at the foot of the stairs with a tray of mugs and a tin of biscuits.

'I love the mermaid,' Judith said, stroking the carving.

'We're arguing over the name,' Debra said. 'Neither of us could remember what the Little Mermaid was called, so I want to call her Morvenna.'

'Morvenna?' Judith asked.

'Mm. It's from an old folk-tale. A Cornish fisherman rescues Morvenna the mermaid; then later, when his ship sinks, Morvenna rescues him. It's very sweet.'

'And what do you want to call her?' David asked, giving Jake a supercilious smile, and waiting for him to say 'Ariel, after the mermaid Daryl Hannah played in *Splash*.'

'Psyche.' Despite his promise to Judith, Jake couldn't help himself. 'I know she wasn't actually a nereid, but I like the story.'

David's eyes widened. 'A nereid?'

'Sea-nymph,' Jake translated with a grin. 'Nereids are the same as dryads, or hamadryads – but they're nymphs connected with water, not trees.' He nodded at the coffee tray. 'Anyway, drinkies.'

He deliberately didn't meet Debra's or Judith's eyes, knowing that he would have burst out laughing, and swept through into the sitting room, propping the tray on the rung of the step-ladder. 'Help yourself to biscuits.'

Judith rummaged in the tin. 'Chocolate hob-nobs. Yes!'

Debra grinned. 'Jake's addicted to them, too.'

'Yeah, well.' Jake shrugged. 'Sorry we don't have anything to sit on, but we don't want to move any furniture in here until we've finished decorating.'

'I don't blame you, Judith said. 'Otherwise Deb would just sit around reading obscure Victorian novels, while you do all the work.'

'And to think she gets paid for it. A career in reading,' Jake said wickedly. 'I dunno. I suppose that's what I pay my taxes for, keeping the education system going and letting students and lecturers sit around on their backsides, reading all day.'

David glared at him. 'Debra works very hard. So do Judith and I, for that matter.'

'Of course you do.' Jake sipped his coffee.

'Just because you can't see a tangible product, it—' David began, reddening.

Judith nudged him, cutting in. 'Calm down. Jake wasn't being rude. He was just teasing.'

'Hm.' David's eyes narrowed.

'All I'm saying,' Jake smiled sweetly, 'is that I'd rather read for pleasure.'

'And I just happen to get paid for doing something that gives me pleasure.' Debra gave him a sly look. 'Mind you, at least I don't show off by reading Plato in the original – and quoting it by the page.'

'Plato, in the original?' David frowned, not seeing where Debra was leading.

Judith couldn't resist it. 'Didn't I tell you that Jake has a First in Classics, from Cambridge?'

David stared at Jake in amazement. 'But I thought you were a builder!'

'I am.' Jake took another sip of coffee. 'Well, you know what they say – never judge a book by its cover.'

'Right.' David swallowed hard.

'No hard feelings.' Jake clapped him on the shoulder. 'I just wasn't cut out for the academic rat-race, so I joined the family firm. So I get the best of both worlds, really.' He smiled disarmingly. 'And I'm sorry about the coffee. We're not actually living here at the moment, so we haven't bothered with a fridge. Once the bathroom's sorted and the kitchen's done, we'll live here, and it'll all be sorted more quickly, and then we'll be able to give people decent coffee instead of this muck.'

'No problem.' David gamely swallowed a mouthful of coffee. 'It's quite nice, actually.'

'So what's the verdict, Jude?' Debra asked.

'One-all, I think.'

Debra laughed. 'I meant on the house, not male chest-beating and humble pie.'

'It's a wreck,' Judith said, 'but it's got potential. Lots of potential.'

'And lots of original features,' Jake added. 'Just as well we both like Victoriana.'

'You know, this man actually has a decent reproduction of *The Hyacinth Girl*,' Debra said.

'So that's why you're moving in with him – to get your hands on his pictures!' Judith quipped.

Debra grinned. 'That's part of it, yes.'

Jake took another mouthful of coffee, and grimaced. 'Actually, this stuff really is foul. If you don't mind drinking out of mugs, why don't I nip round to the shops and get us a bottle of wine? The local offie usually keeps a few bottles in the fridge.'

Judith smiled. 'Now you're talking. I'll go with you, if you like – we can get some nibbles, as well.'

Debra read Jake's smile accurately. 'No, I'm not going to finish this bloody wall before you get back. David and I will wash up the mugs.'

'See what I have to put up with? When we move in, she won't help me paint, in the evening. She'll claim that she has to write her book instead.'

'Because if I do help you, you'll start moaning that I haven't met the exacting standards of Matthews and Matthews, and do it again yourself anyway, so I might as well work on my book instead of wasting my time,' Debra retorted. She kissed him lightly. 'Go and get some goodies.'

'Yes, boss.'

'Tactfully done,' Judith said when they'd left the house.

'I thought David could do with a breathing-space. Give

him time to get used to the idea of me not having cement instead of brain-cells; and then maybe he'll be easier with me when we get back.' Jake gave her a sidelong look. 'I hope not all Debra's friends are going to take that attitude with me.'

Judith shook her head. 'I doubt it. There are one or two, but I think you could shut them up pretty easily. Your little homily on nymphs . . .' She chuckled. 'Mind you, David's a historian. The English lot would have known about nymphs, from poetry.'

'Hm. Well, let's forget it. Chardonnay okay with you?'

'Lovely,' Judith said. 'And tortilla chips?'

'And some of those gorgeous little garlicky things.'

She smiled at him. 'You know, Jake, you're right. We're going to get on famously.'

Later that evening, in his flat, Jake lay in bed beside Debra, one hand idly playing with her breasts. 'I really like your friend Judith,' he said.

'Mm. She can be a bit intimidating, but I liked her from the moment she came into the department. She was like a hurricane, full of energy and ideas – all the fusty Shakespeare scholars just couldn't cope with her!'

Jake grinned. 'I can imagine.'

'Anyway, she popped her head round my office door and suggested going to lunch together. We started chatting, and that was it! Over the past four years, she's become my best friend.'

'I know. She told me.'

'About when we met?'

'No, that you're her best friend. I had the subtle warning that I'm to treat you properly.'

Debra snorted. 'Jude, subtle? I think not!'

'Well. I like her, anyway.'

'I knew you'd get on.' She smiled at him. 'What about David?'

'No comment.'

'He's all right, really.'

'Underneath the rampant intellectual snobbery, you mean?'

Debra turned to face him. 'And who played on it by saying that he was going to put up woodchip paper? I'm surprised you didn't suggest one of those doorbells which play fifty tunes!'

Jake laughed. 'I would have done, if I'd thought of it!'

'Jake, he's okay, at heart.'

He gave a noncommittal murmur. 'Mm. Anyway, let's shut up about him.'

'Did you have something in mind?'

His other hand travelled up her thigh. 'Maybe.'

'Such as?' She turned over luxuriously, widening the gap between her thighs as he stroked her skin.

'Talking about what we're really going to do with the house.'

'Well, we've had all the rewiring done. Once we've sorted the kitchen and bathroom, we can move in and finish all the rest of the decorating. Say, the sitting room, first, then our bedroom, then the dining room, the hall, and finally the spare room.'

'What about flooring?' Jake asked.

'I'd like pamments in the hall.'

'Or black and white chequers. Period, of course. I can probably find some reclaimed tiles.'

She nodded. 'Polished floorboards in the dining room and the sitting room, with some big rugs.'

'Once we've replaced the rotten boards.'

'So that's sorted, then.' She wriggled as his fingers came into contact with her quim, tracing the contours of her labia. 'Was that all you wanted to talk about?'

He smiled. 'Who said I had just talking in mind?' He slid one finger into her quim. Debra sighed, and closed her eyes; he began to move his hand back and forth. He shifted to give himself better access, then brought his other hand round to tease her clitoris. A second finger joined the first, pistoning in and out of her while he rubbed her clitoris, first back and forth and side to side, then in a figure of eight motion.

Debra tipped her head back against the pillows, moaning softly with pleasure; her hands came up to stroke her breasts, playing with her erect nipples. Jake watched her, abandoned to pleasure, and thought that he'd never seen her look so beautiful. Unable to resist, he bent his head, rubbing his face against her midriff and inhaling her scent.

'Oh, yes,' she said softly, bringing her hands up to tangle in his hair, then drawing his head down towards her lap.

He grinned. 'Greedy girl.'

'Please?' she asked, her voice husky.

'Seeing as you ask so nicely . . .' He rubbed his cheeks against her thighs, loving the softness of her skin against his face and the musky scent of her sex, only inches away from his nose.

'Jake, don't tease,' she said plaintively.

'Okay, okay.' He drew his tongue down her satiny cleft. She tasted sweet-salt, of honey and sea-shore; it was a taste he was becoming addicted to. His tongue flickered against the hard bud of her clitoris, and Debra writhed beneath him, tipping her pelvis to give him greater access. His hands grasped her bottom, supporting her weight as he sucked and kissed her sex-flesh.

He heard her cry out, and then her sex pulsed beneath his mouth, her internal muscles contracting sharply. He waited until the first shocks of orgasm had died down, then dropped a gentle kiss on her labia, and kissed his way back up over her abdomen, still holding her thighs apart with one hand.

'Mm,' she said, half-opening her eyes and stretching languorously. 'Second helpings?'

'Different course,' he said with a grin, taking her hand and curling it round his cock.

'Sounds good to me.' She positioned him at the entrance to her quim, then pushed upwards before crossing her ankles around his waist, pulling him into her.

He smiled against her shoulder, and began to move slowly, pulling almost completely out of her, and then sliding back into her, filling her to the hilt. Her hands came up round his neck to tangle in his hair, and she kissed him, nibbling at his lower lip until he opened his mouth under hers, letting her explore his mouth properly.

'I love the way you feel inside me,' she whispered, pulling her mouth away from his again. 'So fuck me to paradise and back.'

Her words made the last vestiges of his control snap, and he began to thrust harder. Debra thrust up to meet him, and their bodies slammed together. The only sounds he could hear were their ragged breathing and the soft wet sound of his cock sliding in and out of her.

Debra began to use her internal muscles, gripping at the head of his penis as he withdrew, then opening herself wide as he pushed back into her. His thrusts grew deeper, filling her to the hilt, and she cried out as orgasm flooded through her, making her sexual muscles clutch round him and tipping him into his own release.

Jake didn't withdraw immediately, but stayed inside her, supporting his weight on his elbows and rubbing his cheek affectionately against hers. When he finally slipped from her, he lay on his back and pulled her into the curve of his body, linking his hands round her waist. Her head rested comfortably on his shoulder, one arm curved round his midriff.

'I'm glad you played hooky from work, that time,' she said.

'Hm?'

'Well, if you hadn't, we'd never have met.'

'You reckon? Supposing you'd bought the house on your own – you could have decorated it on your own, but you'd have needed a builder to sort out some of the heavy work. So you might have chosen our firm.'

'Or one of the hundreds of others in London. Or even a friend of a friend, cash in hand.'

He stroked her face. 'Don't you believe in Fate?'

'I don't know,' she said. 'Do you?'

'I don't know either, to be honest. But I think we were meant to meet. If it hadn't been at the bookshop, it would have been somewhere else. A friend of a friend's party we

He shook his head. 'Not yet. Apart from the fact that I want to do a bit more work, first – and I'm so grubby that the water would be filthy within five seconds – the paint has to dry before we have a bath in here.'

'So you're turning me down, then?' She slid one hand to his groin, cupping his genitals through his worn denims. She smiled to herself as she felt his cock stiffen instantly.

'Yes, I am – for the next couple of hours, that is,' he said, gently removing her hand from his body and twisting round so that he could kiss the tip of her nose, to take the sting from his action. 'If you keep distracting me, we'll still be living in a wreck in five years' time!'

'Exaggeration. Tut, tut.'

'Hyperbole, you mean.' He stuck his tongue out at her.

She started laughing. 'Oh, for goodness' sake! You're such a purist!'

'But not a puritan.'

'You just turned me down.'

He kissed her lightly. 'Not flat, though. Give me a couple of hours' more work.'

'I might not be in the mood, then.'

He grinned. 'Then I'll seduce you.'

'How – by showing me your doodle?'

'Hm?' Jake was lost.

'*My Secret Life*,' she explained. 'Walter – he's the "author" – thinks that any woman will fall for him, as long as he "talks bawdily" to her and shows her his "doodle" – that is, his cock.'

Jake burst out laughing. 'No!'

Debra rolled her eyes. 'Whoever said that Angel Clare

was the most tedious man in fiction had obviously never read this one – and there are eleven volumes of the stuff!'

'How far have you got?'

'Halfway through volume two.' She grimaced. 'I don't think I'll be going much further, somehow. It's an interesting social comment, but I don't find it particularly erotic reading about a man whinging because he can't pull his foreskin back and keeps getting the clap from his "gay ladies". And it's always the same old story – how he catches a glimpse of his mother's servant's thigh, then gets her to let him feel her, shows her his cock, and fucks her. He doesn't even vary his language, to make it interesting!'

'Right.' Jake rubbed his cheek against hers. 'Is there a female equivalent?'

'Not that I've found.' She was thoughtful. 'I've read a diary of a Victorian parson's daughter – she has to choose between two men – and there are a few things hinted. She says "we had fun upstairs", which could mean just about anything, but there's no real equivalent to Walter's diary. I mean, there are a few passages in the Brontës and Eliot – and, of course, there's *Goblin Market* – but other than that, women novelists and poets just weren't supposed to be interested in sex. In any Victorian novel, you'll find that if the heroine is sexually attracted to some-one, she either marries him, or she dies at the end of the novel. Maggie Tulliver, Tess of the D'Urbavilles, Catherine Earnshaw—' She stopped, flushing. 'Sorry. I'm being a boring academic.'

'No, you're not.' He kissed her. 'Come and talk to me while I finish off that bit of plastering in the sitting room.

You'll still be working, because you'll be talking to me about your book.'

'Are you sure you won't find it boring?' she asked.

'Absolutely.' He grinned. 'If you want boring, I could talk to you for *hours* about the correct consistency of plaster.'

She laughed, and they went downstairs, hand in hand.

'So why,' Jake said, 'are Victorian women not supposed to be interested in sex?'

'That's just how it was. The "angel in the house" – that was how women were idealised. Mind you, that was only in public.'

'And in private?' Jake carefully began to plaster the wall.

'I suppose it's every academic's favourite fantasy. You're working in the British Library – or some other collection – and you find a book which hasn't been opened for a hundred years. And inside, there's a letter or a part of a diary . . .' She smiled. 'I've probably got more chance of walking on the moon or winning the lottery!'

'Mm. All the other scholars have probably beaten you to it. But there are always antique sales, and in a secret drawer of a desk, there's a small bundle of paper in tiny script . . .'

She laughed. 'I wish! Mind you, there might be a trunk in the corner of our attic.'

'But it won't be Victorian, will it? If the old lady who owned this house was ninety-odd when she died, she still wouldn't have been alive when Victoria was on the throne, let alone been a sixteen-year-old nymphet.'

'True. Edwardian, at best. And that assumes that she could read and write.'

'And had the courage to write down her sexual fantasies.'

Jake gave her a sidelong glance. 'How about faking it? If we find the right sort of paper, age it a bit, and you can copy Victorian script . . .'

She laughed. 'Oh, Jake!'

'There must have been a female equivalent to "doodle".'

'There was. Motte. Which was the female pudenda – or a lower-class prostitute.'

'Exactly. So you could have *My Secret Motte – by Walterina*.'

Debra couldn't help giggling. 'You're completely mad!'

'Well.' He was unabashed. 'Or maybe you could find the sexy novel that Jane Austen wrote in secret.'

She pulled a face. 'I'm not an Austen fan.'

'One of the Brontës, then. Or Eliot. She wrote a science-fiction one – so why not a sexy one?'

Debra frowned. How come you know so much about English literature, when you did a classics degree?'

'I did *Middlemarch* for A-level,' he retorted. 'One of my girlfriends at college had her complete works, and I'm as nosy as you are when it comes to other people's bookshelves.'

'Right.'

'So, given that you know Victorian style like the back of your hand, you could write Emily Brontë's or George Eliot's lost erotic novel . . .'

Debra thought about it. 'It's a nice theory.'

'But you're not convinced?'

Debra shook her head. 'The erotic writers were men, writing for men. You can tell by the language and structure of their books. And I'm going to shut up, now, because I'm going to get really boring on the subject!'

'Okay. That gives you a choice: go away and work on your book, or talk to me about something else.'

'The house,' Debra said. 'How long do you think it'll take us to finish it?'

'Well, the plaster needs a couple of weeks to dry before we paint it. Then there are the floorboards – you can say at least three days for each room, to sand them down and seal them and let the varnish dry. Then we have the windows and the ceilings. And then, the garden . . .' Jake shrugged. 'So it'll be the end of the summer.' He smiled at her. 'It depends on how you spend your three months off. If you spend it all in the British Library, it'll take ages; if you spend some of it painting . . .'

She laughed. 'Slave-driver.'

'Well. Or we could hold a painting-party instead of a house-warming.'

She shook her head. 'I want it to be all our own work.'

'Now who's being a slave-driver? he teased.

Five

'Our own place,' Debra said happily.

'Mostly a wreck, still,' Jake said, 'but yes, our own place.' He looked at her. 'It's not a very nice place for you to work in.'

She smiled. 'The book can wait for a bit. Until we've done a couple more rooms, anyway.'

'Then,' he said firmly, 'you'll work on it properly, and leave me to do the physical stuff.'

'Bully,' she said affectionately.

'So now what?'

She raised her eyebrows. 'Do you remember when we looked round the house for the first time?'

He caught her train of thought. 'And I made love to you in the hall?'

'Mm.' She smiled. 'You said it was a good way to christen the house. And how it's ours, and we're finally moving in . . .'

'It's not finished yet, though.'

Debra grinned. 'We'll just have another "christening", when it is!'

'Right.' Jake caught her round the waist, pulling her to

him and kissing her. 'Well, seeing as you chucked out all the carpets and curtains—'

'Well, they were in a state, and we're having varnished floors in any case,' Debra defended herself.

'—we'll either have to pin a sheet up at the window of our bedroom, or christen the kitchen or the bathroom,' he said, ignoring her comment.

'How about all three?' Debra tempted.

He laughed. 'You have a high opinion of my stamina! Tell you what – why don't we pin a duvet cover up at the window, and take a bottle of something nice to bed?'

'Something nice?'

'Go and have a look in the fridge.'

Debra went into the kitchen, and came back with a bottle of champagne. 'When did you buy this?'

'This afternoon, when I went to get some more paint. You obviously didn't notice.'

'I was busy stripping paper!'

'I know.' He kissed the tip of her nose. 'So what do you think?'

'I think it's one of the best ideas you've had today.' She took his hand, and led him upstairs. 'You can sort the window,' she said, 'while I do the futon.'

'As soon as our bedroom's decorated,' he warned, 'we're having a proper bed.'

'Futons are good for your back.'

'My bones are older than yours. Anyway, I thought we'd agreed on a king-size pine bed?'

'With lots of pillows. And then we can spend the whole of Sundays in bed, curled up with the papers or a good book.'

Jake cleared his throat. 'Is that all?'

She gave him an over-the-top pout. 'No. Good coffee, as well, made freshly every half an hour or so.'

'Right!' Jake took the bottle from her hand, stood it on the floor, and started tickling her.

'All right, all right!' she said, squirming and laughing. 'I meant having sex as well. Lots of sex. In between reading the papers and drinking good coffee. Oh, and having bacon and avocado sarnies for lunch.'

'And who's going to make the coffee and the sarnies?' he asked, his tone mock-threatening as he stopped tickling her, but kept his hands only millimetres away from her ribs.

'We'll take it in turns.'

He smiled, and stooped to kiss her. 'Correct answer. I'll do the window, then.'

'Right.' Debra deftly sorted out the futon, and stood watching Jake put an old duvet cover across the window, fastening it with drawing pins. 'Our neighbours are going to think that we're completely mad,' she said, laughing.

'Unlike our friends, who *know* that we are!' He smiled at her. 'You know what we forgot. Glasses.'

'We can swig it from the bottle. Okay, it's common, but who cares?' Debra gave him a smile which intrigued him and made him slightly suspicious at the same time. She was obviously planning something – but what? 'Come to bed,' she said.

'I'll open the champagne, first.' He swiftly removed the foil from the neck of the bottle, undid the small cage, and removed the cork without spilling a drop.

'Show-off,' she teased.

He grinned, placing the bottle on the floor next to the futon. 'There's an art to it. You twist the bottle, not the cork.'

'I wonder what other arts you've mastered?' she teased.

'How about the *Ars Amatoria*?'

She rolled her eyes. 'That's unfair. You know my Latin's not up to your standard. Or any standard, for that matter.'

'Maybe I can teach you.'

Debra shook her head. 'I don't think so.'

'Mm. You'd run the risk of being teacher's pet.'

'More like the teacher would have his hand in my knickers when he was supposed to be teaching me the finer points of Latin grammar. Or translating,' she added pointedly.

'All right. *Ars Amatoria* is Ovid. The art of love,' Jake said with a grin. 'And now who's being boring?'

She nodded. 'You are. Very. And there's only one way to make amends.'

'Mm.' He stretched his arms out. 'I'm completely in your hands. Do with me what you will.'

'That,' she said, that same intriguing and suspect smile on her face, 'is an offer I'm certainly not going to refuse.' She unbuttoned his shirt, stroking his hard pectoral muscles and slipping the garment from his shoulders. Jake stood perfectly still, but his breathing grew slightly ragged when she unbuckled his belt, then slid the zip of his jeans downwards.

Debra eased the material over his hips, then helped him to wriggle out of his clothing. When he was standing in just a pair of navy silk boxer shorts, she surveyed him.

'What?'

'Very, very nice,' she purred.

He pouted at her. 'I'm still partially dressed.'

'Not for long.' She curled her hand round his erection, rubbing the silk of his boxer shorts against him. 'Mm. You feel as nice as you look, too.'

'I'm glad I pass muster.'

'Oh, yes.' Debra picked up the champagne, took a swig, and handed the bottle to him. He did the same, and handed it back to her.

'Like you said, it's very common, drinking out of bottles.'

She grinned. 'So?'

He spread his hands. 'You tell me.'

She hooked her thumbs into the sides of his boxer shorts, and slowly drew them down. He made his cock twitch slightly at her, making her smile; she patted the futon. 'Bed.'

'Aren't you joining me?'

'Not fully clothed, no.' She rolled her eyes. 'I thought you said you were completely at my disposal?'

'I am.'

'Then get on the bed.'

'Any particular position, Mistress?'

She grinned. 'There's an answer to that! Luckily for you, I'm not into CP . . .'

He grinned back, and got onto the bed, lying on his stomach with his legs kicked back, his heels virtually on his buttocks, and propped his chin up on his hands so that he could watch her.

Debra undressed slowly, peeling off her T-shirt and dropping it on the floor. Her leggings followed suit; as usual, in the summer weather, she was barefoot. Jake looked at her navy lace bra and matching knickers with interest. Was she planning to stay semi-dressed when she came to bed with him, or was she going to strip totally?

Almost as if he'd spoken the question aloud, Debra smiled at him, then reached behind her back to unclasp her bra. She let it fall to the floor, and sashayed out of her knickers, kicking them to one side.

'Roll over,' she said softly.

Jake moved swiftly so that he was lying on his back, his head resting against the pillows.

'Good.' She smiled at him, and came to kneel next to him on the futon, picking up the champagne again. 'Now. I christen this house, and those who live in her – may we be happy here.'

'May we be happy here,' Jake echoed.

Debra took a swig of champagne from the bottle, then bent her head, sliding his cock quickly into her mouth so that she didn't spill the wine. She swooshed the wine round his cock, sucking hard at the same time; Jake groaned with pleasure. Debra released his cock, swallowed the champagne, and took a fresh swig, putting his cock back into her mouth and letting the bubbles burst against the sensitive skin of his glans.

She repeated the action twice more, chasing the bubbles with her tongue; then, finally, she soothed his skin with her tongue-tip, licking over his glans and the less sensitive skin of his shaft, before taking him fully into her mouth and sucking.

Her thumb and forefinger ringed the base of his shaft; as she lowered her mouth, she raised her hand, and as she raised her mouth again, she drew her hand back down to the root of his cock, increasing the pleasure for him.

At last, Jake cried out, the salty taste of his semen replacing the champagne in her mouth. She swallowed every last drop, then released his cock, taking another swig of champagne to rinse out her mouth. 'Happy days,' she said softly.

'That was one hell of a christening,' he said, his pupils still dilated. 'I wasn't expecting that.'

She couldn't help asking. 'Nice?'

'Very nice.' He sat up and kissed her lingeringly. 'Thank you. Now, your turn, I believe?'

'Mm.' She smiled at him. 'What did you have in mind?'

'Something like this.' He caught her round the waist and pulled her on top of him, then gently moved her so that she was kneeling astride his shoulders. Debra placed her palms flat against the wall for support, and Jake gave her a lazy smile before stretching his tongue out and drawing it along her satiny cleft.

'Mm,' she said, her eyes closing.

Jake smiled again, and began to lick her in earnest, loving the musky scent of her arousal and the way she tasted.

'In Victorian times,' she informed him, her voice catching slightly as he made the tip of his tongue into a hard point and flicked it rapidly across her clitoris, 'this was the height of perversion. It was called the "French Perversion", actually. Or *cunnilictus*.'

Jake said nothing, but varied the pressure and pace of his tongue against her sex-flesh, pushing her to the height of arousal. Debra, who had been about to continue her lecture on Victorian sensuality, gasped as orgasm suddenly flooded through her, her internal muscles contracting sharply under his mouth.

He continued to nuzzle her throughout the small aftershocks, then gently manipulated her down his body until she was half-kneeling, half-lying astride him. Gently, he eased one hand between them positioning the tip of his cock at her entrance; Debra sank down onto the rigid shaft.

'Mm,' she said, flexing her quim round him. 'I love the way you feel inside me.'

Jake gave her an impish grin. 'Funny, that. So do I . . .' He let her set the pace, raising and lowering herself on him; he loved watching the way she moved over him. And the way she felt: her vaginal walls like warm liquid velvet around his cock, her skin as smooth as alabaster under his fingertips as he stroked her breasts, then her puckered, erect nipples in sharp contrast to her soft flesh.

'You're so beautiful,' he said softly, cupping her breasts with both hands and raising his upper body slightly so that he could kiss them. 'I love you. Everything about you from the way you walk to the way you smell to the way your quim ripples around me.'

Debra gently pushed him back against the bed, leaning down to kiss him. 'You, too,' she told him quietly.

'Except that *I* don't ripple round you.'

'You know what I mean.'

He smiled up at her, inviting her to tell him more, and she laughed. 'Okay. I love the way your balls slap against me, and then lift and tighten just before you come: and the way your cock throbs, deep inside me.' She rubbed her nose against his. 'Happy?'

'Very.'

'Me, too.'

'Tut, tut – from an English graduate, too.'

'Hm?' Debra, who was concentrating more on the sensations rippling through her body, looked at him, her eyes slightly unfocused.

'Shouldn't that be "I, too"?' Jake teased.

'How you can be so bloody pedantic when we're both on the point of coming is beyond me,' she said, stroking his face, then gave a soft husky murmur as she reached orgasm again.

Jake's eyes, too, became unfocused, and he held her tight as his seed pumped into her.

Jake ran the bath, humming, and poured a liberal quantity of Debra's favourite seaweed mineral bath-oil into the water. He tested it, added a little more hot water, and wrapped a towel round his waist before padding down the stairs. Debra was working at the computer in the sitting room, cross-referencing material for her book. He slid his hands across her eyes.

'Come on, sweetheart. Time to stop,' he said, licking her earlobe.

'Five more minutes,' she pleaded.

'Nope. You lose all concept of time when you're working. Jude's coming over for dinner, shortly, and we both need a bath.'

'In other words, you want some attention.'

'Considering that I've spent all afternoon replastering our bedroom – yes.'

She sighed, pulling his hands away from her eyes. 'Just one more paragraph?'

'Absolutely not.'

'Bully.' She saved the file, then closed the programs before switching off her computer. 'Do you want the first bath?'

He shook his head. 'What I want is for you to wash my back.'

'Oh yes?'

'Yes.' He took her hand, and led her upstairs. When they reached the bathroom, he pulled off his towel, and struck a pose for her.

Debra burst out laughing. 'Oh, really!'

He grinned, and stepped into the bath. He held up the bar of soap, and waved it invitingly at her. Debra rolled her eyes, and walked over to the side of the bath, kneeling down. She rolled her sleeves up, flexing her hands, and took the soap form him.

'Your back,' she said.

He smiled, and leaned forward. She worked the soap into a lather, and scrubbed his back, sluicing the suds off his skin; Jake closed his eyes in bliss as her hands worked up and down his back, kneading out the tense knots caused by the plastering. He gave a small sigh of pleasure as she finished, and leaned back against the tub. 'Is that all?' he asked.

'What do you want me to do?'

'How about washing the rest of me?'

She grinned, noticing the erect state of his cock. 'Did you have in mind a particular piece of your body, by some chance?'

'How did you guess?' he mocked.

'Hm.' She picked up the soap again, lathering her hands, and grasped his cock with her left hand. Her fingers were slippery against his skin, and moved easily up and down his shaft as she began to masturbate him. As she manipulated his foreskin, he gave a small moan of pleasure, and his fingers gripped the side of the bath.

Smiling, Debra lathered her hands again, this time working on his cock with her right hand while her left hand fondled his testicles. As Jake's breathing grew harsher, she let her hand drift slightly lower, her fingers stroking the length of his perineum. Gently, she probed the puckered rosy hole beneath her fingertips, massaging it until his balls lifted and tightened.

Jake's legs were splayed, pushing out at the constriction of the bath; still, Debra worked him with her hand, prolonging his pleasure. With a gasp, he came, a creamy jet of fluid spraying the surface of the water. She bent to kiss the end of his cock, then sat back on her haunches. 'Well?'

'Rather good. Nine out of ten.' His cock twitched at her. 'From both of us, that is,' he added, laughing.

She grinned. 'I suppose you deserved it. You've been working hard, all afternoon.'

'So have you,' he pointed out. He eyed her breasts through her thin shirt. 'I really think you ought to join me.'

'Lecher.'

'Jude won't be here for *ages*. We've plenty of time.'

'Oh yes? And who was it who wouldn't let me have just another five minutes on my book?'

'That's different.' He blew her a kiss. 'You know, you

were absolutely right about this house. There is something about it.'

'Oh?'

'Mm. It makes me randy.'

'That,' she said, taking off her shirt, 'is just your rampant libido talking.'

'Maybe.' He smiled at her. 'In the meantime, this water's getting cold. Why don't you undress and join me, while it's still tolerably warm?'

She smiled, and unzipped her jeans, easing the soft faded denim over her thighs. She stepped deftly out of them, kicking the material to one side, then tossed back her hair and reached back to unclasp her bra. She covered her breasts with one arm while she removed the lacy garment, then splayed her fingers like a fan so that one erect rosy nipple peeped out. Slowly, she lowered her arm again, giving him full view of her generous breasts, then removed her knickers. 'Well?'

He clapped. '*Bellissima*.'

'Ahem.' She coughed, and nodded at the taps.

He groaned. 'Why do I *always* have to have the tap end?'

'Because you're a gentleman.'

'Don't you believe it.' He remained where he was, leaning back against the roll-top bath.

'Jake . . .'

'Come and sit with your back to me. That way, neither of us has to sit with our back to the taps,' he suggested.

'Hm.' She climbed into the bath and sat down, leaning back against him; he rubbed his cheek against her shoulder, wrapping his arms round her body. 'So how's the book going?' he asked.

'Quite well.'

'Good.' He paused. 'Sitting hunched over a computer . . . your muscles are probably really tight.'

'Probably,' she agreed.

He kissed the nape of her neck, sliding his hands back along her ribcage before cupping her breasts, his thumbs and fingers teasing her nipples into hardness.

She smiled. 'So *that's* what you call a neck massage, is it?'

'Oh yes. I forgot.' He released her, grabbing the soap and lathering his hands. 'Put your head forward a bit, then.'

She did as he asked, and he soaped her shoulders, his fingers working along her muscles and loosening them. He worked down her spine, playing along the vertebrae and letting his fingers splay across her back. Each movement up or down her back brought his fingers closer to her breasts: but he never quite touched her there. He remained tantalisingly close, with the intention of arousing her fully before working on her erogenous zones.

The movement of his fingers made her feel deliciously languorous; at the same time, she wanted a more intimate caress. Eventually, she straightened up, leaning back against him, and took his hands, placing the heels of his palms on her ribcage and his fingers on her breasts. Jake took the hint, and began to stroke the soft undersides of her breasts in the way she liked best.

He buried his mouth in the corner between her neck and shoulder, taking tiny nibbles at the skin which made her shiver. She could feel the hardness of his cock thrusting between them, the shaft engorged and erect, and she longed to feel it pushing inside her, blindly exploring her.

She reached one hand between them, caressing his cock. 'Jake . . .'

'Mm?' He licked her shoulder.

She flushed. 'You don't feel like reading my mind, do you?'

'Nope. If you want something, you have to tell me exactly what you have in mind.'

'I'm feeling really randy.'

'I wondered about that.' He nibbled her earlobe. 'Tell me – when you're looking at one of the steamier passages for your book, does it turn you on?'

'Sometimes,' she admitted.

'So while I'm slaving away on the house, you're sitting at your computer, typing one-handedly?'

She flushed. 'No!'

'What about if you'd closed the curtains – to stop reflections on your screen, of course?'

'Maybe,' she muttered.

'Hm. So you do touch yourself, when you're working.' He continued stroking her breasts. 'You could always come up and see me about it, you know, when you're feeling particularly randy, and you want my cock inside you. All you have to do is take the brush or trowel out of my hand . . .'

She reached behind her, stroking his cock. 'The thing is, you're not always very good about taking hints.'

'Oh?'

'I just told you that I'm feeling randy, and all you're doing is wittering on at me.'

'Indeed.' He stood up. 'And what you want is action, is it?'

'Mm.'

He climbed out of the bath, then lifted her out, wrapping her in a towel. 'What are you planning?' she asked suspiciously.

'The lady said I wittered on. Obviously she thinks it's time for action,' he told her, his eyes glittering with a teasing light. 'So . . .' He patted her skin almost dry with a towel, then spread another one on the chequered lino. He guided her down to her knees on the dry towel, then placed her hands on the side of the bath before kneeling behind her.

Debra shivered in anticipation as he kissed down the length of her spine, stroking her buttocks; she spread her thighs as his mouth drifted southwards, and sighed in delight as he drew his tongue along the silky furrow of her quim. She leaned forward, resting her head on her hands, and Jake shifted forward, his cock easing gently into her hot, moist tunnel.

'Oh,' she breathed softly, closing her eyes.

Jake slid his hands over her hips, and began to thrust in earnest, moving his body in small circles to increase the friction. Each time he drove into her, Debra gave a small sigh of pleasure, the sound growing louder as her arousal increased. She could feel the familiar rolling waves of warmth starting in the soles of her feet, then moving up her calves. As Jake slid one hand round to start playing with her clitoris, she came loudly, her internal muscles spasming wildly.

He continued thrusting into the small aftershocks of her orgasm, not letting her stop, and Debra found the waves of pleasure building again into a climax that seemed to last for hours, making her whole body quiver with ecstasy. She could feel his cock throbbing, and his seed pumping into her; she groaned aloud, the sound echoing through the bathroom.

Jake kissed the nape of her neck, and withdrew. 'Good acoustics, too,' he remarked.

Debra smiled, standing up and turning round to kiss him. 'Mm, not bad.'

'I would love to take you to bed, right now,' he said softly, 'but it wouldn't be fair to Jude. Particularly as I haven't actually made dinner yet.'

'Mm.' She curled her fingers round his cock. 'I need another bath now. And so do you.'

He smiled and got back into the bath, sluicing himself down, then lithely climbing out again. 'That's me done.' He kissed her. 'See you downstairs.'

'Huh. Talk about double standard,' Debra teased.

'How do you mean?'

'It's all right for you to wheedle me into making love to you, but when I try it . . .'

He grinned. 'Just keeping you on your toes – and exercising a gentleman's right to say no!' He gave her a sidelong look. 'I could pander to your whims, if you really want me to, but then you'll have to explain to Jude how come we're not feeding her.'

Debra rolled her eyes. 'Okay, you win.'

'But later,' he promised, his voice husky. 'I'll be entirely at your disposal.'

'It's brilliant,' Judith said, smiling. 'You've worked really hard on it – I can't believe how quickly you've done all this!'

'Jake's been playing hooky at lunchtimes,' Debra told her friend. 'Not to mention doing a couple of hours at night, and all weekends – I don't even get a lie-in, nowadays!' She pulled a face.

'Do I or do I not bring you coffee in bed?' Jake asked.

'Yes, but you always bring a paintbrush or something with it!'

He grinned. 'Just to get you in the mood.'

'You've done wonders with the place,' Judith said. 'If I hadn't seen it when you first bought it, I'd never have believed what a mess it was.'

'There's still a long way to go,' Jake said. 'I mean, now that the bathroom and kitchen are finished, and we've done our bedroom and the sitting room, it's becoming a bit more comfortable, and it's nicer to have friends round. But there's still the dining room, the spare room and the hall to do. Still, we'll get there.'

'I love it. If you ever decide to move, I want first refusal on this place.'

'Of course,' Debra said, 'but I think you'll have to wait until hell freezes over before I give up this house.'

Jake grinned. 'And that goes for me, as well. I've done it once, but doing up wrecks to sell them, and then moving to the next old dilapidated house to start again . . . I know people who do that, and I don't want to spend the rest of my life like that.'

'Neither do I,' Debra said. 'So it looks like we'll be staying put.'

'Do you know anything of the history of this place?' Judith asked.

Debra wrinkled her nose. 'It was owned by a little old lady who lived here for eighty-odd years, and it was built in 1870. That's about all I know.'

'I wonder who lived here before then?' Judith sipped her wine.

'We could always start researching it, once Debra's finished her book,' Jake suggested.

'Mm. It might be connected, though,' Debra said thoughtfully. 'I've just been reading about the publishers of the day – a few of them lived in Islington. One of them might even have owned this place. Or one of the type-setters.'

'You never know. I was hoping for a secret hoard of Victorian sovereigns in the attic, and Debra was hoping for an erotic diary or some letters,' Jake said.

'Every academic's favourite dream,' Judith agreed. 'I was so sick when that chap at Oxford found a forgotten Shakespearean sonnet! I suppose we all want it to be us. Not for the fame, or even the fortune – just to be the first to find it and read it, and to know you've seen something that's been lost for years and years and years.'

'Mm. Though all we found in our attic,' Jake said ruefully, 'was a pile of dust. There wasn't even a sign of an ancient newspaper!'

'Never mind. Maybe the next house?'

Debra laughed. 'Nice try, Jude. I can't see us moving, though.'

Judith grinned, and took a sip of wine. 'It was worth a try.' She gave Jake a sidelong look. 'Deb tells me that you're cooking dinner, tonight.'

'Yes.'

She coughed delicately. 'Is it something that takes hours and hours?'

Jake rolled his eyes. 'Okay, okay, I can take a hint. It's nothing too exciting – just lasagne, salad and garlic bread. I've been busy plastering, so I haven't had time to do the proper gourmet job for you.'

'As long as it's pasta and not plaster for dinner, I don't mind.'

He laughed. 'Now *there's* an idea . . .'

'Jacob Matthews, behave yourself,' Debra admonished him, laughing. 'Don't ever dare him to do anything, Jude. He has this incredibly warped sense of humour.'

'Moi?' He fluttered his eyelashes at them. 'I'll go and dress the salad, and put the garlic bread in. In the meantime, if you two want to sort the table out?'

'Okay.' Debra blew him a kiss, and she and Judith moved the small table from the side of the room to the centre. Debra went into the kitchen to fetch the cutlery, lingering just long enough to snatch a kiss from Jake, and returned to Judith.

'I really like him,' Judith said. 'Does he have a brother, by any chance?'

'Two. But they're both very happily married, with children.'

'Pity.' Judith took a sip of wine. 'How about a clone?'

'Don't look at me. I do a Mickey Mouse arts subject. I'm not a mad scientist.'

'Well, if you ever get bored with him . . .' Judith smiled at her. 'Actually, it's nice to see you looking so happy. I can't imagine Marcus ever doing up a house for you – even if he was capable of doing it in the first place, he'd be too selfish to do what you wanted.'

'I know. Just promise you'll slap me if I get too smug about it.'

Judith grinned. 'With pleasure!'

Six

Jake lifted the floorboards, throwing the rotten ones to one side and checking the others to see if the rot had spread. The damage didn't seem too bad, but he decided to check underneath the other floorboards, just to make sure. He lay flat next to the hole he'd uncovered, then shone a torch into the darkness. It looked sound enough, but he supposed that he ought to do it properly. He levered another board out of the way, making a big enough hole for him to drop into, and shone the torch into the gap, checking how much room he'd have to work in.

It was then that he saw the package. Old sacking, worn and rotted through in parts; something like oil-cloth showing through the gaps. Frowning, he reached down and removed the bundle. He unravelled the sacking slowly, and then the oil-cloth. What he uncovered made his eyes dilate; he rushed to the phone, and dialled Debra's number at the university.

He drummed his fingers impatiently against the wall, waiting for one of the departmental secretaries to answer and put him through to Debra's extension; at last, he heard a voice. 'English department.'

'Debra Rowley, please.'

'Who's calling?'

Jake suddenly recognised the clipped tones as those of the secretary that Debra and Judith both referred to as 'the dragon' – on her nicest days. Both of them said that she must have been a doctor's receptionist, at some point, because of the way she interrogated anyone who rang. Jake couldn't risk her saying that Debra was working and couldn't accept personal calls, not this time. It was too important. 'It's Dr Matthews,' he said, trying to make his voice sound dry and academic.

'And what's it about?'

Jake was dying to say, 'Oh just shut up and put me through, you nosy bitch,' but he knew that that was the quickest way to make her cut him off. 'The research we discussed last week. I've found some more information.'

'Just a moment. I'll see if she's free.'

There was another long pause, and then at last he heard Debra's voice. '*Doctor* Matthews now, is it?' she said, teasing him. 'With more information about my research?'

'I wanted to make sure that that dreadful woman put me through.'

She noticed the urgency in his voice, and frowned. 'What's wrong, Jake?'

'I think you ought to come home. Now.'

'Why?'

'Just get here, Debra. It's important.'

She frowned again. Jake was never less than courteous; something was obviously badly wrong. 'I'm supposed to have a tutorial in ten minutes, Jake.'

'Ask Jude to cover for you. *Please*. I wouldn't ask you if it wasn't important.'

That was true. Jake had always respected her work. 'Okay. I'll be home soon.' She paused. 'Are you all right?'

'At the moment,' Jake said slowly, 'I'm not too sure.'

'I'm on my way.' She put the phone down, and went into Judith's office. 'Jude, can you do me a favour?'

'Of course.' Judith noticed her friend's white face. 'What's up?'

'I don't know. Jake's just phoned me and asked me to go home. Something's wrong, but he wouldn't say what it was over the phone.' She swallowed. 'I've got a tutorial in ten minutes, my second years and Hardy, but . . .'

Judith hugged her. 'Don't worry. I'll handle everything, here; just ring me later, and let me know what's going on.'

'Thanks, Jude. I owe you one.'

'I'll remind you of that, next time I get the freshers from Hell and have to teach them the finer points of Milton,' Jude said with a grin. 'Now, off you go.'

The tubes were running perfectly, to Debra's relief; even so, the journey seemed to crawl. She almost ran home from Islington station. Jake was waiting for her by the front door.

'Are you all right?' she asked, seeing his white face.

'I don't think so,' he said.

Then she noticed tears in his eyes. 'What is it?'

He swallowed. 'I . . . Oh, God, Debra, I can't quite believe it myself.'

'Your brothers? Your parents? There's been an accident?'

'No, nothing like that.'

Her temper suddenly frayed. 'Then tell me what the hell's

going on, you bastard! I've been worrying myself sick, all the way home!'

'I can't.' He took her hand. 'You'll have to see for yourself.' He led her into the dining room, and Debra's eyes widened as she saw what was lying on the floor.

'Jake? Where did you get these?'

'I found them under the floorboards.' He was shaking slightly. 'All those stupid jokes about us finding treasure in the attic, and this lot was under our feet, all the time . . .'

'Buchan.' She breathed the name softly, reverently, as she looked at the paintings. 'My God. No wonder you flipped.'

'It was just a bundle of sacking and oil-cloth.' He shook his head. 'I had no idea what would be in it, and when I opened it and saw the pictures . . .' He shivered. 'I felt like the first time I saw *The Hyacinth Girl*, in the gallery at Birmingham. Her face . . . I felt shivery all over when I saw it.'

Debra couldn't help touching the surface of the water-colour. 'It's the same model – the same pose, even.'

'But not hyacinths.' In the original painting, the girl had been sitting in a field of hyacinths, with a flat oval basket of the flowers on her lap, and holding another just below her nose. In this much smaller water-colour version, she was still in a hyacinth field, but the way that the flowers had been painted, with the stems thick and the clusters of purple petals forming almost a mushroom cap, they looked more like penises. And instead of sitting with a basket on her lap and holding a hyacinth below her nose, she was kneeling and holding the erect cock of a customer, her mouth slightly open as though she were about to fellate him.

A second picture showed a young man naked by a pool, masturbating; semen sprayed from the tip of his cock over a bunch of tiny white daffodils, the fluid dripping from the petals like tears. At the side of the picture, a young woman, also naked, was looking longingly over her shoulder at him. A rosy flush mottled the alabaster skin of her breasts and face, and her hand was firmly between her legs.

'*Echo* and *Narcissus*,' Jake said softly, tracing the flowers with his fingertips.

'*Leda and the Swan*,' Debra added, turning to the third picture. 'Like the Yeats sonnet. I wonder if he ever saw it, and this is what inspired him to write it?' A young woman, with her face in the rictus of orgasm, stood with her legs apart, the swan's wings dipping to reveal her naked breasts but covering her loins. The swan's head wasn't visible, but the position of his curved neck hinted that his head was firmly lodged between Leda's thighs, giving her pleasure.

'And *Nimuë*.' Naked and beautiful, with glossy black hair streaming down her back, the woman knelt at the side of a naked Merlin, his legs splayed and his weight supported on his outstretched arms behind his back. His eyes were closed and his head thrown back, as she rubbed his cock. Nimuë herself had her mouth open as though reading aloud from Merlin's book of spells, dropped carelessly at his side as he abandoned himself to sexual pleasure – and left his secrets in her sight . . .

'Incredible, aren't they?' Jake breathed.

Debra nodded. 'I'm not surprised you rang me in a flap. If I'd been the one who found them, I'd have done the same.'

'Do you think they're really Buchan?'

'They look like it. The women's faces are typical of his work. And I think they're the same model.'

'The same as *The Hyacinth Girl*,' Jake confirmed.

Debra swallowed. 'I can't believe this. After what we were saying to Jude, the other day . . .'

'I know. There are books, too. Illustrated ones – line drawings, not colour plates – but some of them look like Buchan's work.' He indicated the slim volumes stacked carefully at the side of the paintings. 'And there are some handwritten papers, mainly poetry. I haven't studied them properly, but I wouldn't mind betting that they're Buchan's, too. Maybe first drafts of some lost poems.'

A shiver ran down Debra's spine. 'You don't think that he was the one who used to live here, do you?'

Jake shook his head. 'I've no idea. I thought he lived in Cheyne Walk, near Rossetti – or so it said in all the biographies I've read. But he must have known someone who lived here, to leave the paintings with him.'

'His publisher, maybe?' she suggested.

'Could be. I had a look through the title pages, and the publisher's someone called Sykes. Does the name mean anything to you?'

'Apart from Bill Sykes, you mean?' she said, suddenly laughing.

'And Nancy, and his dog?' He laughed back, catching her reference. 'What was the dog's name?'

Debra shook her head. 'I can't remember. But I howled my eyes out over the bit at the end, where the dog dies.'

'Soppy.' He stroked her face. 'Mind you, it upset me, too. I'd like a dog. A boxer. We could call it Sykes.'

'Or a mongrel from Battersea.'

'Whatever.' He paused. 'Joking apart, have you heard of Sykes?'

'Well – no. But I could do some research into it. There's bound to be something in the library at work.'

'And in the meantime – what do we do with these?'

'Well, we bought the house,' she said. 'They came with the house, so they must belong to us, too.'

'I'm not so sure. What about Buchan's descendants? Or even Sykes, if there's a bill of sale for the paintings somewhere.'

Debra shrugged. 'I'm not a lawyer. I wouldn't know.'

'No.' Jake was thoughtful. 'I wonder what Jude will say, when we tell her?'

'Jude! I promised I'd ring her and let her know that everything was all right.' Debra scowled at him. 'You put me in a hell of a panic, when you rang.'

'I was in a bit of one, myself,' he reminded her.

'I thought there had been an accident or something.' She smiled ruefully at him. 'Sorry for snapping. But you did give me a scare.'

'I'm sorry.' He stroked her face. 'Go and ring Jude, then we can decide what to do with these.'

Debra was thoughtful. 'Do you think we should tell anyone else about them, yet? I mean, until we find out a bit more – like if they're really Buchan, and who Sykes is, and what his connection was with Buchan?'

'Maybe not. Though Jude is your best friend.'

'True. She'll keep it quiet, if I ask her to.' She kissed him lightly, and went to ring Judith; Jake, meanwhile, stayed looking at the paintings. He'd seen dozens of Pre-Raphaelite paintings where the sexual tension between the figures was obvious, but never anything so explicit. Particularly from Buchan, who had never painted even semi-naked figures, to Jake's knowledge.

He crouched down on the floor, studying them. The brushwork was perfect. Buchan had been as painstaking in these small watercolours as he had in his larger canvases; the sheer detail of the emotions on the faces of his subjects made Jake shiver. He still couldn't understand why Buchan was always overlooked: he had as much talent as Rossetti, and was a better draughtsman. These pictures, Jake thought, would catapult Buchan very firmly into the public eye.

A light touch on his shoulder made him jump. He looked up at Debra. 'Sorry. I was miles away.'

'So I see.' She smiled at him. 'I've spoken to Jude. She won't tell a soul.'

'Great.'

'She did want to see them, though. I told her to drop in on the way home from work.'

'Good idea.' Jake was still preoccupied with the paintings. A dozen questions were whirling round his mind: he desperately wanted to know the truth about them. Why Buchan had painted them – for money, or for love? Who was the model? Why had no one guessed the existence of the 'lost' Buchan paintings?

'I'll get us a coffee,' Debra said, ruffling his hair.

'Thanks.'

She smiled to herself, recognising that he was on automatic

pilot. She could ask him anything, and he'd make polite noises in the right places, but not pay the slightest bit of attention to what she was really saying . . .

Judith came round, a couple of hours later. 'Well?' she asked, as Debra opened the door.

'Jake's walking around like he's on a completely different planet, so don't expect any sense out of him,' Debra warned.

'Buchan's his favourite artist, isn't he?'

Debra nodded. 'And the pictures . . . Well, they're not what you'd expect from a Victorian artist, put it that way!'

'So you said on the phone. I've been thinking about it all the way here,' Judith said.

'Come through.' Debra ushered her friend through to the sitting room.

'Hello, Jake.' Judith went over to him and kissed him.

'Jude.' He gave her a hug. 'Well, what do you think of our treasure-trove?'

Judith's eyes widened as she saw the watercolours. 'Jake, they're obscene!'

'I know. But they're beautiful. Pure – well, impure,' he corrected with a smile, 'Buchan.'

She nodded at the book by his chair. 'Is there anything about them in the biography?'

'Not so far. It's a while since I've read it, but I can't remember anyone ever saying something about lost paintings. There's nothing in the index, either. I still can't quite believe it. I mean, after what we were saying, the other night . . .'

'Mm, it's very ironic.' Judith smiled at him. 'Jake, are you sure they're Buchan?'

He nodded. 'Gut feeling. Apart from the fact that the faces are typical Buchan – and they're the same model as in *The Hyacinth Girl* – the pictures are painted in exactly the same sort of colours he used. Same brushwork, everything.'

'There's no way he could ever have sent that to the Royal Academy,' Judith said, pointing to the one of Leda and the swan.

'Mm. That's the puzzle. Buchan didn't even paint semi-nudes – not like Waterhouse or Burne-Jones. He always had the reputation of being a bit po-faced. And as for these . . .' Jake bit his lip. 'It's proof that he had some sort of sexual relationship with his model. How else would he be able to paint her in orgasm?'

'Imagination?' Debra suggested.

Jake shook his head. 'It's too . . . too real.' He frowned. 'What I'd like to know is *why* he painted them. Was it because he wanted to, or because he needed the money, so he painted what Sykes wanted for his books?'

'Who's Sykes?' Judith asked.

'The publisher. At least, we assume he is,' Debra said. 'All the books have his name in them.' She gestured to the slim volumes next to the pictures.

Judith picked one up, and skimmed through it. 'Victorian porn. Borrr-ing.'

'Not all of it is.'

'Oh, come on. That stuff you had on your desk, the other day—'

'Was, I admit, exceedingly boring,' Debra admitted, with a grin. 'But some of it isn't bad.'

'You haven't shown me anything to convince me, yet,'

Judith said, grinning back. She skimmed through a few more pages, and raised an eyebrow. 'Nice line drawings, though. Buchan again?'

Jake nodded. 'I think so.'

'If you can prove that it's him, this stuff must be worth a bomb,' Judith said slowly. 'Obscene pictures from a respected, if minor, Victorian artist.'

'And then there's the question of who they belong to,' Jake added. 'Us, Buchan's relatives, or Sykes' family.'

'So what are you two going to do, now?'

'Tomorrow, I'm going to do some research on Sykes,' Debra said. 'Once we know a bit more about him, we can take it from there.'

'They're pretty amazing.' Judith tipped her head to one side. 'I wonder how he did the Narcissus one? Did he have a male model, masturbating, or did he paint his own reflection in a mirror? And if it was his reflection, how come he managed to toss himself off with one hand, and still keep the other hand steady enough to draw?'

'Trust *you* to think that! The other thing is,' Debra added, 'did Sykes live here, or did Buchan?'

'Or even both?' Jake's eyes lit up. 'If they did, could Narcissus even be Sykes, and Buchan painted his friend giving himself a little light relief?'

'Calm down, you two,' Judith ordered, laughing. 'You may never find out the truth.'

'We're going to have a damn good try, though,' Debra said. 'This could be the academic scoop of the decade. Even if the pictures don't belong to us, we've got a moral right to do the research on them, because we found them.'

'And if they do belong to us, as owners of the house . . .' Jake smiled. 'I can remember having an argument with someone about whether it's better to own an original or a good copy, and how you'd know the difference.'

'And?' Judith asked.

'I stand by what I said at the time: I'd rather have an original. Even good copies can't capture all the tone and the colour.' Jake touched one of the watercolours reverently. 'I still can't quite believe this.'

'I think I know how you feel,' Judith said. 'It'd be like if I found proof of the Dark Lady's identity, or another lost sonnet. Or a bunch of obscene sonnets by Milton.'

'Exactly.' Jake smiled at her. 'You'd want to know more – like how it had all stayed hidden for so long, and why.'

Judith laughed. 'Spoken like a true academic. You've missed your vocation, Jake.'

'I wouldn't have found these,' he pointed out, 'sitting in a cramped university office.' He smiled at her. 'And if you want to argue it further, stay for dinner.'

'I'd love to,' Judith said regretfully, 'but I've already promised to be elsewhere. In fact, I'm going to have to leave now, or I'll be late.'

'Not David?' Jake asked.

Judith flushed. 'Yes, actually.'

'You could always ring him and put him off,' Debra said.

'Or even stand him up,' Jake tempted.

'Stand him up?' Debra grinned. 'You obviously haven't heard about Jude's ex-flatmate. Someone once stood her up, when she'd prepared this wonderful gourmet dinner for him. So she delivered the food to his house.'

'And?'

Judith laughed. 'She delivered it through the letterbox! She'd put extra garlic in the salad dressing, stuffed it in a wine bottle, and just tipped it onto the carpet. Followed by three glasses of red wine, two cups of coffee, and six After Eights.'

'No.' Jake smiled in amused disbelief.

'Yes, indeedy,' Judith said. 'The man in question had to have professional cleaners out to clear up the mess and get the smell of garlic out of the carpet. It took them weeks!'

'Yuck. David wouldn't do that to you, would he?'

'I,' Judith said, 'am not taking any chances.'

Jake gave her a hug. 'Well, thanks for coming round.'

'I wouldn't have missed this for the world.' She winked at him. 'And don't worry, I won't say a word to anyone about it.'

'Thanks.'

When Judith had gone, Jake turned to Debra. 'I don't know about you, but I don't feel like cooking, tonight.'

'Neither do I,' she agreed.

'Chinese or pizza?'

She gave him a sidelong look. 'Chinese – in bed.'

He grinned. 'Buchan's pictures having an effect on you, are they?'

She glanced at the obvious bulge in his groin, and smiled. 'I'm not the only one.'

'Who do you see yourself as? Leda, or the Hyacinth Girl?'

She laughed. 'Nimuë, actually. And it's interesting that you don't see me as Echo.'

'That's because if you'd been in Echo's place, you'd have

gone to join him. You wouldn't have lusted and longed from afar.'

'Says who?'

He burrowed under the hem of her loose top, stroking up over her midriff until he reached her breasts. Through the thin stuff of her bra, he could feel how hard and erect her nipples were. 'Says these, for a start.'

She grinned. 'Okay, I admit it. If I saw you masturbating by a pool, I'd probably come and help you out.' She gave him a sidelong look. 'And which one are you?'

He smiled at her, still stroking her nipples. 'The swan.'

She laughed. 'Bragging, now, are we?'

'No. But I couldn't be Narcissus, with you around. I'd rather make love to you than to me. Merlin's a possibility – but he's the one getting all the pleasure, and he's oblivious to Nimuë. It doesn't work like that, with us. So therefore I must be the swan.'

Debra rolled her eyes. 'Why did I forget that you studied logic, for a while?'

'Must be me builder's kit,' he said, hamming up his accent.

She grinned. 'Minus the bum cleavage . . .'

He let one hand slide round to her back, and deftly unclasped her bra. 'What do you think Nimuë would do with the swan, then?'

'She'd probably turn into a swan, herself. Or magic him back to his proper form.' Debra arched her back as he released her breasts, replacing the lacy constriction with his fingers. 'Mm, that's nice.'

'Let's forget the Chinese,' he said softly.

'Good idea.'

He kissed her lightly, picked up one of the books, and waltzed her out of the room.

Debra eyed him suspiciously. 'And what are you planning to do with that?'

'Bedtime reading,' he said, a wolfish smile on his lips.

She gave a theatrical sigh. 'And there was I thinking that you wanted to do other things, in bed.'

'Oh, but I do.' He handed her the book.

'Jake?' She frowned, puzzled, not sure what he was planning.

'I need my hands free,' he said with a grin, picking her up.

'Jake, you'll give yourself a hernia!'

'No, I won't.' He kissed her forehead. 'Stop growling, and humour me. I feel like being macho.'

'A macho swan called Jupiter, perchance?'

'Zeus,' he corrected, smiling, carrying her up the stairs. 'It's a Greek myth, not a Roman one.'

Debra pulled a face at him. 'You're being pedantic.'

He nibbled her earlobe. 'Are you trying to tell me that you're not?'

She grinned. 'Only sometimes.'

'Hm.' He set her down gently on the bed, and went to close the curtains.

Debra put the book on the bedside table, then stretched out, lying back among the pillows.

'Glad we went for a proper bed, now?' he teased, turning round and seeing the expression on her face.

'There was nothing wrong with my futon.'

'Apart from giving me chronic backache, no.' He wrinkled

his nose at her. 'You have to admit, it's nice having more space – and not being quite so close to the floor.'

'Yes.' She smiled at him. 'Though I still liked my futon.'

He came to sit next to her on the bed. 'Well, you can always sleep on it in the spare room, if you miss it that much,' he teased.

'Jake?'

'Mm?'

She sat up, putting her mouth close to his ear. 'Why don't you just shut up and fuck me?' she asked, her voice husky.

'Well, seeing as you put it so nicely . . .' He unbuttoned her loose tunic, sliding it off her shoulders and tossing it onto the floor, removing her unfastened bra at the same time. Then he lifted her slightly, easing her loose navy trousers over her hips and sliding the material down her legs.

'Have I ever told you that you've got great legs?' he said, his eyes crinkling at the corners as he smiled at her. 'They're perfectly shaped.'

Debra, who thought of herself as slightly on the dumpy side, simply smiled disbelievingly.

'And your skin's so soft . . .' He began to stroke her ankles. 'I love just touching you.' His hands drifted higher, his fingers caressing the sensitive skin at the back of her knees. Automatically, her thighs parted, giving him access; he moistened his lower lip with his tongue, and stroked the soft skin of her inner thighs. 'Touching you – and kissing you. I love the way you smell, the way you taste.'

Slowly, he bent his head, letting his mouth travel the same path as his fingers. Debra shivered as he licked the hollow behind her knee, and then moved up so that his cheeks rubbed against her thighs. He'd shaved earlier, so she was spared the discomfort of stubble feeling like sandpaper against her skin; she closed her eyes, her mouth opening slightly in anticipation as she waited for his mouth to reach her moistening quim.

When the expected contact didn't take place, she opened her eyes and frowned. 'Jake?'

He blew her a kiss, and she realised that he was stripping swiftly. 'I got a bit carried away. I forgot I was wearing so much – and I'm not going to insult you by just unzipping my fly and giving you a quickie.'

She smiled. 'So what did you have in mind, exactly?'

'Turn over, and close your eyes.'

'This sounds interesting . . .' She tipped her head on one side. 'Aren't you going to tell me more?'

He shook his head. 'Roll over, sweetheart, and close your eyes. If you put your arms above your head, it'll probably be more comfortable.'

'The mind boggles!' she teased, but she did as he asked.

Jake opened the drawer of his beside cabinet, bringing out a small bottle of oil, and tipped a few drops on his hands. Then he knelt beside Debra on the bed, and drew his palms down her back.

'Mm. Nice,' she said, suddenly realising what he had in mind.

'Well. Your muscles are all tense; I thought you could do with a bit of relaxing.'

Debra decided not to point out that she was tense because of a certain phone-call; she just made a noncommittal murmur, and settled down against the pillows.

Jake continued to massage her back, his palm flat against her skin on the downstrokes, and his fingertips moving in small circles on the upstrokes. Debra gave a sigh of pleasure and flexed her shoulders; he smiled, pushing the hair away from the nape of her neck and kissing her. 'You've got a gorgeous bum, as well.' He squeezed her buttocks to emphasize his point. 'All soft and warm and round.'

'I'll take that,' she said drily, 'as a compliment.'

'That's how I meant it.' He rubbed the backs of her thighs, then let his hand drift between them, his fingers burrowing between her labia.

'Jake,' she protested lazily, 'that isn't very comfortable.'

'Sorry.' He lifted her hips, guiding her up onto her knees, while her forehead remained resting on her hands. 'Better?'

'Mm.'

'Good.'

He knelt between her thighs, unable to resist taking a small bite at the soft curve of her buttocks; she wriggled, laughing. 'Behave!'

'Being a good boy,' he said, his voice growing husky at the sight of her glistening quim, 'isn't at all what I had in mind.'

'Tell me more,' she invited. 'Or, even better, show me.'

'I thought you'd never ask.' He bent his head, drawing his tongue along her exposed furrow.

'Mm. That's nice,' she said softly.

'Glad Madam's enjoying herself.' He shifted position so that the tip of his cock touched her vaginal entrance; Debra pushed back against him, and he slid slowly inside her.

He was still for a moment, simply enjoying the feel of her

quim gripping his cock, like wet silk wrapped round his skin; then he began to thrust with long, slow strokes.

Debra groaned with pleasure, muffling the sounds in the pillow, and Jake's thrusts grew harder and deeper in response. He rested one hand on her hips, guiding her body back towards him as he thrust into her, increasing the tempo of their love-making. His other hand reached round her body to stroke the erect tips of her breasts; he bent his head to kiss the nape of her neck. 'God, I love you,' he whispered hoarsely.

Her answer was muffled by the pillow, but he felt her quim tighten round him, her internal muscles contracting sharply as she came. It was enough to tip him into his own release, and he cried out as he came, resting his cheek against her back and breathing in her scent.

Eventually, he pulled out of her, and lay on his side next to her, turning her round so that she lay in his arms. 'Well?'

Her eyes glittered mischievously, 'Not bad, Zeus, not bad at all!'

He kissed her lightly. 'Mm, and, for an enchantress, you're not so bad yourself . . .'

They both laughed, and settled back against the pillows.

'Are you hungry?' he asked.

Debra wrinkled her nose. 'Not really. Are you?'

'Not exactly.'

'But?'

'I've got this craving for a bacon and avocado sandwich.'

'Tough. We're out of bacon, let alone avocados.'

'Looks like I'll have to do without.' He slid one hand up her thigh. 'Or have an alternative.'

'Such as?'

He smiled. 'The first time I met you, I fell in love with your voice. It was quite simply the sexiest voice I'd ever heard.'

She tipped her head to one side. 'I don't follow.'

He stroked her face. 'I'd like you to read me a bedtime story.'

'From Buchan's book?'

He nodded. 'It's killing two birds with one stone, really. A bit of research for your book – and doing something special for me.'

'If you put it like that . . .' She smiled at him, and reached over to pick up the book.

Seven

'The French have a saying, "staircase wit",' Debra said. 'You know, when you suddenly think of the retort you wish you'd made half an hour earlier.'

'And?' Judith asked.

Debra grinned. 'For once, my timing was impeccable. The best put-down *ever*.'

Judith's eyes narrowed. 'Dare I ask what exactly you've been up to?'

'Guess.'

Judith rolled her eyes. 'I've spent all day marking exam papers. I'm too knackered to guess anything. Tell me.'

'Marcus.'

'*Marcus*?' Judith was surprised. Debra had been careful to steer clear of him ever since they'd split up – including avoiding any parties where he might be, with a woman in tow. He worked in a different department, on a different floor, so they were unlikely to meet at work. Just what had Debra been up to?

'Mm. He just paid me a visit, in my office.' Debra's eyes sparkled. 'The bastard still thinks he's completely irresistible, you know.'

Judith nodded. 'Let's face it, if you didn't know what his personality was like, you'd think he was gorgeous. He is sex on legs, Deb. He's got a gorgeous bum and, if half the rumours are to be believed, a gorgeous cock as well, and he knows how to use it.'

'True enough. Unfortunately, the package goes with the personality of a first-class bastard.' Debra's tone was dry.

'So what happened?'

'Someone's obviously told him that I'm with someone else. So he decided that it was his duty to save me from myself.'

Judith laughed. 'No! Are you telling me that he tried it on with you?'

Debra nodded. 'We've screwed on the desk in my office before now, with the door locked – and with a horde of students due to descend on me within ten minutes. Marcus likes to live dangerously. And knowing him, he's probably had other women there, too.'

'Not in *your* office, surely.' Judith was faintly shocked.

'I wouldn't put anything past him, not now.' Debra smiled. 'Anyway, in he waltzed, and leaned against the wall, trying to look seductive. He said that he'd heard about my new man, and said that obviously it was just for sex; why else would I be knocking about with a mere builder?'

'Did you tell him Jake's background?'

'No. I simply smiled at him, and said that yes, Jake was very good – and could teach him a thing or two.'

Judith was delighted. 'You didn't!'

'Mm-hm. Anyway, then he told me that it would never work out, because I needed someone who could stimulate my mind, as well as my body.' Debra pursed her lips. 'I asked him if he was volunteering.'

'Dangerous.'

'Mm. But I rather enjoyed it. Stringing him along, for once. Anyway, you know Marcus. He immediately assumed that I was only with Jake because I was on the rebound from him – and that I was still gagging for him to put his cock in me.'

'Which,' Judith asserted, 'you're not.'

'That's not what he thought.' Debra smiled. 'Then he started rambling on about how much he'd missed me, and how I was made for him – I had the right body, the right intellect, the right sort of personality. Just like I was some little decoration to sit in his flat.'

'Did you tell him to fuck off?'

Debra shook her head. 'I should have done, I know – but something just came over me. I keep thinking of those pictures Jake found, and it makes me well, hot.' She sighed. 'It's dreadful. I have masturbatory fantasies about them, and it's as much as I can do to resist ringing Jake and talking dirty to him down the phone.'

'So he caught you at a randy moment, and you let him have you.'

'I didn't say that,' Debra said with a grin. 'I just decided to teach him a teensy lesson. Bits of me still can't believe I've just done something as wicked as that, but . . .'

'You didn't let him have you?'

Debra spread her hand, and gave her friend a mischievous grin. 'Much, much, much better than that.'

'I'm not with you.'

'Well . . .' She moved over to Judith's office door, and locked it. 'Just in case he susses out where I am, and barges in.'

'He wouldn't dare do that with me.' Marcus and Judith had had a couple of spats before, and Marcus was slightly intimidated by the redhead – which was one of the reasons why he was always so rude to her.

'Maybe. Anyway, he was wittering on about how good we used to be together, and how good it could be again. I simply licked my lips; and he took it as an invitation. He pulled me out of my chair, sat me on the edge of my desk, and kissed me.' She frowned. 'I must say, he does know how to kiss. It's the way he does it, those little nibbly kisses which make you open your mouth under his.'

Part of Judith wanted to pull a face and make some comment about only opening her mouth for Marcus so she could be sick over him, but she wanted to hear exactly what her friend had done, so she remained silent.

'While he was kissing me, he slid one hand under my shirt, stroking my breasts through my bra. He pulled down the cups, so that he could play with my nipples.' Debra smiled. 'Either he uses the same technique on all his women, or he remembered just how I liked being stroked. Anyway, I responded, and he took heart, bunching up my skirt and slipping his hand under the hem. He stroked my thighs, nudging his way ever so gently upwards until I opened my legs for him.

'Then he pushed the gusset of my knickers aside. I'd been thinking about Jake and those pictures, so I was already wet; Marcus assumed that it was what he was doing to me.' Her lips curved. 'The arrogant sod. Anyway, he remembered what I like. He started stroking my quim, very slowly, his finger travelling full length up and down it until I pushed against him. Then he pushed one finger inside me, while he rubbed my clitoris with his thumb. He made me come twice like that, and then he went down on me.'

Debra's eyes shone with sudden lust. 'He hasn't shaved today, so his skin was ever so slightly rough against my thighs. He burrowed his head under my skirt, licking me and sucking my clitoris until I was wriggling on the desk. I could feel my whole body quivering, and then I came, my whole sex throbbing in his mouth.'

Judith whistled. 'I thought you said you didn't let him have you?'

Debra gave her a feline smile. 'Oh, it got better. Believe me. When I'd calmed down a bit, he unzipped his fly. His cock was large and hot and dry, and I knew he wanted to fuck me. Then I smiled, told him I wasn't on the pill, didn't have a condom, and didn't want to take the risk.'

'A teensy lie?' Judith suggested.

Debra grinned. 'Just a little. Anyway, he took my hand, placing it on his cock, and asked me if I remembered what he felt like. That's when I thought about being *really* wicked.'

'The mind boggles!'

'I said I could remember what he tasted like, too. He went very red at that – I'd say with lust, not with embarrassment – and turned my chair round so he could lean against it. Then he asked me if I'd like to refresh my memory.' Debra grinned. 'So I said yes.'

'You didn't!' Judith rolled her eyes. 'Oh, honestly.'

'I haven't finished,' Debra reminded her. 'Anyway, I got off the desk, and knelt before him. I pulled his pants down a bit further, to give me better access to his cock, then I started stroking it. He asked me – very nicely – if I'd stop teasing him, and use my mouth on him. So I did, licking the sensitive groove under his glans, just the way he used to like it. He started gripping the back of my chair very hard, and I worked my mouth up and down his shaft.

'Then I started stroking his balls, and the little silky crease between his thighs. He pushed against me, so I let his cock out of my mouth, just long enough to wet my ring finger, and started massaging his anus. He started moaning, then, when I eased my finger inside him, pushing it back and forth. I could feel his balls lifting and tightening, and he was just about to come – then I stopped.'

'You stopped?'

'Mm. I sat back on my haunches, looked at him, and said, "I'm sorry, Marcus. But after Jake, you just don't feel big enough." Then I said, "You're right about needing intellectual stimulation as well as physical. Lucky for me that Jake's got a First."' She grinned. 'Marcus got an upper second, and he's paranoid about it. Anyway, then I stood up, and walked out of my office.'

Judith burst out laughing. 'No! I wish I'd seen his face.'

'I wish I'd had a camera,' Debra admitted.

'Bloody hell. Telling him his cock was too small, and that your new man was brighter than him, as well . . . Didn't he go mad?'

'I think he was too shocked,' Debra admitted. 'Though I hate to think what he's done to my office. Probably wanked over my keyboard, to get his own back.'

Judith was still shaking her head and laughing. ' Oh, Deb. That's brilliant. Stopping just as he was just about to come, and telling him he was inadequate . . . You're right, it's the best put-down ever.'

'And well-deserved.'

'I trust you're not going to tell Jake?'

Debra shook her head. 'I haven't told him about Marcus – though I know you've primed him, a bit.'

'With the best intentions,' Judith said.

'I know. But I don't think he'd appreciate what I just did, somehow.'

'No.' Judith's nose twitched. 'Next time I see Marcus, I'm just going to say "hello, big boy" – and watch him go puce!'

Debra grinned. 'Just make sure I'm with you, when you do it!'

'I will.' Judith stretched. 'Fancy a coffee?'

Debra shook her head. 'I'm afraid I have some research to do – on a certain Mr Sykes.'

'Right.' Judith smiled at her. 'Well, keep me posted on anything you find out.'

'Well?' Jake looked over his shoulder, his paintbrush stilling, as Debra walked through the door.

She blew him a kiss. 'Well, what?'

'Don't tease.' He came down from the ladder. 'Did you manage to find out anything about Sykes?'

'Well, apparently there was a publisher called Richard Sykes, towards the end of the last century. He lived in

Islington, and—' she beamed at him '—he specialised in erotic books and prints.'

'So he could have lived here?'

'Or nearby, and asked a friend to hide the stuff for him. Don't forget the laws in Victorian times – publishers and even typesetters could be jailed. Annie Besant was prosecuted, would you believe, for publishing birth control pamphlets! It's no wonder they used to hide the stuff. Besant hid some of her pamphlets under someone's cistern; God knows how many other Victorian houses have books and papers hidden under the floorboards in one of the rooms.' She shrugged. 'Things that were considered illicit then, but would be quite tame, nowadays.'

'Maybe we ought to take up the rest of the floors.'

Debra wrinkled her nose. 'I shouldn't think we'll find anything else.'

'Maybe not.'

'Nothing as good as we've already found, anyway.'

'You're probably right.' Jake's eyes were dark and intense. 'So what else did you find out about him?'

She breathed on her nails, and polished them against her T-shirt. 'Just that he published some of Buchan's early line drawings in his books. Which, I might add, were Victorian melodramas and epic poems.'

Jake was delighted. 'I *knew* it!'

'So they were probably friends for years.'

'Mm. And because he helped Buchan out when he was a struggling artist, Buchan repaid him by doing those paintings for him. Probably a birthday present or something. Though Sykes couldn't exactly have had them framed and on show.'

'No. Though I should add that Sykes died in 1895,' Debra continued. 'Penniless.'

'Penniless?' He frowned. 'Buchan's minor now, I know, but his work was quite popular, at the time. Besides, you told me that the Victorian erotic books were mostly aimed at the aristocratic market, and collectors paid a lot of money for "exclusive" editions.'

'I haven't finished, yet,' she said. 'The house where he was found – and no, the address wasn't given, before you ask – was completely empty, except for a mattress and fifty chloral bottles. So he probably lost all his money through drug addiction.'

'Unless someone wanted him out of the way. Someone in Buchan's family, who didn't want his reputation ruined – which it would have been, if the general public had known about his erotic drawings. He'd have been thrown out of the Academy, and only a very broadminded and influential patron would have been able to buy his work.'

She nodded. 'It's a theory, yes.'

'But one which you don't buy.'

'Not until I know a bit more. Anyway, I did quite a bit of research on our Mr Sykes. It seems that his wife left him, with their son, either when she found out what he really did for a living, or when she discovered his alleged drug habit. She went back to her family in Norfolk, the year before he died.'

'His descendants might still be there,' Jake said. 'Do you know whereabouts in Norfolk?'

'The north coast, somewhere. A little fishing village. I can do some more digging, if you think it's worth going to see them.'

'Definitely. They must have some papers which will shed a bit of light on it for us.'

'What about the prints?'

Jake looked thoughtful. 'Well, if they really are Buchan, they're worth quite a lot of money. If they're not, we're on a wild goose chase, and we might as well forget it now and get them framed nicely.'

'For our bedroom?' Debra suggested, a wicked smile curving her lips.

He nodded. 'Where else?'

'In the living room. To shock the parents.'

He grinned. 'I think mine are past shocking.'

'Mine, too,' she admitted ruefully. 'At least, if they were shocked, they'd hide it.'

'So what do you think we should do now?'

She spread her hands. 'There's only one way to find out the truth.'

'Take them to an expert,' he agreed. 'Do you know anyone at the university who could look at them?'

'There's a History of Art department, but I don't really know anyone in there.' She wrinkled her nose. 'Wouldn't we be better off taking the pictures to a professional valuer?'

He thought about it. 'Probably.'

'Right. You sort out the valuer, and I'll see what I can dig up about Sykes' family.' She smiled at him. 'We can book into a little hotel as Mr and Mrs John Smith.'

Jake smiled back. 'Or even Mr and Mrs Fred Bloggs.'

'And make a proper weekend of it. Long walks on the beach, a lazy lunch on the seafront, a paddle at sunset, that sort of thing.' She paused. 'I haven't been to Norfolk, before.'

'Neither have I, actually.' He curled his fingers round hers. 'So let's make it a long weekend. Thursday to Monday.'

'Sounds good to me.' She kissed him lightly. 'Now, are you going to finish that wall, while I sort out dinner?'

'Okay. Give me a few minutes' warning, though, so I can have a shower first.'

'You mean you're not going to work for the rest of the evening?'

Jake laughed. 'Actually, I had plans for being a couch potato. We could watch a film, or an old video.'

'Lazy.'

He smiled. 'Alternatively, you could change into some old clothes, grab a paintbrush, and start at the other end of the room.'

She groaned. 'Jake. You know I hate painting.'

'Exactly. So what's it to be?'

'Couch potato,' she said.

'A TV dinner?'

She shook her head. 'I'm not going *that* far. We'll eat in the kitchen.'

Jake smiled, suddenly thinking how convenient that might be. 'Okay.'

Debra didn't see the look in his eyes, and went into the kitchen.

Half an hour later, she called out to Jake. 'Ten minutes, if you want a shower first!'

'Okay.' He finished painting the section of wall, then went upstairs for a quick shower. The shower was the only non-period thing about the bathroom; everything else was either reclaimed Victorian, or a good reproduction. But Debra

133

had said that she couldn't live without a shower to wash her hair with, so he'd regretfully added the electric shower. Though, he thought, sometimes it was very convenient . . .

He scrubbed the paint from his skin, washed his hair, and joined Debra in the kitchen in seven minutes flat.

'Not bad,' she teased, ruffling his still-wet hair.

He caught her round the waist, and kissed her. 'I try.'

'Mm, you can be *very* trying,' she quipped, kissing him back. 'Sit yerself down then, lad,' she ordered in a mock Yorkshire accent.

Jake smiled, and sat down at the small table; as Debra served the cannelloni, he realised just how hungry he was. At last, he pushed his empty plate away. 'Lovely. If you ever get bored with your job, you could always be my cook instead.'

She laughed. 'I don't think that's very likely, somehow! You'd never let me have the kitchen to myself.'

He pulled a face at her. 'I don't know what you mean.'

She grinned. 'Stop doing your hurt little boy act, Jake. You know bloody well you'd be in here, wanting to know exactly what I was doing, and demanding tastes of everything.'

'Hm.' Jake conceded the point. 'Anyway, I can't see you getting bored with your job.'

Debra smiled. 'What do you want for pudding?'

'You.'

'No, be serious.'

'I was.'

'Oh, honestly!' She rolled her eyes. 'Yoghurt and honey okay?'

'Perfect.' For more than one reason, he thought, smiling to himself.

'It's better than perfect, sunshine, so you'd better appreciate it.'

'Oh?' Jake was intrigued.

'This,' she said, spooning yoghurt onto two plates and adding a dollop of thick dark honey, 'is proper Samian wild thyme honey. It's like liquid toffee.'

She passed him a plate; Jake tasted it, and his eyes widened. 'This is gorgeous! How did you come across it?'

'Jude and I went to Greece together, one year.' One year when Marcus had said that he had piles of work to do, and she'd be better off going on holiday with a friend – and not to feel guilty about him, because it was his own fault for not working hard enough during term. She'd gone away with Judith, had a wonderful time, and come back to discover that Marcus had had a house-guest, in her absence. A female one, who had conveniently left a pair of knickers under her pillow . . .

Her face tightened at the memory; Jake, who had been told about Marcus by Judith, had a fairly good idea what caused the sudden cloud in her eyes. He knew better than to ask her, and he knew that she certainly wouldn't discuss it: so there was only one way to take the hurt from her eyes. He reached over, and pulled her onto his lap. 'Debra?'

'Mm?'

He nuzzled the corner of her neck. 'This pudding is excellent – except for one thing.'

'Oh?' Debra frowned. 'What's that?'

'You're serving it on plates.'

'Well, if you want a bowl, you know where they're kept.'

He shook his head. 'I didn't mean pottery of any sort.'

'What, then?'

He smiled, and removed her shirt.

'Jake, we're in the kitchen, and the blinds are up!' she protested.

He rubbed his nose against hers. 'No one can see, so stop worrying.' He unclasped her bra, dropping the garment on top of her discarded shirt. 'And you did say that you wanted to christen the kitchen properly.'

Debra said nothing; Jake kissed her lightly. 'Relax, sweetheart. You know I'd never do anything that made you feel uncomfortable.'

'True,' she conceded.

'Well, then.' Smiling sweetly at her, he dipped his fingers in the honey on his plate, then smeared it over her breasts.

Debra shrieked. 'Yuck!'

'It's meant to be very good for the skin,' Jake said. 'Lots of Roman women used it as a beauty aid.'

'Oh, really?'

'Really. It's also meant to be one of the best natural face-masks.'

'And how would you know about that?'

'One of my old girlfriends was into natural products before they became fashionable. She used to make her own cosmetics,' was the surprising answer.

'So you're doing this for the good of my skin, are you?' Debra asked, a smile quirking her lips.

'But of course,' Jake said, rubbing the honey into her skin and anointing her nipples with it.

'And you don't have any ulterior motives?'

'Nope.'

'Liar.'

He grinned. 'All right, so I did have something else in mind.'

'Such as?'

He bent his head, and began licking the honey from her skin. Debra closed her eyes and tipped her head back as his tongue worked over her nipples, the honey dragging slightly against her skin and creating a delicious friction.

Taking advantage of her position, Jake slid one hand between her thighs, rubbing back and forth. He could feel the heat of her quim through her leggings, and smiled to himself. By the time he'd finished, he and Debra were going to have the best fuck yet.

He continued working on her breasts, licking every scrap of honey from her skin and then smearing a second helping over them. The scent of the honey, combined with the scent of her skin, was like paradise, and he murmured with pleasure as he lapped at her skin.

Debra tangled her fingers in his hair, urging him on as he suckled first one nipple then the other, drawing fiercely on the hard peaks of flesh before running the tip of his tongue along her dark areolae.

'Jake?' she said softly.

'Mm?' he mumbled against her flesh, not wanting to take his mouth from her.

'This is very nice, but . . .'

'What?' His voice was still muffled against her breasts.

She pushed her quim against his hand.

Jake sat up straight again, laughing. 'Talk about pushy, woman!'

'You started it.' She unbuttoned his shirt, sliding her hands against the crisp hair on his chest. His nipples were hard and flat; she traced the areolae, amused by the difference between their bodies.

'Actually, you started it. By giving me honey.' His lips twitched. 'Which is, as every Roman housewife knew, an aphrodisiac.'

'If you're going to be a show-off academic,' she warned, laughing, 'I'll get Jude to lecture you on Renaissance symbolism and metaphysical poetry. You'll be Donne to death.'

'That,' Jake informed her, 'is about the worst pun I've ever heard.'

'So what are you going to do about it, then?' she asked, removing his shirt and tossing it lightly onto her own clothes.

'There's a Roman poem which demands a thousand kisses, then a hundred, then another thousand . . .'

'Could be fun.' Debra giggled. 'Though it depends where the kisses are!'

He laughed back. 'Now you're being lewd.'

'No – you just think you know what I'm thinking, and you're assuming it's lewd because either you want it to be, or you're thinking those thoughts yourself.'

'Debra.'

'Mm?'

'Shut up,' he told her cheerfully, and kissed her.

'Nine hundred and ninety-nine to go. And then another eleven hundred,' she quipped. 'According to your Roman poet.'

Jake dropped a trail of tiny rapid kisses across her

shoulders. 'How many was that?'

'I lost count. You'll have to do it again.'

'Mm.' He urged her gently to her feet, then knelt beside her and peeled down her leggings, licking and kissing her skin as it was revealed.

Debra shivered, and arched her back. 'Tease,' she murmured.

'If my lady tells me what she requires . . .'

She smiled. 'I wonder if Buchan ever stood in this kitchen like this with his model?'

'I doubt it,' Jake said.

'How can you be so sure?'

'Because women,' he pointed out, 'didn't wear leggings. Or shoes like this, especially without stockings. Tut, tut. And you're supposed to be the Victorian specialist!'

She pulled a face at him. 'I didn't mean *literally* like this. I meant "in this fashion", as you well know!'

He grinned. 'I just like teasing you.'

'So I noticed.' She smiled. 'So are you going to be nice to me, or what?'

Jake rocked back on his haunches, and gave her a mischievous smile. 'Guess.'

She groaned. 'I swear, Jake Matthews, if you keep me waiting much longer, I'll murder you.'

'We are not amused,' he quipped solemnly.

'Actually, the Royal sense of humour was more along the lines of Jeremy Beadle. They thought it was hilarious if someone pretended to trap their finger in the door or fell over.'

Jake nibbled her inner thigh. 'Is that how you're going to

murder me? Bore me rigid with little anecdotes about po-faced Queen Vic?'

Debra grinned. 'And now you're waiting for me to make some comment about how I'd much rather see a particular part of you rigid.'

He drew one finger along her quim, parting her labia. 'Wouldn't you?'

'Guess,' she retorted.

'Hm.' He dabbled one finger in the syrupy juices of her quim, then anointed her clitoris with the musky fluid. He licked his finger, savouring the taste as though it were some expensive and rare wine. 'Judging by the feel – and the taste – of this . . .'

'Jake.'

'Mm?'

'Shut up,' Debra said, twining her fingers in his hair, to guide his face towards her quim; she squatted slightly so that her musky sex-flesh was only millimetres away from his mouth.

'I can take a hint,' a muffled voice, filled with laughter, informed her.

She closed her eyes as, at long last, he drew his tongue down the length of her quim, moving it slowly between her labia. She gave a small sigh of pleasure, and at once his tongue began lapping at her. He found her clitoris and flicked his tongue across it in a figure-of-eight motion until her breathing had become ragged; then he took the hard bud of flesh into his mouth and began sucking it, gently at first and then harder as she dug the pads of her fingertips into his scalp.

The combination of his warm breath and the expert ministrations of his tongue soon had Debra pushing hard against him, longing for a deeper penetration. Jake had no intention of stopping just yet, but slid one finger in her to help ease the ache, sliding it back and forth until she began to moan and rock gently, supporting herself by holding on to his shoulders.

The familiar warm feeling of orgasm began at the soles of her feet, a buzzing glow which travelled up her legs and pooled in her solar plexus. She gripped his shoulders more tightly as the sensation deepened; Jake's mouth grew more urgent, licking and caressing until she gave a muffled cry and came, her flesh contracting wildly against his lips.

Debra had half expected him to stop there; to her surprise, he lowered her to the floor, unzipped his jeans, and slid his cock inside her, its hard length acting as resistance to her internal muscles and lengthening her orgasm. And then he began to move, very slowly, sliding deep inside her and then pulling out until his cock was almost out of her.

He stroked her face, smiling at her; she relaxed again, and smiled back, wrapping her legs round his waist so that he could achieve maximum penetration. She still felt lazy with post-orgasmic indolence, but the rhythm he was setting up as he thrust into her was irresistible, making her thrust back up towards him. She didn't care that he was still half-dressed: all she wanted was to feel him inside her, loving her, needing the shared release as much as she did.

'Oh, Debra,' he breathed. His cock seemed to swell again, and then she felt him spurt inside her. He buried his face against her shoulder, and she wrapped her arms round his neck, stroking his hair with one hand.

'Even your coffee isn't going to match up to that,' she murmured against his ear, laughing.

'No.' He withdrew from her, kissing her breasts, and winced as he realised that he was still wearing his jeans. 'Um. Sorry about that. I got a bit carried away.'

'No problem.' Debra grinned at him. 'And I bet Buchan never did that – even in the Victorian equivalent of jeans!'

'I don't know. Remember the look on Leda's face . . .' He stood up, and helped her to his feet. 'Actually, that's probably how he managed to get the figures right.'

'Hm?' Debra hadn't followed him.

'The model was standing up; then either he set up a mirror so that he could watch himself giving her an orgasm orally, and see how her body moved, or he asked a friend to do it.'

Debra rolled her eyes. 'Buchan wasn't like Rossetti's set, you know.'

'That's in the official biography. But until we found the pictures, we had no idea that he did erotic work, did we?' Jake dressed her tenderly. 'It'll be very interesting to see if Sykes' family can shed any light on it. Someone must have some papers, somewhere – letters, a diary or whatever – which tell the full story.'

Debra smiled affectionately at him. 'Well, Sherlock, we'll just have to hope that I can dig up some information.'

They didn't mention the subject again until the following evening. Jake, who had been to see the valuer, was late home, and Debra was sitting working at her computer when he walked in. She tipped her head back to look at him. 'Hi. How did you get on?'

He stooped to kiss her. 'He'll let us know in about a week to ten days. How about you?'

She smiled. 'Let's put it this way – we're off to Norfolk, on Thursday.'

'Whereabouts?'

'A little place called Blakeney. Apparently it's popular with tourists because of the trips out to see the seals. It's marshy, full of rare birds, and used to be a fishing village.'

'And now, it's the playground of the rich?' he guessed.

'Not exactly, but there's a quay there, so I imagine that the yachting types probably moor there and head for the local pubs.'

'Right.'

She picked the atlas up from her feet. 'Here,' she said, flicking to the page which covered Norfolk and pointing out the tiny village.

Jake smiled at her. 'So are we going to book somewhere, or take pot luck?'

She thought about it for a moment. 'Pot luck. If we can't stay in Blakeney, we could always go on to the next village and stay in a pub or hotel there.'

'Okay. If we leave here at about ten, we can have lunch somewhere on the way.' He gave her a sidelong look. 'And then, Mrs Smith, we can look up the Sykeses.'

Eight

Jake pulled into the car park of the Red Lion with a sigh of relief. 'They have accommodation here,' he said, 'so staying right here's fine by me. I need a beer,' he added, licking dry lips. 'A really, really cold one. And a shower.'

Debra smiled at him. 'Anyone would think that we'd driven for hundreds of miles without a break.'

'It bloody well feels like it! Honestly, I'd rather drive for six hours on a motorway, than for three hours on these tiny narrow roads that aren't really big enough for two cars to pass. And I don't think I've ever come across so many cyclists.'

'Not even in your Cambridge days?' Debra teased.

Jake rolled his eyes. 'At least you could *see* them. Here, they're hidden by hedges and reeds and whatever.'

'Come on,' she said, climbing out of the car. 'You get the case – I'll book a room and get you that nice cold beer you're rabbiting about.'

'That's about the first sensible suggestion you've made all day!' Jake informed her, closing his door and stretching.

She pulled a face at him, and sauntered into the pub. By the time that Jake arrived in reception with their suitcase,

Debra had already booked their room, and a pint of ice-cold beer was waiting for him on the gleaming mahogany bar. She patted the bar stool next to hers. 'Come on. Drinkies.'

He grimaced, flexing the muscles in his back. 'I need a shower, after that drive.'

'You can have one in a minute. Beer first.'

Jake drained the glass in fifteen seconds flat, and placed it on the bar. '*Now* can I have a shower?'

Debra laughed. 'Honestly, men!' She finished her glass of mineral water and smiled at the barman. 'See you later, Steve.'

'See you, Debra,' he said with a smile.

Jake frowned as Debra led the way to their room. 'Do you know him or something?'

She shook her head. 'I only met him when he checked us in.'

'So how come you're on first name terms with him, as though you're long-lost pals?'

Debra rolled her eyes. 'Oh, Jake, don't over-react. The guy was just being friendly. He's probably like that with everyone. No doubt being nice to tourists is the best way to get handsome tips from them.'

'Hm.' Jake wasn't convinced. Debra was very attractive; it stood to reason that just about any man would want to proposition her. Hadn't he done that, himself, when he'd seen her in that second-hand bookshop?

'Jake, stop being grumpy. We're on holiday.'

'Sorry.' He put his arm round her. 'When I've had a shower, I'll be out of jealous axe-fiend mode.'

'I'm glad to hear it,' she said lightly.

Much to her delight, the narrow window in their heavily beamed room had a view of the quay, and their bed was a double rather than the standard hotel twin singles. The flowered curtains with the matching bedspread, the sloping ceiling and the pitcher and bowl on the oak dressing-table gave the room a cottagey feel; Debra bounced on the bed, smiling happily. 'This was an inspired choice, Mr Matthews.'

'I can't take the credit, I'm afraid – I'd just had enough of driving!' he said, setting the case on the bed next to her and pulling out his wash-bag. 'Anyway, I need a shower.'

'Actually, I could do with one, too.' She gave him an impish smile. 'Fancy sharing a towel?'

'What if I said no?'

She grinned. 'I'd just have to ignore you, wouldn't I?' She went over to close the curtains, then stripped swiftly, making it into the bathroom before Jake did.

'That's unfair,' he protested.

'No, it isn't. Just think – I can wash your back for you.'

'Just my back?'

She grinned at the hopeful note in his voice. 'Well, I suppose you did all the driving. Though I did offer to take over,' she reminded him.

'I know, and it's my own stubborn fault for refusing.'

'Exactly.' She took the wash-bag from him, hanging it on the end of the towel rail, and stripped him slowly. 'So you don't really deserve this, but . . . I think I'll make allowances.'

Jake smiled to himself. In other words, she was feeling randy; and even if she hadn't admitted it, he would have known by the physical signs. Her breasts had become slightly swollen, and her nipples were hard and dark.

His own physical reaction to her was equally obvious; Debra gave him an over-the-top pout, stroked his erect cock, took the soap from their wash-bag, and climbed into the bath. She beckoned to him, wiggling her hips; grinning, he joined her, pulling the shower curtain across behind her and switching on the water.

She held the soap under the water, then lathered her hands and began washing Jake's back. He closed his eyes, leaning against the wall; she smiled to herself at the look on his face. He really was tired after their journey. But she knew a way to revitalise him . . .

She lathered her hands again, and gently washed his penis, rubbing it back and forth; Jake gave a soft murmur, and began stroking her breasts. As her movements became quicker, he slid one hand between her thighs.

'Debra?'

'Mm?'

'How about we finish this shower pretty quickly, and have a little lie-down before dinner?'

She nuzzled his shoulders. 'And there I was thinking that you were going to offer to fuck the arse off me.'

He laughed. 'Apart from the fact that neither of us happens to be into that particular sexual delicacy . . .' He gently removed her hands from his penis, and picked up the soap, lathering her body swiftly and then sluicing her skin clean again. Then he switched off the water, stepped out of the bath to grab a towel, and wrapped it round her before lifting her out of the bath.

'That's a bit macho, isn't it?' she teased.

'No. It's selfish, actually, because you'll be *ages* if I let you do this yourself,' he retorted, briskly rubbing her dry. She pulled a face at him as he towelled himself dry, but allowed him to lead her back into the bedroom.

He took the case from the bed, then pulled back the covers. 'Mm. Nice crisp cotton sheets. It seems a pity to crumple them, really.'

Debra shook her head. 'No. It's like when you were a child, and you woke up in the morning and saw snow everywhere – you just *had* to make as many tracks in it as you could. Or if you see a steamed-up window – how can you resist drawing a face on it, or writing a stupid comment?'

He chuckled. 'Mm, I know what you mean.' He struck a pose. 'Sheets, prepare to meet thy crumpled doom!'

She couldn't help laughing, and collapsed into an unceremonious heap with him in the middle of the bed. He tickled her until she squirmed, then bent to kiss her. He nibbled at her lower lip; as she opened her mouth, the kiss became more passionate, with Debra's tongue exploring his mouth.

Within a few moments, they had changed position, so that Debra was lying on top of Jake, straddling his thighs. She rocked back slightly, so that she could put the tip of his cock at her entrance, then slowly lowered herself onto it.

He gave a murmur of pleasure, and closed his eyes. 'God, you feel good,' he said softly.

'You don't feel so bad, yourself,' she replied, starting to move her hips in small circles as she raised and lowered herself onto his cock. She loved the way he felt inside her, the way he filled her to the hilt: with Jake, she had quality *and* quantity, she thought gleefully.

She arched backwards, changing the angle between their bodies to give them both maximum pleasure. As she came, her quim rippling round him, she felt his balls lift and tighten, and his cock twitching as he reached his own orgasm.

She bent her head to kiss him lightly, then climbed off him, settling happily by his side. He shifted to cuddle her, his face against her hair.

'One duly crumpled pair of sheets, methinks,' he said, smiling.

'Definitely.'

They lay in silence for a while; then Jake drew a hand down her body. 'So, now we're in Blakeney, what's the plan about finding Sykes' family?'

'Well, I was intending to ask the barman if he knew anyone by the name of Sykes, but you insisted on coming up here.' She stroked his midriff. 'Anyway, now you've had what you wanted—' Jake grinned, and kissed her breasts '—perhaps we can go back downstairs and I can have another go at asking about Sykes.'

'Okay.' He delivered a slap to her rump which made more noise than pain. 'Up you get, then, wench.'

When they finally dressed and returned to the bar, the barman had obviously gone off duty; a middle-aged woman, whom Jake assumed was the landlady, was polishing glasses.

Debra nudged him. 'Your turn.'

'Hm?'

'You'll be better at charming information out of her than I will.'

'How do you mean?'

'Just give her one of your knockout smiles, Jake. She'll tell us everything, then.'

'That's assuming that she knows everything. Blakeney isn't exactly a tiny village, is it?'

'Mm, it's not the "one-eyed, blinking sort o' place" I was half-expecting,' she agreed. 'But it's worth a try.'

'A joint effort,' Jake suggested. He took Debra's hand, and sauntered over to the bar with her.

'Good afternoon,' he said, smiling.

'Good afternoon. You're our new guests, aren't you?'

Jake nodded. 'Jake Matthews and Debra Rowley.'

'I'm Susan Wetherby, the landlady.'

'Nice to meet you.' He smiled again. 'Can we have a pint of beer and a dry white wine, please? And one for yourself, of course.'

'Thank you. I'll have an orange juice,' Susan replied. 'Is this your first visit to Blakeney?'

Jake nodded. 'Our first ever to Norfolk, actually. We just fancied a weekend away from London.'

'Mm. We get a lot of Londoners up this way. They come for the peace and quiet,' the landlady told him. 'Well, make sure you get a boat trip to see the seals at Blakeney Point. The coast road between here and Cromer is quite pretty, too, if you wanted to drive somewhere a bit livelier in the evening.'

'Thanks.' Jake took a sip of his beer. 'Actually, we're here on business, as well as pleasure.'

'Oh?' Susan Wetherby's little black eyes, which reminded Jake of a starling's, glittered with interest.

'My fiancée's writing a book,' he explained, 'about the life of a Victorian poet. We think he might have connections in the area, and maybe there might be some old papers we could look at.'

'One of his friends was called Richard Sykes,' Debra added. 'He's the one we're really interested in. His wife came from around here, and after he died, she came back here with her son. We're not sure if she remarried, though.'

Susan Wetherby thought for a moment. 'Well, there's old Dicky Sykes, who lives in the estate at the other end of the village. I don't know if he'd be a relative, but it might be worth a try.'

Debra and Jake exchanged a glance. Dicky Sykes. Richard's son, maybe? Or his grandson? 'Er – how old is he?' Debra asked.

'Somewhere in his eighties.' Susan smiled at them. 'He's as deaf as a post, when it suits him, but he's always willing to chat if you buy him a pint.'

'Right.' Jake nodded.

'Actually, his granddaughter Melissa works in the bar at lunchtimes,' Susan continued, 'and on Friday and Saturday nights. She might be able to tell you something, if Dicky can't.' She gave them the address, which Debra carefully wrote down. 'I'd have your trip out to Blakeney Point first, if I were you, then pop down and see him in the afternoon.'

'We will.' Debra smiled broadly at her. 'Thank you.'

'It's no trouble at all.' Susan returned her smile. 'Will you be eating here, tonight?'

Jake nodded. 'We thought we might have a wander along the quay, first.'

'There's a nice walk across the marshes, to Cley, but it's maybe a bit too hot for that, today.' Susan laughed. 'Not that you'll need to work up an appetite. The Norfolk air and the sea breeze will do that for you!'

'This place is timeless,' Debra said happily as they walked along the narrow path by the quayside. 'You can completely forget that London even exists, here.'

'Mm. It's a shame that there isn't a proper beach. I don't fancy walking barefoot in that mud.'

'It's sandy mud – clean really.'

'Clean mud?' Jake scoffed.

She ignored him. 'Susan told me that it's tidal; that's why you can only get the boat out to see the seals in the morning.'

'Right.' Jake slid his arm round her shoulders. 'Actually, I know what you mean. This place is so quiet, so still – no rush hour, no commuters, and no crowded tube trains. Bliss.'

'And it's probably always been like this. Most of these little flint cottages must have been here when Sykes first met his wife. Oh, by the way, I found out that her name was Mary.'

Jake nodded. 'The question is, did he meet her here, or in London?'

'London, I should think. I can't imagine him coming here – unless he was a local, too – so she must have been staying with family or friends in the city.' Debra shrugged. 'Do you think Dicky might be Richard Sykes' son?'

'Not if he's eighty. Remember, Sykes died in 1895. He might be the grandson, though.' Jake frowned. 'That's assuming that Mary didn't remarry or change her name back to whatever her maiden name was.'

'True. I hadn't thought of that.' She sighed. 'And if Dicky isn't Sykes' grandson?'

'Then we've reached a dead end, and we'll just have to forget about it.' He dropped a kiss on her cheek. 'In the meantime, let's live in hope.'

Debra nodded. 'And Susan was right, there's definitely something about the air, here. I'm starving!'

Jake grinned. 'I might have guessed. Come on, let's go and have some food.'

When they got back to the pub, the waitress told them that the food was all local, the poultry and beef, as well as the fish. They were spoiled for choice; eventually, Jake chose the baked crab with Stilton, and Debra opted for mussels in garlic. Neither of them could resist the skate in butter, or fresh local strawberries and cream.

'I think we should retire here,' Jake said, eating the last mouthful of baked crab with Stilton. 'We could have fresh fish every day for dinner, with our own home-grown vegetables. And then fresh fruit for pudding, or local home-made ice-cream. We could eat it on the terrace, looking out over the quay, and then sit there drinking good wine until the sun goes down. Oh, and my boxer dog called Sykes. He'd come boating with us, or swimming in the sea.'

'There's only one flaw with that idea.'

'What – that we'd get bored with fish? Or that we haven't got a dog?'

'I could eat fish every day, and I'm happy to get a dog any time you want.' She smiled at him. 'No, just a tiny thing. Like the fact that we're not rich enough to retire.'

Jake spread his hands. 'We might be.'

Debra sighed, knowing exactly what he meant. 'I don't really want to think about that, for the moment. Anyway, I thought you'd want to retire to Greece. Or Rome.'

'So I could make love to you in olive groves and deserted ruined temples?'

She grinned. 'You've got a one-track mind, Jake Matthews.' She took a sip of wine, and then looked at him. 'By the way, what was all that stuff you told Susan about my being your fiancée?'

'Well, I thought you'd rather be semi-respectable, instead of having her think that you were just here for a dirty weekend with me.'

'And that's all you meant by it?'

Jake nodded. 'I'm not proposing to you in the middle of a pub.'

'Does that mean you're planning to do so in some other place?'

'And at some other time, yes.' He took her hand, and kissed her fingertips. 'When I think you might accept.'

'It must be all this fresh air going to your head,' Debra quipped.

Jake leaned across the table. 'Not to mention another part of my anatomy,' he whispered, and was gratified to see Debra's face going a beautiful shade of red.

Their trip to Blakeney Point, the next morning, was every bit as good as Susan Wetherby had said it would be. Debra fell in love with the seals, and informed Jake on the way back to the quay that she might go along with his idea of retiring to Norfolk, on condition that they had their own boat and she had a lap-top computer, so that they could picnic on Blakeney Point every day and she could write academic books among the seals. And on their return, their children could sit on the quayside and catch crabs with the aid of a line and a net, putting their booty into a red plastic bucket filled with sea-water.

Jake groaned. 'And you said that the fresh air had gone to *my* head? Come on, Deb, we're supposed to be going to see Dicky Sykes.'

'True.' She fished in her handbag, and brought out the address Susan had given them the previous afternoon. 'Well, Sherlock, let's go hunting clues to Richard Sykes – and what really happened.'

Dicky Sykes' house turned out to be one of the small flint-faced terraced houses at the other end of the village from the quay. The house looked shabby, the white paint peeling from the windowsills and doorframe, and the front garden laid to a slightly scruffy lawn instead of being filled with hollyhocks and lavender and Canterbury bells like its neighbours.

Debra looked at Jake. 'This isn't what I was expecting. He can't possibly be anything to do with Richard Sykes.'

'We won't know unless we try,' Jake reminded her, taking her hand. 'We're here, now. It's stupid to turn around and go away without even asking him, Deb.'

'I suppose so.' She swallowed hard, and rang the doorbell.

They waited for a while, and they were just about to think that no one was in when the door opened slightly. 'Who is it?' a cracked voice asked in a strong Norfolk accent.

'Mr Sykes? My name's Debra Rowley, and this is Jake Matthews. We wondered if we could come in to talk to you.'

'I haven't got anything to sell. And I haven't done anything wrong, either, if you're the police,' he added. His voice was slightly querulous and slightly aggressive, at the same time.

'Er – we're not the police, Mr Sykes,' Debra said. 'We just want to talk to you about someone we think might have been your grandfather.'

The door opened slightly wider, and he gave them a suspicious stare. 'Why do you want to know about him?'

'My fiancée's researching a book about a Victorian painter called Henry Walter Buchan,' Jake said. 'And we think your grandfather might have known him. So we wondered if you knew anything about him?'

The old man gave them a calculating look. 'I might do.'

Debra gave him her sweetest smile. 'We wondered if you might like to come to lunch with us. Our treat. Maybe we could talk more easily over a pint of beer.'

'Eh?'

She smiled to herself. Deaf as a post, when it suited him, according to Susan Wetherby. 'Or maybe a tot or two of whisky, if you'd rather?'

'Well, that's as may be. You'd better come in.' Dicky Sykes shuffled backwards, letting them into the house. The sitting room opened straight onto the street, and was as small and dingy as the outside of the house had been. It was untidy, too, as though Dicky Sykes had never heard of throwing things away, and a thick layer of grime coated the skirting boards and the dingy picture-frames on the walls. Debra wouldn't have minded betting that the wallpaper behind the pictures looked almost white in comparison.

'I haven't got anything in the house, so I can't offer you

anything to drink. Lissa doesn't do the shopping till Saturday,' he warned.

'Lissa?' Jake prompted.

'Lissa's my granddaughter. She lives with me.'

'She works at the Red Lion, doesn't she?' Debra asked.

Dicky eyed her with suspicion. 'What do you want to know that for, eh?'

Jake and Debra exchanged a glance. 'We don't mean any trouble, Mr Sykes. We're just trying to follow up a lead, that's all,' Debra said. 'We're not spying on you, or anything like that.'

'Hm.' He motioned to them to sit down. 'So what do you want to know about the family, then?'

'Well, anything you can tell us about your grandfather. When were you born, Mr Sykes?'

'1913. I've lived all my born days in this here cottage,' he said, a note of pride in his voice. 'And my father lived here before me, and his mother before him.'

'Was your father called Dicky, as well?'

He shook his head. 'No, my father was called Henry. His father was called Richard, though I don't know as anyone called him Dicky. He never lived in Norfolk. He was a London man, see. My grandmother came home to the village when he died. That was just after my father was born.'

Henry. Debra shot Jake a look of delight. Could Dicky's father have been named after Henry Walter Buchan, perhaps?

'And do you know anything about what your grandfather did?' Jake asked.

Dicky shook his head. 'No one ever talked about it, and I didn't ask. My grandmother didn't like questions.' He shrugged. 'She never married again, I know that much. She just lived here with my father.'

'When was your father born?'

'1894, or thereabouts.' The year before Sykes' death, Jake and Debra thought, looking at each other in hope. 'He married in 1912, but he died in the Great War, when I was still a babe in arms.' Dicky looked slightly wistful. 'My mother wasn't long after him, so my grandmother brought me up. She never said much about the family, or London. We kept ourselves to ourselves – she didn't like to see the family, except at Christmas. Then I married our Nelly – God rest her soul – and we had Mary. I named her after my grandmother,' Jake and Debra exchanged another glance of delight – 'but she was nothing like her.' He sighed. 'Nothing at all. Our Mary was trouble, right from the first. She ran away to Norwich, and brought Lissa back with her a year later. Then she was off to Norwich again, leaving Lissa with me and Nelly. You never really hear from her now, unless she wants something.' Dicky shrugged, looking disapproving. 'Not that I've got anything to give her. Just my pension – and that's not enough to keep a flea alive. And to think I fought in the war for that.'

Debra squeezed his hand. 'Will you let us take you out to lunch, Mr Sykes?'

'You might as well call me Dicky. Everyone else does.'

'Dicky. We'd like to buy you lunch.'

'What for?'

'Because you've helped us,' Debra said simply. 'We wondered what happened to Richard Sykes' family, and now we know.'

'There's just me and Lissa – and our Mary, though God only knows what she's up to, in the city. I don't ask, she doesn't tell, and that's the way I like it.'

Debra smiled to herself. She rather liked the old man. He was a bit crusty, but she admired his independence. And he was her link with Sykes – and Buchan. 'So where would you like to go, for lunch?'

'Not the Red Lion. Lissa's busy, and I don't want her feeling obliged to come and chat to me,' was the immediate answer.

'How about the Quay Point Hotel?' Debra suggested.

Dicky nodded. 'I'll just have a quick wash and brush-up, then,' he said. 'If you'll excuse me?'

Debra smiled at him. 'Of course.'

Dicky went to change; Debra looked round the room, and wrinkled her nose. 'This Lissa person doesn't believe in keeping her grandfather comfortable, does she?'

Jake shook his head. 'I can't see Susan Wetherby employing someone scruffy or dirty, though.'

'No.' Debra's voice was full of disapproval. 'And fancy letting him stay here with no food in the house!'

'I know.' Jake's attention was suddenly caught by a photograph. 'Deb, look at this!'

Her eyes widened as she saw the picture. 'She looks familiar,' Debra said, frowning. 'I know her from somewhere.'

'Of course you do! She's the Hyacinth Girl,' Jake hissed.

'What?'

'That's the woman who was Buchan's favourite model, I'd swear it on my life. He painted her dozens of times. *The*

Hyacinth Girl, Guinevere, Ophelia – half his paintings are of her.'

'But what's she doing here?' A shiver ran down Debra's spine as she made the connection. 'My God. Mary Sykes. Dicky's grandmother was the Hyacinth Girl. And the woman in our pictures.'

Jake nodded. 'No wonder she didn't want to talk about her husband, or London. You know what everyone thought of models, in Victorian times.'

'That they were all whores, yes,' Debra nodded. 'And she wanted to be respectable, here, so she just pretended that London had never happened.' She paused. 'Did she meet Buchan first, do you think, or Sykes?'

'It could have been either.' Jake's voice was shaking slightly with excitement. 'Buchan was married. Maybe Mary had modelled for him, fallen in love with him a bit. Maybe she had an affair with him, but knew that it would go nowhere because Buchan couldn't or wouldn't divorce his wife.'

'And then Sykes came along. He was in the same set, a friend of Buchan's, and if she was married to him, it meant that she could continue to see Buchan without people being suspicious,' Debra added thoughtfully. 'Supposing they really did have an affair, and because she still slept with Sykes, he either turned a blind eye to it or kidded himself that nothing was going on.'

'Then Dicky,' Jake finished quietly, 'might actually be Buchan's grandson, not—'

A noise at the door cut him short. Dicky had obviously spruced himself up specially for lunch – he was at least clean, although his clothes had seen better days, and Lissa

161

obviously detested ironing as much as she detested dusting.

'We – er – we were admiring the picture,' Debra said, feeling guilty, replacing the photograph.

Dicky came over to them, and nodded in approval. 'That's Mary. My grandmother, that is, not my daughter. She was a beauty,' he said. 'My Lissa takes after her.'

'Right.' Debra felt a slight twinge of unease. Bearing in mind how much Jake loved the painting, who was to say that he wouldn't fall for a woman who was her double, in the flesh?

Jake, as if sensing her fears and wanting to reassure her, took her hand, squeezing her fingers. 'Come on, then. I don't know about you two, but I'm starving!'

Despite a couple of pints and a glass or two of whisky over lunch, Dicky remained tight-lipped about his grandfather. Either he really did know nothing about Richard Sykes and his publishing business in London, or else his grandmother, who had brought him up, had conditioned him never to talk about his grandfather.

If there were any papers in the loft of the tiny little cottage, Dicky didn't know about it, or didn't want to know. There were dozens of questions Debra wanted to ask him, but she knew that there was no point. He'd already warned her that his grandmother never talked about London, and Dicky obviously took his lead from his grandmother.

Even so, her mind raced with the possibilities. If only there was a way to find out, for sure. She'd do anything to find out the truth. Anything.

Nine

'She doesn't look anything like her grandmother. I don't know what Dicky was talking about,' Debra said quietly to Jake, nodding at the barmaid in scorn.

'That might not be Melissa Sykes.'

'Yes, she is – I heard someone at the bar call her Lissa,' Debra informed him tartly. She looked at the woman with dislike. Lissa Sykes was tall and slender, with a bust which owed a great deal to a push-up bra, a skirt that was just that little bit too short, and permed shoulder-length blonde hair which reminded Debra of a poodle's curls. The simile was rendered even more apt by the red ribbon, tied at the top with a bow, which Lissa wore in her hair.

Debra found it difficult to see the relationship between the beautiful model of *The Hyacinth Girl* and the tarty and rather obvious woman behind the bar. Her dislike of Lissa increased even more when Jake went up to the bar and spent nearly fifteen minutes talking to her. Debra couldn't see Jake's face, but she could see Lissa's very clearly – and there was a lot of flirting going on. They were obviously also talking about her, as Lissa kept glancing over in her direction. Debra was sure that she could see a mixture of amusement and pity on the woman's face – so what the hell was Jake saying?

By the time that a smiling Jake returned, bearing a glass of cold white wine and a beer, Debra was in the sort of mood to throw the drink over him.

'All right?' he asked, seeing the scowl on her face.

'You took your time, didn't you?'

'I was talking to Lissa. Dicky's granddaughter.'

'I know who she is,' Debra said tightly. 'What did she want?'

'Well.' Jake smiled at her. 'I think we might have another lead.'

'Oh?' Despite her bad mood and the twinges of jealousy, Debra was interested. Disdain fought a brief battle with curiosity – and lost. 'What sort of lead?'

'Well, Dicky obviously told her that we'd been to see him, and took him out to lunch. She said that he never liked talking about her grandmother, but her mother had told her a few stories which had made her wonder.'

'I thought she never saw her mother?'

'Apparently, it upsets Dicky, so she sees her mother in secret. She tells Dicky that she's going shopping in the city.'

'I see.' Debra's voice was frosty.

'Anyway, there might be some letters in the loft.'

'Letters?' A shiver ran down Debra's spine as she thought of the possibilities. 'You mean letters from Mary Sykes?'

Jake shrugged. 'Lissa isn't sure whether they're to her or from her.'

'Letters.' Debra's eyes gleamed. 'If they're to her – maybe they could be from Buchan?'

'Maybe.' Jake agreed. 'And I was thinking. Dicky said that Mary Sykes came back to Blakeney in 1894, just after his grandfather died. We know that Richard Sykes died in 1895 – and also that Henry Walter Buchan died from cholera in the winter of 1893.'

'Which leaves three possibilities. One, Mary knew about Sykes' erotic publishing, and couldn't cope with it. So she left him, and came back here with her son. She pretended to her family that he was dead, so they still thought that she was respectable because she was a widow.'

'That's quite plausible,' Jake agreed.

'Two, Dicky's dates are wrong, and Mary came back to Blakeney in 1895, after Sykes died – not in 1894. That makes her a devoted wife to Sykes, having nothing to do with Buchan apart from model for a few pictures, because her husband asked her to do it as a favour to his friend. Buchan used a different model for the bodies of his obscene pictures, just putting Mary's face on them from other sketches he'd made of her, because he fantasized about Mary, and his feelings weren't reciprocated.'

'Also plausible.'

'Or three . . .' She took a sip of wine. 'Dicky was right about the date, and Mary told the truth – Dicky's grandfather died before 1894. Now, as Richard Sykes died in 1895, he couldn't have been Dicky's grandfather. Which means that Buchan, who died the year before, was his real grandfather, even though Sykes let the child have his name,' Debra said.

'Though why would he do that?'

'Sykes was an erotic publisher. Maybe he'd had a wild life before his marriage, and had caught the clap so many times that he couldn't give Mary the child that she so desperately wanted. He loved Mary, and wanted to see her happy, so he arranged with his best friend, Henry Walter Buchan – who would do anything to help him, and was also in love with Mary, who'd modelled for him – that Henry would make her pregnant.'

Jake smiled affectionately at her. Sometimes, he thought, she was more of a romantic at heart than she let on. 'And which do you think it is?'

'Guess.'

'You'd like it to be the third. Which would explain why they called the child Henry.'

'And I bet Buchan was the godfather.'

'If he'd lived long enough to see the child. Henry Sykes was born in 1894 – and Henry Buchan died in 1893.'

'Pedant,' Debra said, pulling a face.

'Yep.'

'So when is she going to meet us with the letters?'

Jake coughed. 'Um. She's meeting me tomorrow morning.'

As his words sank in, Debra frowned. 'Meeting you. Not us.'

He winced. 'I know, I know, it sounds bad. But you're an academic, Deb. Loads of people are scared of intelligent and academic women. Whereas me, plain old Jake the builder, well, I don't pose a threat to anyone.'

Debra wasn't mollified in the slightest. Apart from the fact that Jake was just as academic as she was, and had a better first degree than she did, Debra didn't think that Lissa Sykes looked the sort of woman who'd be scared of anything. 'Oh, really?'

He sighed. 'Look, Debra, we want to know the truth, don't we? So let's just play it her way. She meets me tomorrow, we get the letters, and everybody's happy.'

'So what does she get out of it?'

Jake rolled his eyes. 'Don't be so suspicious.'

'Come on, Jake. A handsome stranger chats you up in the bar—'

'I was *not* chatting her up!'

'Yes, you were.'

'Oh, and who was it who told me that I was being ridiculous when Barman I-think-I'm-Tom-Cruise Steve chatted you up, yesterday?'

'You were.' Debra scowled at him. 'Okay, we'll take another tack. A couple of people have been talking to your grandfather about his grandfather. Are you going to offer him your great-great-grandmother's letters, simply out of the goodness of your heart?'

He spread his hands. 'Okay. If the letters are any use to us, there's a chance that the university might buy them. Which means that she'll split the money with Dicky.'

'I see.'

'Which is only fair, as she's the one who's brought the letters to our attention – Dicky didn't tell us anything about them.' He smiled at Debra. 'You can't blame her, really, for wanting to make something of herself. She doesn't want to be a barmaid for the rest of her life, stuck in a remote seaside village which is only lively in the tourist season. If she gets some money together, she and George can go to London.'

'George being the boyfriend?' Dicky, who had taken a

shine to Debra, had told her over lunch that he wished that Lissa was as steady as her, and had a nice boyfriend like Jake instead of a rough long-haired layabout who spent all his time tinkering with motorbikes and playing in a band.

'Yes.' He finished his drink. 'Do you want another?'

Debra shook her head. 'I'm hungry. Let's go out to eat.'

'Where?'

'How about that fish restaurant we saw this afternoon?' Anywhere except the Red Lion. Despite what Jake had just told her, Debra still distrusted Lissa's motives, and the last thing she wanted was to have the barmaid watching them all evening.

'Fine.' He took her hand. 'Let's go.'

The next morning, Jake walked over to the car park by the quay. Lissa Sykes was waiting there for him, clad in a pair of faded denims which looked as though they'd been sprayed on, four-inch black patent stilettos, and a low-cut top which revealed the generous curves of her breasts.

She smiled at him, tossing back her hair. 'I didn't think you'd come.'

He shrugged. 'We had an arrangement, didn't we? I always keep my word.'

'I see.' She eyed him up and down. 'Let's walk. We can talk more easily, then.'

They walked along to the far end of the car park. It was too early for the tourists to have come for a day trip to the beach, and slightly too late for the villagers to be taking their labradors for a stroll along the quay; the whole place seemed deserted. In London on a Saturday morning, Jake thought, the whole place was buzzing; here, it was like being in another time.

Lissa was silent; Jake eyed her capacious handbag, wondering whether there was a bundle of letters in it. A bundle of letters, written in faded brown ink, in Victorian copperplate handwriting. Letters to Mary from Buchan – or even letters to Buchan from Mary, letters which he'd generously sent back to her to avoid all risk of a stain on her name. Letters tied with blue ribbon, and interleaved with lavender.

Eventually, he coughed.

Lissa looked at him. 'What?'

'Did you – er – manage to find the letters?' he asked.

She shook her head. 'They weren't where Mum said they were. I couldn't exactly start poking round in the loft last night – Dicky would have been suspicious. He'd have wanted to know what I was doing, and if I'd told him . . .' She shrugged. 'So I'll just have to wait a couple of weeks, until he's forgotten about it, and forgotten you.' She licked her lower lip, implying that although Dicky might forget Jake, she certainly wouldn't.

'I see.' Jake strove to keep the disappointment from his face.

'He's protective about his grandmother. Remember, she brought him up. I suppose that's why he agreed to bring me up, in the end, when Mum dumped me on his doorstep and buggered off back to her fancy man in Norwich.'

Jake winced, not knowing what to say.

'I'll have another look. I could always send them on to you. Or maybe I could even come up to London for the day, deliver them in person so I know they get to you all right. You know what the post office are like, always losing things.'

'I work fairly long hours,' Jake said. 'And I wouldn't be able to see you at work.'

'Why not?'

'Because I never know where I'll be, until the evening before.'

'So you could ring me and let me know where to meet you.'

He shook his head. The way Lissa was talking, it sounded like she was trying to make some kind of romantic assignation with him. He didn't need that sort of complication – even if he did find her attractive. There was Debra to consider. 'You can always send the letters by recorded delivery. I'll give you some money to cover the costs.' He smiled. 'I'd better give you our address, then.'

The word 'our' obviously registered with Lissa, though she looked as if she couldn't give a damn. She opened her handbag, tipping it towards Jake while she rummaged for a pen. There was a packet of condoms near the top – she obviously meant him to see it – but he swallowed hard and looked away, pretending not to have noticed.

She smiled, then, handing him the pen and an old envelope. 'Write it down on the back of that.'

He wrote swiftly, and handed both the pen and the paper back to her. She dropped the pen, and bent down to retrieve it, deliberately giving Jake an eyeful of her cleavage. As she stood up again, her hand ran lightly along his thigh, cupping his groin and the soft swelling within for a brief moment.

Jake flushed beetroot, embarrassed.

'What's the matter, Jake?' she asked. 'No one saw. Stop worrying.'

He didn't answer.

'No one can see us, Jake.' Her eyes raked up and down his body. 'Look, we may as well put our cards on the table. I find you attractive,' she said, 'and I don't think I'm alone. Otherwise you wouldn't have met me on your own, would you?'

'Melissa,' he said, hoping that his use of her full name would somehow bring her back to her senses, 'I'm with Debra.'

'So? What difference does that make?'

All the difference in the world, Jake thought. And even if he hadn't been with Debra, Lissa was too obvious to be his type. 'Anyway, I thought you said you had a boyfriend – George?'

'Yes.' She smiled. 'And he's very, very . . .' She paused. 'Shall we say, accommodating? He says he doesn't mind what I do, as long as I'm happy.'

Jake swallowed hard.

'Well.' She shrugged. 'Maybe I won't be able to find the letters.'

His eyes narrowed. 'What are you saying?'

'Isn't it obvious?'

'If you're saying what I *think* you're saying . . .'

She gave him a sensual pout. 'No fuck, no letters. If you want it in black and white.'

Jake was appalled and aroused at the same time. He'd never been in this sort of situation before. Sexual blackmail. Even the strongest come-on he'd had, from a bored housewife when he was doing some small building work for her, had never been like this. There had never been the implication: *do what I want, or else.* He didn't like it at all – particularly as he had no choice in the matter.

He looked at her. 'How do I know that there are any letters?'

'You just have to trust me,' she said. 'Take my word for it.'

'And if I don't believe you?'

'Then walk away. It's your choice.' She laughed. 'But then you'll never know the truth, will you?'

'And if I do believe you?'

'Then you know what I want.'

He thought about it for a moment. Hard-bitten trollop that Lissa Sykes was, she couldn't be lying about the letters. She couldn't have made something like *that* up. There had to be something which would tell the truth about Buchan and Sykes and Mary. There just had to be.

He nodded, finally. 'Okay. You win.'

'Good.' She urged him towards a deserted corner of the car park. 'There's a little hollow over here. All the courting couples in Blakeney know about it. No one can see you.'

Jake didn't like the idea of being the other half of Melissa Sykes' courting couple, but he had no choice in the matter. Not if he wanted to know the truth about Buchan. And since he'd found the pictures, discovering the truth about them had become the most important thing in the world. It was what had brought him to Blakeney in the first place, with Debra – because they wanted to know the truth.

He knew that Debra felt the same. He just hoped that

she'd see it his way, if she ever found out about it, and understood his reasons. Though maybe there was a way out of it . . . 'I – er – I haven't got a condom,' he said. 'And considering that we barely know each other, we ought to be on the safe side.'

She grinned at him. 'I agree. Lucky I've got some, isn't it?'

Shit, Jake thought. There was nothing more he could do now. He had to go through with it.

Lissa unzipped his jeans, pushing them down over his hips, and was gratified to see the bulge of his cock through his underpants. She pulled off her top, tossing it down onto the grass. She was wearing a black lace bra underneath, which she unclasped swiftly and tossed to one side; then she unzipped her jeans, peeling them down to reveal her black lace G-string. She had a good body, Jake acknowledged. She was thinner than Debra – and Jake preferred his women to be curvy – but her small, shallow breasts were firm, and her nipples were richly dark against her pale skin.

She smiled at him, and dropped to her knees in front of him. Taking the condom out of her bag and ripping the wrapper open, she placed the small rubber disc expertly in her mouth. Then, to Jake's mingled horror and arousal, she rolled it over his cock with her mouth.

She fellated him for a moment, until she saw his eyes dilate, then silently urged him to sit down on her discarded top. He smiled wryly to himself. It was Raleigh and Elizabeth the First, in reverse. Though her intentions towards him were far from chivalrous.

Straddling him, she squatted until her quim just rubbed

against his cock; then she pushed the gusset of her knickers to one side and curled her fingers round his cock, placing its tip at her entrance. Then she lowered herself down, pushing hard so that she sank all the way down onto him. Despite the condom, Jake could feel her internal muscles working round him as she began to move slowly over him, swaying in small circles as she lifted and lowered herself onto his cock.

She took one of his hands, placing it round her breasts and urging him to rub her erect nipples. Jake's eyes met hers. She shrugged. 'Either you do it my way, or you don't get the letters. You agreed, remember.'

'Yes,' he said, his voice dull. It was the first time that he'd ever been in a situation where he thought that he'd be going through the motions rather than enjoying a sexual encounter. Dutifully, he stroked her breasts, his thumbs playing with her nipples. Then he had an idea. The quicker he could make her come, the better. Smiling, he eased one hand between their bodies, sliding his fingers under the satin of her knickers and seeking her clitoris.

She gasped as he found it, and began to manipulate the hard little button of flesh deftly, his finger moving rapidly in a figure-of-eight shape. 'Oh, yes,' she said, leaning back and caressing her own breasts. 'Oh, that's good.'

Images blurred in front of Jake's eyes. Debra, straddling his body and smiling at him as she lowered herself onto his cock. The Hyacinth Girl, kneeling in front of her customer, about to fellate him. And Lissa Sykes, her face contorted in a mixture of arousal and triumph . . .

At last, he felt her quim ripple round him; the tiny rocking movements tipped him into his own orgasm and he came, his semen filling the tip of the condom. She deftly stood up, took a tissue from her bag, and removed the condom from his cock, wrapping up the contraceptive in one quick movement and shoving it back into her handbag.

She dressed again, swiftly; Jake stood up, handing her the black top, and pulled his jeans up. Part of him wanted to turn away from her while he zipped up his flies, but he knew that she'd only laugh at his false modesty.

'So,' she said, giving him a smile. 'I'll be in touch.'

'I'd better give you some money, for postage.' He fished in his jeans pocket for his wallet, and extracted a ten-pound note.

'Thanks.'

Why did he feel that he'd just paid her for a fuck? he wondered, hating himself.

She walked off down the car park; Jake waited for a moment before following her. He felt used. All he wanted now was to have a good shower, scrub every trace of her off his skin. At the same time, he knew that Debra was either waiting in their room for him, or waiting downstairs, in the Red Lion. How could he possibly explain to her why he wanted a shower so desperately?

When he got back to the Red Lion, Debra was sitting in the garden, a half-full glass of freshly squeezed orange juice by her side, pretending to be absorbed in the paper.

'Hi.' He slid into the rustic seat opposite her. 'All right?'

'Yes.' Her voice was expressionless, and although she didn't say it, he knew what she was thinking. You've been a bloody long time, just getting those letters from that woman. What else have you been doing?

She looked at him. 'So did you get them?'

'The letters? Er – no.' He swallowed. 'Lissa couldn't find them. She – er – she's going to have another look for us in another couple of weeks, when Dicky's forgotten about us, and then she'll send them on to us.'

'You mean to say you gave her *our* address?'

'Yes.' He curled his fingers round hers. 'Our address. Anyway, enough of her. What do you want to do today?'

'Well, it's Saturday. We're going home tomorrow.'

So much for staying until Monday, he thought.

'As it's our last full day in Norfolk, let's go into Norwich for the day. There are some beautiful buildings there, and the cathedral's worth a look.'

He understood exactly what she meant. She didn't want to spend the day in Blakeney, where she'd have to come face to face with Lissa Sykes. And where Lissa might be more than happy to enlighten her as to what had actually happened in the car park.

'Okay. I'll just change first, if you don't mind.'

'Change?'

'It's meant to be hot today, so if we're going to be walking round, I'd rather wear a loose shirt than a T-shirt.'

'Right.' Her voice was toneless, but he knew that she knew exactly why he wanted to change and shower.

By the time he came down again, feeling clean and refreshed, Debra had finished her orange juice and had made serious inroads into the crossword. She didn't smile when she saw him, merely walked to the car with him in silence.

She didn't speak much in the car, either; in the end, Jake gave up trying to make conversation, and switched the radio on, retuning it to Radio Three. Gregorian chant was playing, and although it annoyed him, he knew that Debra liked it, so he left it playing, concentrating on the drive.

Eventually, they arrived in Norwich, and parked in one of the multi-storey car parks. They spent the first part of the afternoon wandering round the small cobbled streets – Debra having said that she was too hot to eat – peering at the antique shops and art galleries and old-fashioned jewellers' shops.

Jake's eyes lit up as he looked in one particular window. There was something there that would be perfect . . . He coughed. Debra?'

'Mm?'

'This is probably the worst time I could pick, and I honestly intended to ask you some other time, but . . .'

'What?'

He took her hand. 'Have you seen that ring in the corner?' He nodded to the ring which had caught his eye: it was a plain band of gold, with a half hoop of sapphires and emeralds made into a tiny garland of forget-me-nots on the top.

'What about it?'

'I'd like to buy it for you.'

'A ring.'

'With all the connotations that go with it,' he said, his voice soft and intense.

'You're right,' she said. 'This is probably the worst time you could pick.'

'If you don't want it as an engagement ring, then how about as an eternity ring – for your right hand?'

She looked at him. 'Jake Matthews, do I detect a tiny note of panic in your voice?'

'No. It's a very large note of panic.'

She grinned. 'I don't think Lissa Sykes is worth all this, do you?'

His eyes widened. 'So you don't mind, about—?' He turned the rest of the question into a cough.

'I do mind. Very much so. But – she's not your type, so I guess you had a good reason. Like putting her in the right frame of mind to get us the letters.'

'Mm.' He swallowed. 'So how about it, then?'

She tipped her head to one side. 'If it fits, you're on.'

It turned out to be a Victorian ring, made in London. Debra tried it on the ring finger of her right hand and, to their amazement, it fitted. 'I told you,' Jake said. 'Fate. It's made for you.'

'Maybe.'

'So you're keeping it on your right hand?' Jake asked, as they left the shop.

She nodded. 'You haven't actually asked me to marry you, in so many words – so it's staying on this hand.'

'Right.'

They visited the cathedral next; Debra fell in love with it, exclaiming over the Victorian stained glass windows. 'That's definitely a Burne-Jones,' she said, pointing to one window.

'Maybe Buchan did one, too,' Jake suggested.

She shook her head. 'We don't know that he ever came to Norfolk.'

'True.'

Debra was equally taken by the sheer peace and quiet of

the cathedral close, and the way that the sunlight fell, dappled, on the pale stone of the building. They were lucky enough to catch the hourly chimes, the mournful minor key of the five-note phrase sending a shiver down their spines as it repeated itself with tiny variations.

Neither of them could resist the second-hand bookshops; after an hour of poking round musty, dusty shelves, they emerged triumphantly with an armful of books each.

'I'm hungry now,' Debra said.

'Funny, that, how you're always starving after a shopping frenzy. So do you want to go back to the Red Lion for dinner?'

Debra shook her head. 'I'll be really starving, by the time we get back. Let's eat here.'

'Okay. The first place we come to that looks nice . . .'

They ended up in a crowded and lively Mexican bar, eating plate after plate of nachos.

'Debra.'

'What?'

'About earlier.' He sighed, reaching over to take her hand. 'I'm sorry. Really, really sorry.'

'I don't want to talk about it,' she said crisply. 'All I can say is that those letters had better bloody well turn up, now.'

'Right.'

She smiled sweetly at him, removing the melted cheese from his side of the plate and eating it.

'I saw that!'

'Did you, now?' she teased, licking her fingers. 'And what are you going to do about it?'

'Hm.' He contented himself with adding guacamole to his

nachos. 'I've been thinking. About Dicky.'

'Oh?'

'He's got a moral right to those paintings. I mean, his grandmother was the model, and his father was probably the painter. Either way, his grandmother's husband owned the pictures.'

'We don't know that for sure.'

'Come on, Deb. You saw it, too.'

'True. But can you imagine Dicky's reaction to the paintings? You know how fastidious he is about Mary – and he doesn't see Lissa for the cheap little trollop she is. He'll never be able to accept them.'

Jake sighed. 'I suppose you're right.'

'Besides,' Debra added, 'I don't want her getting her sticky little paws on the money.'

Jake frowned. 'We must be able to do something for him, though. Pay for someone to come in and do his ironing and the housework, and cook him a decent meal once a day.'

'We'll do something, definitely,' Debra said. 'Though we have to see what happens, first. Don't forget, we don't even know that the pictures really are by Buchan.'

'Come off it. We both know it.'

'Gut feeling, yes – but we need the valuer's opinion. Supposing he says that they're fakes?'

Then, Jake thought to himself furiously, everything had been for nothing. 'We'll see.'

Eventually, they left the city and returned to Blakeney. Jake was amused to notice that as they pulled up in the car park, Debra switched the ring onto her left hand. She was obviously intending to make a point where Lissa Sykes was concerned; though he wisely said nothing.

'I'll get the drinks,' she said sweetly. 'Go and sit down.' She marched over to the bar; Lissa lingered over a customer, but was eventually forced to come over and serve Debra.

'What can I get you?'

Debra leaned on the bar, resting her chin on her left hand so that the ring was visible. 'A pint for my fiancé, a dry white wine for me – and whatever you're having.'

'Right.' Lissa poured the beer with obvious bad grace.

'It's so sweet of you to help us with our research,' Debra cooed. 'I've been working on the book for some time, but Jake's been a real help. He finds out all the difficult things for me.'

'I see.' Lissa banged the drinks on the bar.

'He has such a charming way with him, don't you think?'

Lissa gave her a look of pure malice, and took Debra's proffered money.

Debra gave her one of her sweetest smiles, and went over to Jake. Jake didn't dare ask her why she looked so pleased with herself; he only hoped that she hadn't upset Lissa enough to make the woman burn the letters.

Ten

'So what happened?' Debra asked, her eyes gleaming with suppressed excitement as Jake laid the portfolio on the table.

'The valuer's had a look at them.'

'Yes, I know that. You said he'd let us know today.' She couldn't keep the impatience from her voice. 'What did he say?'

'He said . . .' Jake spread his hands and smiled at her. 'Guess.'

She glared at him. 'Don't tease.'

'Okay.' Jake blew her a kiss. 'They're genuine Buchan.'

'Bloody hell.' Debra swallowed.

'Come on, Deb, we already knew that.'

'Or we thought we did.'

'And now it's been confirmed.'

Debra bit her lip. 'So how much are they worth?' Jake named a sum which took the colour from her cheeks. 'You're kidding!'

'I'm not.'

She wiped a hand over her face. 'Bloody hell,' she said again, her voice a mixture of shock and pleasure.

'So what, now?' Jake asked.

'Well, we can't keep them.'

'Why not?'

'Number one,' she said practically, 'they'd cost a fortune to insure, and the insurance company would insist on God only knows what security measures to protect them. Number two, we'd always be paranoid about being burgled.'

'We could deposit them in the bank – but there's no point in that, because they'd just be hidden away again,' Jake said. 'Or we could give them to one of the art galleries, so the whole world could see them.'

'Bearing in mind what the subjects are, can you see them being on display?' Debra asked.

'Well, I suppose not.' Jake wrinkled his nose. 'So what other options do we have?'

Debra thought about it. 'We could sell them.'

'Which would wipe out our mortgage and give us enough money to plate the entire house in gold and platinum, if we wanted.' Jake looked wistful, and took the pictures out of the portfolio, spreading them out on the dining room table. Seeing them sent shivers of pleasure down his spine. 'I think I'd rather have the paintings.'

'Me, too, but we've got to be sensible about it.'

'I know.' He sighed. 'Okay, suppose we sell them. What then? I mean, Sykes' family could claim that they should have the money, as the pictures really belonged to them.'

'Or to Buchan's family. Moral rights, as he was the artist, and there aren't any bills of sale or anything to prove that Sykes bought them.' She paused. 'Though that's pretty unlikely. I mean, why else would the pictures have been hidden under the floorboards in Sykes' house?'

'If it really was Sykes' house. We haven't proved that yet, either,' Jake reminded her. 'Maybe Sykes was one of his drinking cronies and just let Buchan keep the paintings here, away from the eyes of his family and his more conservative patrons.'

Debra smiled. 'Considering who the model was, I don't think so. Anyway, if we do sell them, we ought to give some of the money to Dicky. It's only fair.' She bit her lip. 'It'll make his last days a bit more comfortable.'

'If Lissa doesn't get her sticky mitts on it first.'

Debra scowled. 'That bitch.'

'I know you think that I'm completely out of my tree—'

Debra rolled her eyes. 'Not your conspiracy theory, again!'

He smiled good-naturedly at her. 'Indeed. But don't you think there's something weird about the way Sykes died in such poverty, when he had a goldmine hidden under the floorboards? Buchan died before him, and you know how prices shoot up once an artist dies. Why didn't Sykes cash in on the price-boom?'

'Maybe he was too soaked in drugs to remember about them.'

Jake shook his head. 'Once seen, not forgotten. No, I reckon that someone put the frighteners on him so he couldn't sell them.'

'But who? And why?'

'I haven't,' he said with a rueful smile, 'worked that one out yet. Maybe it was because he didn't want to embarrass Mary.'

'Nope.' Debra wasn't convinced. 'Okay, his wife was the model in the pictures. But if he'd sold them, it wouldn't have been to someone who'd keep the stuff on show. It would have been to a private collector, who wasn't likely to come into contact with Mary's family.'

'So we're back to my conspiracy theory. Maybe Buchan's wife found out about them. Maybe she found Mary's letters to him, after he died, and warned Sykes that if he ever let anyone see those pictures, or sold them, she'd tell the police about his erotic publications.'

'I know we're talking about the end of the Victorian period, when women were becoming more emancipated – at least, the wealthy and educated classes – but I can't imagine that. She'd have just destroyed them, surely?'

Jake sighed. 'Maybe you're right. I still think that someone put the frighteners on him, though.'

'Well, Sherlock, until you work out exactly what happened, what are we going to do with the pictures?'

'How about we leave them where we found them? At least they'll be safe there.'

She sighed. 'I suppose so. Though it seems a pity to hide them again.'

'Like you said, sweetheart, we're at risk of burglars, if we don't.'

'Yes. But how many people know about them? Jude, the valuer . . .'

'If the letters Lissa was talking about tell her anything about Buchan, she'll probably guess,' Jake added. 'And who knows who was listening when I went to the valuer, or who was watching you in the library when you started researching Sykes?'

Debra shivered. 'Don't. I hate the thought that someone's

been watching me. It makes my skin crawl.'

He slid his arms round her waist. 'It's a possibility, but it's very remote.'

'Good.' She kissed him. 'Now, I have to do some more work on my book, tonight. Why don't you go out for a beer with Adam and Joe?'

'You mean, you're not going to make me slave in the house?'

'Not in this heat. Just put the paintings back, that's all.'

'Okay.' He left the room for a moment, coming back with a crowbar, and lifted a couple of boards at the side of the room. He put the pictures back in the portfolio, wrapped it in a black plastic bag, and lowered it gently into the hole. 'There we go. Safe and sound again – for the moment, anyway.' With a look of regret, he replaced the floorboards. 'Right, then, I'll ring the boys. We'll probably grab a pizza, while we're out. What about you?'

She wrinkled her nose. 'I'm too hot to eat. I'll make myself a salad or something, later.'

'Okay.' Jake went to ring his brothers, and came back to see Debra, on his way out. 'See you later, then. I won't be back too late – probably about ten?'

'Fine.' She smiled at him.

'Don't work too hard.'

She rolled her eyes. 'Don't nag. See you later.'

When he returned, a couple of hours later, Debra was still at her computer.

'Hi. Did you have a good evening?' she said, tipping her head back to look at him.

187

'Yes, thanks. They all send their love, by the way, and they've invited themselves over for Sunday lunch. So we're doing a barbie,' he informed her.

She smiled. 'No problem. I take it the kids are coming, as well?'

'Mm.'

She grinned. 'Don't we sound domesticated?'

'Just a tad.' He licked her earlobe. 'How's the book coming on?'

'Okay.' Debra rubbed her hand over the back of her neck, and grimaced. 'Though I'm still boiling. And I'm wringing wet.'

Jake wiped the sweat from his own face. 'Funny how, when it's cool, we all whinge about the lack of the British summer. And when it's hot, we all whinge that we can't cope with it . . .'

She pulled a face. 'It's not the heat that I can't handle, it's the humidity.'

'Not necessarily. Have you ever been to Kew?'

'Not for years. Why?'

'There's a conservatory with about ten different climates in it. There's a cold and humid area, called a Cloud Forest, and that feels gorgeous – like a late autumn day.' He smiled at her. 'So it's the combination of heat and humidity that gets to you, not the humidity itself.'

'Don't be so pedantic.' She scowled at him. 'I just can't sleep properly when it's sticky, like this. I can't work properly, either, because I'm too hot and grumpy.'

'I'd already gathered that.'

'What's that supposed to mean?' she demanded.

He grinned. 'What you need is something to take your mind off it.'

'I have – the paintings, and what we should do with them. And what you were saying, when we were in Norwich. You're right. We ought to make Dicky's last days a bit more comfortable.'

'Even though you also think that Lissa will wheedle the money out of him – over your dead body, of course?'

Debra looked thoughtful. 'There must be some way we could do something for him and make sure that she doesn't take it from him.'

'We just haven't thought of it, yet,' Jake finished.

Debra grimaced, and lifted the hair from the back of her neck, pulling her hand away damp again. 'Yuck. I wish we'd gone to Norfolk this week, instead. It would have been miles cooler on the coast.'

'And we'd have had to sit in a traffic jam in those horrible narrow and twisty roads, getting hotter and hotter.' Jake wrinkled his nose. 'London's not so bad.'

'Yes, it bloody well is!' Debra scowled.

'I've got an idea.'

She looked suspiciously at him. 'Jake, it's far too hot and sticky to make love.'

'Who said anything about making love?' He took her hand. 'Come with me.'

She submitted to being led upstairs to the bathroom. 'What are you planning?' she asked.

'Something to make you feel a lot better,' he informed her. He undid the buttons of her thin shirt, and removed it, dropping it neatly into the linen basket. Her skirt followed, and then her half-slip, knickers and bra.

'I told you, I'm too hot to fuck,' Debra said grumpily.

'I didn't say anything about fucking you,' Jake retorted, lifting her up and putting her in the bath.

'Ah, that's cold!'

'Indeed.' He smiled at her, then switched the shower on. He fiddled with the head of the shower until the jet was a powerful spray, then directed it at Debra's bare skin.

She shrieked. 'That's *really* cold!'

'Exactly. I'm cooling you down.' He grinned at her. 'Hold your hair up.'

'What?'

'Hold your hair up,' he repeated patiently. 'I want to do your back.'

She rolled her eyes, but did as he asked, scooping her hair up and piling it on top of her head, weighing it down with her hands.

Jake directed the jet at the back of her neck, then down her spine. 'Better?' he asked.

'A bit,' she admitted.

He turned the cold tap onto full, and the jets of water came out almost like needles, the spray bouncing hard off her skin. 'How's that?'

'I'm not sure if it hurts or feels nice,' came the honest reply.

'Both, probably.' He continued spraying the jets of water up and down her back. 'Hydromassage is the term for it, I believe.'

'You've just made that up,' Debra accused. 'I bet you've never been anywhere near the inside of a beauty parlour!'

In answer, Jake moved the shower so that the water sprayed over her breasts. He concentrated on the soft undersides, then, as her nipples became darker and swollen, hardening under the ministrations of the water, he directed the jets onto the erect nubs of flesh.

Debra gasped, and he smiled. 'Open your legs,' he said softly.

'Are you making some perverted offer?' she asked.

He blew her a kiss. 'What do you think?'

She grinned, and brought her knees up, splaying her legs wide. 'Is this what you had in mind?'

'Not quite.' He coughed delicately. 'I need to see something a little more . . .'

She was tempted to make him ask her directly, but the look in his eyes, dark and intense, made her want to humour him. Without a word, she let her hair tumble back onto her shoulders, and slid her hands along her thighs until her fingers touched her labia. Then she held herself open, giving him an uninhibited view of her inner lips, her clitoris, and her vaginal entrance.

'Beautiful,' he said softly – and turned the shower-head so that the spray of water was concentrated in a single powerful jet.

He directed it straight at her clitoris.

Debra cried out as orgasm rocked through her. Jake continued to massage her clitoris with the jet of water; she gripped the side of the bath, closing her eyes and tipping her head back as another orgasm rippled over the first.

Gradually, Jake turned the water off, letting the jet become softer as the fluttering in her quim became softer. 'I told you

I could make you feel better, and take your mind off the heat,' he informed her with a grin.

'And how.' She tipped her head to one side. 'I must repay the favour, some time.'

'I've been sitting in an air-conditioned bar, most of the evening. I don't need cooling down.' He helped her out of the bath. 'So if you fancied returning the favour right this minute by taking me to bed and fucking me silly, that's no problem!'

She smiled at him. 'That can be arranged. I just want to get myself a drink of water, first.' She towelled herself dry, then wrapped the damp towel round herself, sarong-style. 'I'll see you in bed. Do you want anything?'

He gave her a theatrical leer. 'What do you think?'

'Oh, ha ha.' She pulled a face at him, and sauntered out of the bathroom.

When she returned to the bedroom, a glass of iced water in her hand, Jake was already in bed, covered by a sheet. He patted the bed next to him.

She placed the glass on the bedside table, then let the towel drop. Jake tipped his head to one side. 'Have I ever told you how beautiful you are?'

'Even when I'm hot, sticky and grumpy?'

'Even then.' He nodded to the bed. 'Are you going to join me, or what?'

'Ever heard of patience?'

He shook his head. 'Nope. I'm afraid that word isn't in my vocabulary.'

'It's a virtue,' she informed him.

'Not one of mine. Anyway, I'm not feeling even the

slightest bit virtuous, right now.' He held the sheet up invitingly.

She smiled at him, and slid between the cool cotton sheets. 'Mm. Nice.' She stretched luxuriously, and turned to him. 'Jake.'

'Yes?'

'Your turn, I think.'

In response, he smiled broadly, closed his eyes, and lay back against the pillow. 'I'm in your hands entirely.'

'Good,' she said softly.

Jake was fantasizing, wondering what she was going to do to him, so he wasn't really listening; he missed the note of mischief in her voice. Even if he had heard it, her next actions would have lulled his suspicions: she pushed the sheet back, and started kissing her way down his body, licking his skin and savouring the masculine tang of his skin.

He was willing her to start on his cock next, taking it into her mouth and sucking it hard – so he didn't register the slight movement she made behind her, taking an ice-cube from the glass. It was only when he felt her lips moving over his glans, and then suddenly felt something very very cold against his skin, that he realised what she was up to.

'Ah, that's cold!' he said.

Debra, who had her mouth full, didn't answer; she merely moved the ice-cube over his penis with her tongue, swirling it round the head of his cock and teasing it along the sensitive ridge at the base of his glans. Jake moaned, and she moved her head slightly, then held the ice-cube between her teeth and moved it up and down his shaft with long, slow strokes.

When the ice-cube eventually melted, she returned to

sucking his cock, working her mouth over him so that he gasped and started to thrust up to meet her. She stroked his thighs, drawing her nails lightly over his skin, and then eased her hand gently over his perineum, stroking and teasing the sensitive skin until Jake was moaning beneath her.

She kissed her way up his body again; he cupped her face, opening his mouth under hers and sliding his tongue into her mouth. Debra reached behind her for another ice-cube, her movements so subtle that Jake didn't notice them, and kissed her way back down his body to his cock.

A drop of clear fluid stood in the eye of his penis; she licked it, making her tongue into a delicate point and flicking it rapidly across his penis. Then she worked her mouth slowly down to the base of his cock, taking as much of it as she could into her mouth.

Jake groaned again; Debra, had her mouth not been filled by him, would have smiled wickedly. And then she slid the ice-cube over his perineum to his anus, pushing gently on the dark puckered skin until it gave, and the ice-cube slid inside him.

'I don't know whether to kill you for that,' Jake groaned, 'or to fuck you madly.'

Debra removed her mouth from his cock. 'Better than that. *I'll* fuck *you*,' she said.

What she'd already done with Jake had excited her enough to make her wet; she straddled him, tossing her hair back, and slowly lowered herself onto his cock. As she ground her quim against him, moving her body in small circles so that Jake's body moved against the ice-cube, he groaned again. 'Oh, Debra . . .'

'You started it, with the cold shower,' she told him with a grin, riding him harder.

'Two can play at that,' he warned her.

'Indeed.'

As soon as the ice-cube in his anus had melted, he reached across to the glass and took another, putting it between his teeth. He brought his lower body up so that he could brush the ice against her already hardened nipples; Debra gasped at the sensation, and began to lift and lower herself more rapidly on his cock.

Jake cupped her breasts, pushing them up and together; while he moved the ice on one nipple, his thumb and forefinger manipulated the other, until Debra was crying out. He gave a wicked grin against her breast, transferred the ice to his fingers, and began to rub it against her clitoris.

She jerked as he made contact with the sensitive flesh. 'Jake!'

'You asked for that one, sweetheart,' he told her, rubbing more rapidly, then taking one nipple into his mouth again.

The combined stimulation of Jake's cock deep inside her, his mouth on her breasts and the way he was rubbing her clitoris with the ice-cube was enough to make her come; her whole body quivering with the strength of her orgasm.

The way her sex-flesh spasmed round him was enough to bring Jake to his own orgasm, and he pushed as deeply into her as he could, his cock throbbing inside her.

Debra collapsed against him, putting her arms round his neck and burying her face in his shoulder; he rested his hands on the base of her spine. 'Better?'

'Much,' she murmured, nuzzling him contentedly.

'Good.' He licked her earlobe. 'And next time you say you want a drink of water to take to bed, I'll know exactly what to expect . . .'

Debra studiously ignored the wolf-whistle, lifting her chin and striding down the road. Suddenly, arms came round her waist and spun her round.

She shrieked, and looked into Jake's face. 'You bastard! You scared the living daylights out of me!'

He grinned. 'Well, that's what you get for ignoring my wolf-whistle.'

'Oh, so that was you, was it?'

'Mm. Just doing what builders always do, when a pretty girl's around . . .'

She laughed. 'Cut the crap, Jake.'

'Yeah.' He took her hand. 'Though I thought you would have turned round, when I whistled.'

'To simper in appreciation?'

'No, to give me one of your famous icy glares.'

'I do not have an icy glare.'

'According to Jude, you do. If someone dares talk in one of your lectures . . .' Jake's eyes danced with mischief. 'Mind you, I know that you have quite a way with ice.'

'I'm going to treat that remark,' Debra told him firmly, 'with the contempt that it deserves.'

'Ahh.' His fingers squeezed hers. 'So what are we doing, tonight?'

'How about the cinema?' she suggested. 'There's a film I'd like to see at the Barbican.'

'I really ought to be working on the house.'

Debra shook her head. 'It'll do you good to have a break.'

'And you. You're spending about twelve hours a day in the British Library, working on your book.'

'That's an exaggeration.'

'Well, when you're not there, you're thinking about it.' Jake took a bunch of his keys out of his pocket as they reached the bottom of their road. 'Though I can live with it, as long as you continue to do the odd bit of practical research.'

Debra laughed. 'Jake Matthews, you're just a sex-fiend at heart.'

He pouted at her. 'And you love it.'

'Yes.'

They both stared in shock when they turned into their gate. The big sash window in the front had been forced open.

'I don't believe it!' Debra said. 'We've been burgled!'

'Looks like it.' Jake's mouth thinned. 'I wonder if the bastards are still inside?'

Debra read his mind accurately. 'Jake, don't do anything stupid. Let's just call the police. I mean, if whoever's in there has a crowbar or something—'

'I'll use it on them myself,' Jake said angrily.

'Jake, think about it. If there is more than one of them, and they've got a knife, they might stab you or . . .' She caught his hand. 'I don't want you to go in there.'

'They've probably already gone. With the telly, the video and your little CD player from the dining room – and probably your computer, so I hope to God you've taken a backup copy of your files.' He didn't mention his real fear: that the prints had gone.

Eventually, Debra agreed that the burglars were probably miles away, and Jake unlocked the front door.

'You ring the police,' he said. 'I'm going to look round.'

As Debra expected, he went straight into the dining room. The boards hadn't been disturbed; frowning, he went into the sitting room. The television, video and hi-fi were all there. He came back into the hall, mouthed to Debra that he was going upstairs, and checked the upper floor. Again, nothing had been taken – no one had rifled through their drawers in the hope of finding money or jewellery hidden among Debra's underwear.

Frowning, he came downstairs again. Debra replaced the receiver, and turned to him. 'Well?'

'Nothing's missing,' he said. 'What did the police say?'

'They're coming round to take a statement. Though if nothing's missing . . .'

'They were after the prints,' Jake said softly. 'It's obvious. Why else would they ignore the television or the video?'

'Maybe they were disturbed before they could take anything?' Debra suggested.

Jake shook his head. 'It must have been the prints.' He rubbed his hand along his jaw. 'I think we'd better move them somewhere safe.'

'The bank?' Debra asked.

Jake nodded. 'Best place for them. Until we decide what we're going to do with them, anyway.'

'Who the hell was it, though?' Debra asked. 'I mean, hardly anyone knows about the prints. Jude, the valuer . . .' She frowned. 'They wouldn't break in.'

'Maybe you're right. Whoever it was wanted the telly and

the video, and was disturbed before they could take the stuff.' Jake frowned. 'I'll fit a burglar alarm, tomorrow. I should have done it before, really, but you never think it'll happen to you.'

'At least there's no harm done.' Debra's lips thinned. 'I hate to think of someone in here, though. Poking round our home.'

'I know, but they've gone now.' He put his arm round her. 'Let's just try to forget it, hm?'

Later that evening, Debra was curled up on the sofa, wrapped in a thin dressing gown, a glass of wine in her hand.

'Penny for them?' Jake asked as he looked up to see her staring into space, the book on her lap forgotten.

'Hm?'

'I said, what are you thinking about?'

'The pictures.' She frowned. 'What are we going to do, Jake? We can't keep them. Though if we give them to the Tate or something, they'll probably never be shown, because they're just too explicit. So they'll end up mouldering in a basement somewhere.'

'That leaves selling them.'

Debra frowned. 'And what if someone from abroad has the highest bid? I hate to think of yet more of our culture going to America or Japan or somewhere, for some rich collector to gloat over.'

'Well, we can't have everything. It's just a matter of working out which is the least painful solution, I suppose.'

She sighed. 'In some ways, I wish we'd never found them.'

Jake shook his head. 'I'm glad we did,' he said softly. 'We've had the privilege of owning some beautiful drawings by a brilliant artist – if only for a little while. That's more than many people ever have.'

'I know.' She closed her book. 'Though that doesn't make me feel any better.'

'Me neither,' Jake told her. 'Maybe we should just hand them over to Dicky, and let him decide for us.'

Debra shook her head. 'Give me a bit longer to think about it. I'm sure there's a solution – we're just not looking in the right place for it.'

Eleven

Jake looked up and caught the gleam of interest in Debra's eye. 'Obviously not the usual junk mail, then?'

'Hm?' Debra smiled at him. 'Sorry, I wasn't listening.'

'I said, from the look on your face, your post is a bit more interesting than the usual junk mail offering you top class healthcare at just a few pence per day.'

'Mm.' She passed the letter over to him. 'Just look at this!'

'Dear Dr Rowley,' he read. 'I'm currently researching my great-great uncle's life and work, and as you're one of the experts in the field of Victorian poetry, I wondered if you could spare a few minutes of your valuable time—' Jake paused to pull a disgusted face, opening his mouth wide and waving his middle finger at his mouth in a parody of making himself sick '—to talk to me about him. Perhaps you would let me take you to lunch so that we could talk. If you are able to help me, please ring me on this number after seven pm, weekdays. Yours sincerely, Henry Buchan.' He frowned, and looked at Debra. 'It's a bit of a coincidence, isn't it? Just after we get someone breaking into the house, someone who was obviously after the prints, you get a letter from Buchan's great-great nephew?'

She shook her head. 'It's a coincidence, yes, but it's nothing sinister. We get letters like that all the time, Jake. No end of students write, asking for help. It might be anything from recommending a book as a starting point, to reading a dissertation and giving advice on how to improve it.' She pushed the envelope towards him. 'He wrote to me at the university, who forwarded it, so he's got no idea where I live. Anyway, how could he possibly know about the pictures?'

'Hm.' Jake wasn't convinced. 'There are a lot of nutters around.'

'Jake, if your great-great uncle had been a famous Victorian poet or painter, and you wanted to know more about him, where would you start?'

'With the family. I'd take all the aged aunts out to tea at a very nice tea-shop, one by one, and ask them what they remembered about him.'

'Smart-arse,' she said, laughing. 'Seriously. Once you'd exhausted family memoirs and papers, what would you do?'

'Read the complete works, find a book of his paintings or some postcards.'

'And if some of them were out of print?'

'I'd try a library. Or a university.'

'And then you'd talk to a lecturer – one who specialised in that era – to find out some more?'

Jake sighed. 'Okay, I admit that you have a point. Though I'd rather you didn't meet this bloke on your own.'

'If it had been anyone else but Buchan – if he'd wanted to ask me about Rossetti or Hardy or Eliot – you wouldn't have been too bothered, would you?'

Jake shrugged. 'I don't know.'

'It's just a coincidence, Jake,' she repeated. 'That's all. Believe me.'

'Okay, okay. Ring the bloke and let him lunch you. But I'm buying you a mobile phone. The first hint of trouble, and you call me, okay?'

'You,' Debra told him, amused, 'are becoming an old fuss-pot.'

'I just believe in taking precautions. Since we've found the paintings, we've been broken into, with nothing taken—'

'Probably because the burglars were scared off before they could nick anything.'

Jake ignored her. 'And you suddenly get this letter, out of the blue, from Buchan's so-called great-great nephew. I don't like it, Deb. I think it's a bit too much of a coincidence.'

'Well, I don't. And if we're talking platitudes, don't they always say that truth is stranger than fiction?'

'Mm.' Jake still thought that there was something odd about the letter, but it was obvious that Debra wasn't going to listen to him. 'By the way, I have to go away on business, on Thursday. I'll be out overnight. Will you be all right, on your own?'

Debra rolled her eyes. 'May I remind you that I'm over twenty-one, and I lived on my own before I met you?'

He grinned ruefully. 'Sorry. I'm trying to wrap you up in cotton wool.'

'And I don't appreciate it.'

'I'm sorry.' He took her hand, and kissed her fingertips. 'I won't do it again.'

'You'd better not.'

'But I'm still going to buy you a mobile phone, today.'

'Oh, come on, Jake. You're over-reacting.'

'Maybe, but I'd feel happier if I knew you had a phone with you. Then, like I said, if there was any trouble, you could ring me. And I don't just mean Buchan's so-called great-great nephew. Supposing you're out in the car on your own, and it breaks down? Or you have to work late, and there's a problem with the tube so you won't be home for hours?'

Debra rolled her eyes. 'Why don't you just admit that you want to pose with a mobile phone?'

'Rubbish.'

'You, Jake Matthews, are just a gadget freak.'

'Right – just for that . . .' He stood up, and pulled her into his arms, kissing her lightly at first, and then more passionately as she responded, twining her hands into his hair.

'You're going to be late for work,' she said, as he took his mouth from hers and began a trail of kisses down the side of her neck.

'So?'

'And I'm working to a schedule.'

'So we'll both work late, tonight, to make up for it.' He hauled her over his shoulder and carried her up the stairs.

'Jake, put me down!' she said, laughing.

'As my lady wishes,' he quipped, putting her down next to the bed. He slowly unbuttoned her shirt, taking it off her shoulders and placing it neatly beside the cheval mirror. Then he removed her jeans, folding them neatly and placing them on top of her shirt.

Debra undid his shirt, sliding her fingers over his bare chest. He felt good, hard and muscular; she let her fingers drift lower, unzipping his jeans and tracing the outline of his cock. It was gratifyingly large and erect. She smiled at him.

Jake peeled off his jeans, removing his underpants and socks at the same time. He tipped his head to one side, looking at Debra. 'You're so beautiful.'

She curled her fingers round his cock. 'You're not so bad yourself.'

'Turn round,' he said softly.

She did as he asked, giving his cock one last rub between finger and thumb before holding her arms stretched out to the side and giving him a ballerina twirl.

'Perfect,' he said, taking her back into his arms and nibbling at her lower lip until she opened her mouth and kissed him properly. He stroked her back, resting one hand of the soft slope of her buttocks, and undoing the clasp of her bra with his other hand. Debra made a soft murmur, pressing herself against him; he eased one hand between them to stroke her breasts, feeling her flesh swell against his hand and her nipples grow hard and erect.

She arched her back and tipped her head up; Jake couldn't resist licking the hollows of her throat, nipping gently at her skin until she shivered. 'I love the way you taste,' he said softly, nuzzling against her skin. He walked her backwards towards the bed, pushed the duvet to one side, and then lowered her gently onto the sheet.

Debra smiled up at him. 'You're an insatiable sex-fiend.'

'That's your fault. I was celibate, until I met you.'

'In your dreams!' She grinned at him. 'A man as sexy as

you could only be celibate if he was in solitary confinement. And even then, you'd be thinking about it!'

Jake grinned back. 'Just as well I've got a partner who can match me, then . . .'

He sat on the bed next to her, and drew one hand down her body. 'Perfect. Warm and soft and curvy.'

'Who could do with losing a few pounds and going to a gym class, a couple of times a week,' Debra supplied drily.

'And be a gym-obsessive with a flat stomach? It'd be like making love to an ironing board,' Jake said. 'Anyway, making love is meant to be the best sort of exercise. Reaches muscles that other exercise just doesn't touch!'

'Such as?'

He took her hand, curling it round his erect cock. 'This, for a start.' He drew one hand slowly up her inner thigh; her legs parted automatically, and he slid one finger along her labia. 'And here.'

'You're a complete pervert,' Debra informed him, laughing.

He grinned, and bent his head, breathing on her quim. She shivered, widening her stance to allow him access; he kissed the skin on her thighs, ignoring her quim. 'As well as a complete tease,' she added.

'Was there something you wanted, milady?' he quipped; then, before she could make a sarcastic remark, drew his tongue along her inner thigh. She made a small murmur of pleasure, and tipped her head back among the pillows. His breath felt warm against her skin; she made another small sound of pleased anticipation, and bent her knees to give him easier access.

Jake's tongue slid along the length of her quim, exploring

its folds and crevices. As he found her clitoris and began to tease it, lapping at it and then hardening his tongue into a point and flicking it rapidly across the hard nub of flesh, Debra groaned, bringing her hands up to grip the rails of the bedstead. The combination of his warm breath and the expert ministrations of his tongue soon had her thrusting up to meet him, longing for a deeper penetration. Jake slid one finger in her to help ease the ache, sliding it back and forth until she began to moan and rock under him.

The familiar warm feeling of orgasm began at the soles of her feet, a buzzing glow which travelled up her legs and pooled in her solar plexus. She gripped the bedstead more tightly as the sensation deepened; Jake's mouth grew more urgent, licking and caressing until she gave a muffled cry and came, her flesh contracting wildly around his mouth.

'For starters,' Jake promised, adjusting his position slightly so that he could slide his cock inside her. Its hard length acted as resistance to her internal muscles, lengthening her orgasm.

Debra twined her hands round his neck, pulling his head down so that she could kiss him, her tongue exploring the contours of his mouth. And then he began to move, very slowly, sliding deep inside her and then pulling out until his cock was almost out of her.

He stroked her face, smiling at her; she smiled back, wrapping her legs round his waist so that he could achieve maximum penetration. She still felt lazy with post-orgasmic indolence, but the rhythm he was setting up as he thrust into her was irresistible, making her thrust back up towards him.

'Oh, Debra,' he breathed. Just when she thought she was

about to come again, he pulled completely out of her.

She opened her eyes, shocked, to see him leaning over her, his cock glistening with her juices – and a look of sheer determination on his face. 'Jake?'

'So are you going to let me buy you that mobile phone, or not?'

She shook her head. 'I don't believe this! Sexual blackmail, or what?'

He drew his fingers lightly over the tips of her breasts. 'Well? Yes or no?'

'That's not fair, Jake.'

He licked his finger, and touched it to her clitoris, manipulating the sensitive nub of flesh very gently in the way he knew that she liked. 'Yes or no?'

'All right. I give in.'

'And you'll carry it round with you?'

'Yes, I'll carry the bloody thing round with me.'

'Good,' he said, smiling and sliding his cock back into her. 'Oh – and one more request.'

'What?' She glowered at him. 'I thought we were making love?'

'We are.' He bent to kiss the tip of her nose. 'Actually, it's two requests.'

'Go on, then. Tell me your demands.'

'You meet this Henry Buchan bloke in a public place. Somewhere where people know you.'

'All right. Second?'

'Will you marry me?'

She burst out laughing. 'I think I've found your flaw.'

'What?'

'Crap timing.' She grinned at him. 'Jude said there had to be something wrong with you. Looks, personality, brains, cooks like an angel, shags like a donkey . . . there just had to be a flaw, somewhere.'

'Even Achilles had his heel,' Jake said, laughing back. 'Anyway, you haven't answered my question.'

'Aren't you supposed to propose on one knee?'

Jake calculated their positions. 'No, I don't think it would be possible. Not without a great deal of muscle strain.'

Debra grinned. 'In that case, I'll take the woman's prerogative to give you your answer in a week's time.'

Jake groaned. 'That's mean.'

'That's your problem.' She tightened the grip of her legs round his waist, pushing up to meet him. 'In the meantime, shouldn't we be getting on with the business in hand?'

Jake nibbled her ear. 'Don't you mean, "the business in cunt"?'

Debra rolled her eyes. 'You're so bloody pedantic . . .'

Debra arranged to meet Henry Buchan on Thursday, while Jake was away. To humour Jake, she'd arranged the meeting in a small café near the British Library, being a place where people knew her. She also agreed to carry the mobile phone with her, when she discovered that Jake had found a small and unobtrusive model which would fit easily into a pocket as well as a handbag.

She spent most of the day working in the library, and arrived at the café at four o'clock. She could see no sign of an earnest young man – or even an elderly man – on his own. Feeling slightly cross that he wasn't on time, she ordered herself a cup of coffee, and sat down at a table in the corner.

When Henry Buchan didn't show up in the next five minutes, she took a book from her bag and began to read. It was an old favourite of hers – *The Mill on the Floss* – and she quickly grew absorbed in it; it was only when she reached to take another sip of coffee and discovered that it was nearly cold that she glanced at her watch. Half past four.

Five more minutes, she said silently, and that's it. I'm going back to the British Library, and Henry Buchan can find someone else's time to waste. She had just finished the chapter, and was about to put the book back in her bag, when a flustered-looking man came up to her. 'Dr Rowley?' he asked.

'Yes.'

He held out his hand. 'I'm Henry Buchan. I'm so sorry that I'm late – I was held up. I'm so glad that you waited.'

'Right.'

'Can I get you another cup of coffee? Or a cold drink?'

'Coffee would be fine, thanks. Black, no sugar.'

'Right.' He smiled nervously at her again, and went over to the counter.

Debra wasn't sure what she'd been expecting, but certainly not this. From the tone of the letter, she'd judged Henry Buchan to be in his early twenties, at most; whereas he looked about the same age as her. Something, she thought, was slightly odd about all this. She was suddenly glad that Jake had nagged her into having a mobile phone. He had one, too, for business, and he'd programmed his number into her phone. Within seconds, if she needed him, she could press that one button and ring him.

Henry Buchan came back to the table, carrying two cups of coffee. 'I'm so sorry I'm late,' he said again.

'It doesn't matter.' Debra took a sip of coffee. 'Thanks for this. Now, you wanted to talk about your great-great uncle. Are you researching him for a project?'

'Not exactly.' Henry winced. 'You see, Henry was the elder brother. My great-grandfather was always brought up in his shadow, so he rather rebelled against the arts. He became an accountant, and started the family firm.' He swallowed. 'It was expected that I'd be an accountant, too. Anyway, my grandmother let slip, a few months ago, that the great-great uncle that no one ever talked about was *the* Henry Buchan. I saw some of his paintings in the Tate, and there are one or two others at home, and I just wanted to know more about him. His life, his work, that sort of thing.'

'I can give you the name of a good biography,' Debra said, taking out the shorthand pad she used for notes and writing rapidly on it. 'And these are the best editions for his poetry.'

'Thank you.' He sipped his coffee. 'I'm sorry if you think I'm a bit ridiculous, coming to you about the sort of things I could probably find in a public library, but I just want to do it properly.'

'I see.'

'So what can you tell me about him?'

Debra smiled. 'Where do you want me to start?'

'At the beginning.'

She laughed. 'Well, I don't know everything about him.'

'The university said that you were the Victorian specialist.'

'There are an awful lot of other Victorian poets, not to

mention the novelists and the playwrights,' she told him gently. 'You're great-great uncle's one of the minor ones, I'm afraid.'

'Oh.' He looked crestfallen. 'I suppose I've come to think of him as a sort of Victorian Milton or Shakespeare.'

Debra shook her head. 'His poetry's not particularly brilliant, I'm afraid. There are one or two verses in the popular anthologies, and I usually give my students a few of the better and lesser-known poems to study, but you're in for a real disappointment if you think he's something special. His painting, on the other hand – I'd rate him above Rossetti, even. There's a particular painting called *The Hyacinth Girl*, which is a superb example – it's probably my favourite picture ever.'

'Is it in London?' Henry asked hopefully.

'No, I'm afraid it's in Birmingham. But it's definitely worth a visit, if you're out that way.' Debra felt more relaxed with him now; his tale of being a stifled accountant who wanted to know more about his artistic uncle was something she could really identify with. Friends of hers at school had been forced to go out to work rather than going on to university, because their parents had never been students and didn't see why it should be different for their children.

At the time, Debra had burned with indignation on their behalf; she could imagine that the same sort of thing had happened to Henry Buchan. Wanting to read English, perhaps history, but being expected to read accountancy and join the family firm. He'd given in to family pressure: and now was his chance to break free. Debra had every intention of helping him.

'You're a lot younger than I expected,' Henry said suddenly. 'I thought you'd be – well, about fifty, being an expert *and* a doctor.'

'Grey hair in a bun, glasses, and sensible shoes?'

He flushed. 'Yes.'

She grinned. 'I was teasing you, Mr Buchan.'

'Call me Henry, please, Dr Rowley.'

'Debra. Actually, I finished my doctorate in my mid-twenties. On George Eliot and Victorian ethics.' She smiled at him. 'I imagine you're about the same age as me, too. I was expecting an eighteen-year-old, or maybe a man in his sixties.'

Henry smiled back. 'Oh dear.'

'Anyway, you wanted to know about your great-great uncle.' Debra took another sip of coffee, and sat back in her chair. She gave him a brief history of Buchan as poet and painter, his involvement with Rossetti on the fringes of the Pre-Raphaelite Brotherhood, and finished up with a list of the people known to have influenced his work.

She was very tempted to ask Henry if he knew anything about the Sykes connection, although something stopped her. Nice and inoffensive as Henry seemed, she didn't want to tell him about the paintings she and Jake had found. Since the break-in, she'd become much more wary. It seemed more sensible to keep it quiet, until they'd decided what to do with the pictures.

Henry seemed grateful for everything that she could tell him. 'It's so kind of you.'

'No problem. I'd rather talk to someone who's interested in the subject, than give a tutorial to students who'd much rather be elsewhere.'

'In each other's beds, no doubt.' It was out before Henry could stop it, and he flushed. 'Oh dear. I hadn't meant to say that.'

She smiled. 'Don't worry. It's the standard view of students, isn't it? Either that, or that they're a bunch of unwashed layabouts.'

'Yes.' He looked at her empty cup. 'Can I get you another coffee?'

She shook her head. 'I'm fine, thanks.'

'Well – I know it sounds a bit presumptuous – but would you let me take you out to dinner? As a thank-you for helping me in my search.'

'It's very kind of you, but I haven't exactly done much.'

'Oh, but you have.' He looked earnestly at her. 'Please. It would make me feel so much better, considering how much of your time I've taken.'

Debra thought about it. Jake was away overnight, Judith was doing something with David, and her other close friends were either out of the country or furiously writing up doctoral theses. She really ought to be writing her own book, she knew – but if she had dinner with Henry Buchan, there was just a chance that he might tell her a few snippets of family history that would prove her theory about his great-great uncle's involvement with Mary and Richard Sykes. And at least it would be real proof, unlike Lissa's supposed letters.

The thought of what had happened between Lissa and Jake was enough to tip the balance. 'All right. I'd like that. Maybe you can tell me a few things about your great-great uncle that I didn't know, either.'

'Well, I don't know about that. After all, you're the

expert.' Henry looked diffidently at his feet. 'Mind you . . . are draft manuscripts of poems worth anything?'

'How do you mean, worth? Money, or academic value?' Debra asked.

'Well, both, really.' He shrugged. 'The academic value's more important, I know, but I'd also like to know how much I should insure them for.'

'Draft manuscripts?' The back of Debra's neck prickled with sudden excitement.

'I've got a box of papers that my great-aunt gave me. After Gran told me about Henry . . . Well, Great-Aunt Rose has always been one of my favourites. I thought she might be able to tell me something about him, so I asked her. That's when she gave me the papers. She didn't have any children, you see, and she thought that I'd be more likely to look after it than anyone else on my side of the family.'

'A box of papers.'

'Yes. Scribbled notes, a few snatches of verse, letters, that sort of thing.' Henry bit his lip. 'That's what started me thinking about him, you see. When I read the poems, I rather liked them. So I wondered what he was like, what else he did.'

'I see.' Debra swallowed. A box of papers. There could be something in there about Mary Sykes. 'Well, I couldn't really put a price on things like that.'

'Not without seeing them.' Henry stared at the floor. 'Perhaps you could come back to my flat, after dinner, to have a look at them. All strictly on a professional basis, of course. I wouldn't be expecting any – you know.' He flushed a dull red.

It was only then that Debra realised that Henry found her attractive. And he'd offered to take her out to dinner, then show her a box of Buchan's papers in his flat . . . She smiled to herself. Jake would never believe this. Especially if she managed to find out the very information that he was supposed to find out from Lissa, and hadn't.

And Henry wasn't exactly unattractive, underneath his diffident manner. He had light blue eyes, and fair hair which fell over his face in a manner which reminded her of Rupert Brooke. His skin was pale, too – the sort that would quickly show broken purple veins if he took to drinking too much good burgundy with clients. He also had a sensitive mouth, and sensitive, long-fingered hands.

Debra wondered briefly what he would look like without clothes. And would he be so shy, then, or would he turn out to be a surprisingly confident lover? It would be a way of paying Jake back for the Lissa episode, she thought – and a way of maybe finding more of the truth about Buchan. And she was in just the sort of reckless mood to do it.

'I'd love to,' she said, beaming at him. 'And I'd love to see the papers. My friend Jude would be at your feet, begging to see them. She has this dream about finding a lost Milton sonnet.'

'In my great-great uncle's papers?'

'Anywhere.' Debra spread her hand. 'Most academics have the same dream. We'd like to find something that's been lost for years and years. Not for the glory, you understand – just for being the first one to see it again.'

'There might be a lost poem in the box, then.' Henry's face brightened. 'Shall we make it a rather quick dinner? We could maybe get a bottle of wine, for when we're reading through the papers. And then I'll call a taxi, to take you home.'

'I'd like that. Thank you.'

Debra suggested a small pasta bar; they ate quickly, then took a taxi to Henry's Docklands flat. They stopped at a small off-licence, where Henry insisted on buying a bottle of champagne, and then he ushered her into his flat.

It wasn't the sort of place that Debra would have chosen – it was very stark and modern in design – but the view over the Thames was fantastic. Henry smiled at her obvious delight, and uncorked the champagne. It was already chilled, and Debra sipped it with pleasure. 'Thank you, Henry.'

'Now, the papers.' He sat her down at the dining room table, facing the Thames, then came back with a shoebox.

The hairs on Debra's arms stood up, and the back of her neck prickled again, as Henry opened the box and she recognised the handwriting. Buchan.

'It's very good of you to look at these for me,' he said.

'The pleasure's all mine, believe me.' She touched the papers reverently, then picked one up and began to read it. 'It's one of his early poems. A draft from his Lancelot and Guinevere sonnets,' she said. She was unable to keep the excitement from her voice. 'You were asking me about worth, earlier. The academic worth . . .' She shivered. 'This stuff could be really important, Henry.'

'Do you think so?' He topped up her champagne.

'Very much so.' She nodded, and took her glasses from her handbag. 'Too much time spent slaving aver the computer, and too many hours spent reading in dim light,' she told

Henry ruefully as she slid them onto her nose.

She picked up another piece of paper, and almost dropped it again when she realised what it was. It looked like the draft of a letter to someone called Mary – and contained explicit references to the last time they'd seen each other. *Been as one*, Buchan had said. She swallowed hard. This looked like the proof she needed – the proof that Jake hadn't been able to find. If only there was some way of getting Henry to let her borrow it.

'Interesting?' Henry asked.

Something made her lie to him. 'Oh, it's just a letter.'

'Your face went white. I thought it might be important.'

She could have kicked herself; instead, she smiled sweetly. 'Obviously, all papers like this are important, but the poems are the main thing. The letters – well, they're just a bonus.'

'Right.'

She continued sifting through the papers; all the time, Henry watched her, saying nothing. Debra was oblivious to the look in his eyes: all she could think about were the poems – and the letters. There were several letter drafts mixed in with the verse; and some of them looked as though they were in another hand. From a brief scan, Debra thought that the letters were from a woman. Possibly even Mary Sykes . . .

Twelve

Eventually, Henry coughed, making Debra jump. 'So are they any good?' he asked, when she looked up.

She nodded. 'I recognise a lot of them. If I had my copy of Buchan's complete works with me, I could show you which ones were which, and put them in proper date order for you.'

'If it wouldn't be too much trouble for you.' Henry smiled at her. 'I'd really appreciate it if you could do that, some time.'

She thought quickly. He was virtually offering her the papers . . . wasn't he? 'Henry. If you'd let me borrow them for a couple of days, I could do it very quickly for you.'

He looked worried. 'I don't know. I mean, I'm not suggesting for a moment that you'd steal them, but . . .'

'But they're family papers, and you'd feel much happier if they were in your sight.' Debra put her hand over his. 'I don't blame you. Maybe you could think about photocopying them, and letting me have the copies? That way, you'd keep the originals, and I'd still be able to work on the papers for you.'

'I could do that,' he said, turning her palm over and stroking it. 'Yes, I think I could do that.' His fingers curved round her wrist, his thumb stroking the small pulse.

Debra had drunk enough champagne for her body to react to the way he touched her; her hardened nipples were obvious through the thin stuff of her shirt. A small voice in her head reminded her that she was living with Jake: and another one reminded her that Jake had slept with Lissa to get some papers. And what was sauce for the goose was most definitely sauce for the gander . . .

She drew her tongue over her lower lip; Henry bent his head and lifted her hand, kissing the soft skin of her inner wrist. His tongue flickered over her pulse-point, and Debra felt a kick of desire in her loins.

'Henry.'

He looked up, his blue eyes heavy-lidded. 'Yes?'

With her free hand, she began unbuttoning her shirt. Henry swallowed hard as she shrugged the garment off her shoulders, and reached behind her to undo the clasp of her bra. The action thrust her breasts forward, and he moved to kneel in front of her, burying his face in her cleavage.

'I can't believe this is happening,' he murmured. 'This can't be real.'

She stroked his hair. 'It is.'

Slowly, he straightened up again, removing her bra and tracing the curves of her breasts. He toyed first with one nipple, then the other, rolling the hard peak of flesh between finger and thumb. And then, as if unable to resist tasting the sweetness of her flesh, he lowered his head again, suckling hard on one nipple. His tongue flickered over the pimply flesh of her areola, teasing her, and then she felt his teeth gently graze the swollen flesh.

She twined her fingers into his hair, urging him on. 'Oh, yes.'

He caressed her calf; she widened her stance, letting him move his hand up under her skirt until he was stroking her thighs. The way he'd been touching her breasts had made her wet, needing to feel his cock filling her: she pushed her pelvis forward.

He took the hint, pushing the gusset of her knickers to one side and drawing one long tapered finger down the length of her quim. She shuddered, pushing against him once more; he laughed softly, and slipped one finger into her, pistoning it in and out of her while his broad thumb caressed the hard nub of her clitoris. She gasped, and he added another finger, and another, so it felt like a short and thick cock pushing into her.

Debra tipped her head back, moaning as she came, her quim fluttering around his fingers. He nuzzled her breasts again, and removed his fingers. She made a soft murmur of protest, and then he reached forward and took off her glasses, placing them on the table.

'Oh, Debra,' he said, standing up. She could see the hard bulge of his cock through his trousers, and swallowed hard. It would be so, so easy to reach out and unbuckle his belt, then undo his trousers and push them down over his hips, pulling his pants down and releasing his cock. So she did.

Henry almost ripped open his shirt, pushing it off his shoulders. He wasn't as well-developed as Jake, and his torso was milky white, rather than the tan she was used to on Jake, but he was still attractive. His cock rose stiffly from a cloud of dark hair, the head dark and glossy; a small drop of clear fluid glittered in the eye of his cock.

There was only one thing she could do, Debra thought, in the circumstances; she leaned forward and touched it with the tip of her tongue. He tasted clean and male – not quite the same as Jake, but still pleasant – and she couldn't resist the idea of tasting him further. She opened her mouth, taking the bulbous head in first, and then sucking hard.

Henry gasped, twining his hands in her hair and urging her on; as she gradually worked her mouth down his shaft, he lost patience, and thrust into her mouth.

Debra pulled back, frowning; he winced. 'Sorry. I got carried away.'

'That's okay. But let's just take this nice and slow, hm?' she asked. At his nod, she made her tongue into a hard point, licking the sensitive groove at the base of his glans; then she swirled her tongue over his glans, before taking his cock deep into her mouth and sucking hard.

Henry spread his legs slightly, leaning against the table; he closed his eyes and tipped back his head in bliss as Debra stroked his thighs, then eased her hand between his legs to stroke the soft area between his balls and his anus. She ringed his cock with her other hand, squeezing gently to increase the friction as she rubbed the shaft, her hand working in the opposite direction to her mouth.

He gasped as she wetted her little finger, then rubbed it against the rosy puckered hole of his anus. She felt the soft flesh give beneath her touch, and then her finger was inside him, massaging him gently.

'I'm afraid I'm going to come,' he said faintly: Debra smiled to herself. She'd already gathered that, by the way his balls had lifted and tightened, and his cock had started to throb in her mouth. She stayed where she was, letting the warm salty liquid flow into her mouth, and waited until his cock had stopped twitching before letting it out of her mouth and swallowing hard.

He stroked her hair, then knelt down. Debra felt a small shiver of anticipation run down her back: was he going to repay the compliment? As he pushed her skirt up over her thighs, she shivered again. He was. She closed her eyes as she felt his breath, warm against her thighs; he lifted her buttocks slightly from the chair, and eased down her knickers. Then she felt the long slow stroke of his tongue along her quim, exploring her more intimate topography.

She gave a small murmur of pleasure, and settled back against the chair, opening her thighs wider as he lapped at her. Her internal muscles flexed, and she could feel the familiar warmth of orgasm starting from the soles of her feet, and moving up through her legs.

She cried out as she came, her quim spasming beneath his mouth; he stayed there for a moment, then rocked back on his haunches, looking at her. His mouth was glistening with her juices; she stroked his cheek. 'Henry.'

He wouldn't look at her; she suddenly realised why. His cock was hard again, hot and dry. Obviously he was aching to fuck her, but was too shy to say so. Well, Debra thought, I can do something about that. 'Henry,' she said again, her voice calm and soft.

He looked at her, then.

'We've done virtually everything else. Why not—' She paused. Henry was a fastidious man. He responded best to understated language. If she suggested that they should fuck, he'd be appalled, not turned on. 'Why not?' she asked, letting her gaze drop to his cock so that he understood her meaning.

He said nothing; she closed her eyes, wondering if she'd gone too far, and then she felt the tip of his cock nudging against her entrance. She slid forward on the seat, to give him easier access, and his cock pushed slowly into her.

He stayed there for a moment, feeling the aftershocks of her orgasm ripple against him; then he began to move, long slow thrusts which made her writhe against him. She felt his balls slapping against her as he moved, and the root of his cock rubbed against her already sensitised clitoris; at length, she felt his balls tighten and lift, and his cock throbbing inside her. She came again at the same time, her quim flexing wildly round the thickness of his cock.

He still hadn't kissed her; it amused her in a way to think that he was so shy about putting his mouth to hers, when more intimate parts of their bodies had been in such close contact. She stroked his hair as he withdrew.

'I'm sorry,' he said.

'I'm not.' She smiled at him, half-expecting him to lead her to his bedroom. He didn't: merely looked at her, and then at the papers strewn across the table.

She followed his gaze. 'When do you think you can have the papers copied for me?' she asked.

It was at that point that he exploded. 'You bitch! You only let me fuck you to get at them, didn't you?'

'I—' Debra shrank back, thinking he was going to hit her.

'You're all the same. Using a man for anything you can get – you're all whores at heart, aren't you?'

Debra's initial shock turned to anger. She stood up, pushed her skirt down, and threw her shirt on, not bothering with her bra. 'How dare you! You wrote to me, asking if I could help you. I agreed to meet you, and then you asked me to look at these papers. That's why I'm here. What just happened between us – well.' It had been a combination of champagne, missing Jake, and excitement at what Buchan's papers held. 'And now you're accusing me of doing it all for my own good, and calling me a whore!'

It was true that she had fucked him to make sure that he'd give her copies of the papers, but he would be getting the fruits of her knowledge in return, she told herself. It was a fair swap. And now he was whinging about it. 'Well, you can go to hell, Henry Buchan. Which is probably where your great-great uncle is, in any case!' Her temper loosened her tongue. 'Fucking his best friend's wife, having a child with her – oh, he wasn't the paragon that your family might like to make him out to be. You don't hear anything about his obscene paintings, do you?'

'Paintings?'

'Go to hell!' She snatched up her underwear, stuffing it in her handbag.

'What paintings?' He had hold of her wrist, now. For such a slight man, he was surprisingly strong.

'Take your hands off me!'

'That isn't what you said, earlier,' he sneered, shaking her. 'You were practically begging me to put my cock in you.'

The words seemed so out of character that she stared at him, amazed.

'Yes, you wanted it badly, didn't you?' he said, shaking her again. 'And you'll get it again. Or maybe you'd rather feel my hands on your backside? Or a ruler, a cane, a whip?'

Debra stared at him in shock. Was he actually threatening to hit her?

His voice rasped at her. 'So tell me about the paintings.'

She suddenly came back to her senses. 'Take your hands off me,' she repeated, her voice calm and stern. 'If you don't, I'll start screaming, and your neighbours will hear. And when they bang on your door, I'll tell them that you assaulted me.'

'You bitch!'

'Physically, not sexually. Now, take your hands off me,' she said coldly.

He let her go, reluctantly. 'What paintings?' he asked again.

'Go to hell,' she said, marching over to the door, and slamming out of his flat. If he so much as dared to follow her, she knew how to deal with him. She'd done a self-defence course, years before, and although she hadn't practised the moves for a long time, it was like riding a bike – you didn't forget.

It was only when she was sitting in a taxi on her way back to Islington that it suddenly hit her. How stupid she'd been, letting herself get into that sort of situation! She'd never met the man before – and, despite the papers he'd shown her, she had no proof that he was who he said he was. He could have been anyone. And then the way he'd suddenly reacted, turning from a mild-mannered and apologetic man into an arrogant bully who had threatened to hit her . . .

She went cold. And she'd been stupid enough to mention the paintings to him. Obscene paintings. If he tailed the taxi, and found out where she lived . . .

She leaned forward, and tapped on the glass; the cabbie opened it. 'Yes, love?'

'I've changed my mind,' she said. 'Could you take me somewhere else, instead?'

'No problem, love. Where do you want to go?'

She gave Judith's address. At least there, she wouldn't be on her own. So if Henry followed her, she wouldn't have to deal with him alone.

'Do you mind waiting until I'm inside, please?' she asked the taxi driver.

'Of course, love.' He smiled at her.

'Thanks.' She walked up the path to Judith's front door, and rang the bell.

After a lengthy pause, Judith answered the door, wearing only a dressing gown. 'Deb! I wasn't expecting you over, tonight.'

'I know, and I wouldn't ask, normally, but . . .'

Judith noticed her friend's white face, and put her arm round her. 'Come in.'

The taxi driver put his thumb up as Judith closed the front door, and drove off. Judith took Debra through to the kitchen. 'Looks like you need some coffee. Or is something stronger more in order?'

'I don't know.' Debra closed her eyes. 'I'm sorry, Jude. I

know you had plans for tonight, and I'm sorry for interrupting, but can I use your spare bed, please?'

'What's happened? Have you had a fight with Jake?'

Debra shook her head. 'He's away on business tonight. No, I've done something really, really stupid. This bloke – he said he was Henry Buchan's great-great nephew, and he wanted some advice from me, as I'm supposed to be so wonderful on Victorian literature.'

'You are,' Judith said loyally.

'Anyway, he said he had some papers. Drafts of poems, letters, that sort of thing. I thought there might be something in them about those paintings, so I agreed to go back to his flat, and take a look at them.'

'If he laid a finger on you—' Judith began.

'It was at my instigation.' Debra winced. 'Okay, so I shouldn't have done it, but we'd been drinking champagne, I miss Jake – and yes, I know it's pathetic, before you say it – and when I read some of those papers and saw a letter to Mary Sykes which proved my theory . . . I don't know what came over me. I suppose it was a combination of wanting to celebrate, but knowing that I ought to keep it quiet, and something – just went.'

'So what happened?'

'He'd suggested that he could copy the papers for me. So, after we had sex – God, Jude, I was such a tart, we kept most of our clothes on, and I was virtually begging him to do it to me – I asked him when he was going to copy the papers, and he blew a fuse, saying that the only reason I'd screwed him was to get my hands on the papers. I lost my temper, too, and I told him that Henry Walter Buchan wasn't such a paragon.'

She groaned. ' I told him about those bloody paintings.'

'Oh, no! He doesn't know your address, does he?'

'No, the letter came via the university, so there's no problem there. The phone's in Jake's name, and he doesn't even know that we live in Islington, so it won't be easy to track me down.' She swallowed. 'But it won't take him long to work out that if I'm one of the only people who knows about the paintings, I know where they are.'

'You're *definitely* not going back to your place tonight,' Judith said. 'And I suggest you ring Jake pretty damn quick, too, to let him know what's happened.'

'What's going on?' a voice said from the doorway.

Debra turned round, and smiled weakly. 'Hello, David. Sorry to interrupt your evening.'

'Minor crisis,' Judith said, giving David a shortened version of the story.

He frowned. 'So what paintings are these?'

'They're paintings which Jake found under the floorboards, when he was checking out the woodworm.'

'Obscene paintings, and books with line drawings,' Judith added, 'by Henry Walter Buchan.'

'Right.' David looked slightly hurt. 'You didn't tell me about them, Jude.'

'That's because Deb and Jake wanted it kept quiet. Just until they'd had them checked out.'

'The valuer confirmed that they're by Buchan. And the model's Mary Sykes – wife of Richard Sykes, a Victorian erotic publisher. We've been trying to find out the truth about them, which is why we went off to Norfolk, the other week. When this letter came from this bloke professing to be

Buchan's great-great nephew . . . well, it seemed like another chance to find out more.'

'The great academic sleuth, eh?'

'Mm.' Debra looked rueful.

'We'd all jump at the chance, if we had it,' David said, smiling at her.

'I know. Though I've made a monumental cock-up of this one.'

'Well, if he's tracked you here, he'll have me and Jude to deal with,' David said. 'Have you told Jake about it, yet?'

'Give her a chance – she's only just got here!' Judith said.

David patted Debra's shoulder. 'You're an idiot, Deb. You should have asked Jake to go with you – or one of us, since he's on business – when you met him.'

Debra swallowed. 'Jake bought me a mobile phone.'

'So why didn't you use it?' Judith asked.

'Because I just didn't think. The important thing was getting out of that flat.'

'Well, you're safe now.' David looked thoughtful. 'Do you think he really was Buchan's great-great nephew?'

'I don't know. The papers looked authentic, though, and I know Buchan's handwriting.' Debra shivered. 'I just hope no one breaks into the house.'

'You've got a burglar alarm, haven't you?' Judith asked. She nodded.

'Well, then. If someone breaks in, as soon as the sensors hit him, the alarm will go mad, and the whole street will be out, wanting to know what's going on. The box on the wall's enough to deter them.'

'There isn't a box.'

'Even better. Catch the bastard in the act.' Judith smiled at her. 'David will make you a cup of coffee, while I make up the spare bed.'

'Thanks, Jude.'

'Well, what are friends for?' Judith rolled her eyes. 'And next time you get a fantastic lead, do me a favour. Tell me, and take me with you.'

'I will,' Debra promised.

Half an hour or so later, she had a shower, and went to bed, having borrowed a voluminous T-shirt from Judith. She usually slept in the raw, but tonight, she felt that she wanted the extra comfort.

David and Judith were obviously taking up where they'd left off when she rang the doorbell, she realised, hearing the odd groan from the room next door. Knowing that the couple were making love made her suddenly miss Jake even more.

Jake. She sighed. It was about time she rang him, to tell him what had happened. She rummaged in her handbag, and brought out the mobile phone, dialling his number.

'Jake Matthews.'

'Hi. It's me.'

'Where are you?'

'At Jude's.'

'At *Jude's*?' His voice sharpened. 'Are you all right?'

'Yes, of course.' She told him quickly what had happened.

'I bloody *knew* it. Deb, you should have let me go with you, in the first place. You're so stubborn. Have you called the police?'

'He didn't actually *do* anything to me, Jake. If I'd cowered, he probably would have hit me; but because I didn't, because I stood up to him . . .' She sighed. 'Let's forget about it, hm?'

'Maybe.' Jake paused. 'So you had sex with him?'

'Like you did with Lissa,' she retorted sharply. 'I've had a hell of an evening, Jake. Don't bully me.'

'I'm not bullying you. I just wondered what you did, exactly?'

'It turns you on, then? To think of me having sex with another man?'

'No – just thinking of you doing certain things, and remembering how it feels when you do it with me.'

'Oh.'

There was a tiny hint of laughter in his voice. 'Did you suck his cock, then?'

She sighed. 'Yes.'

'What was it like?'

'Smaller than yours.'

'I didn't actually mean that.'

'Oh. "It" as in "the act", not as in "his cock".'

'Exactly.'

She thought about it. 'All right.'

'Did he lick you?'

'Yes. He touched me, first, stroking me and sliding one finger inside me. Then two, then three.'

'Greedy girl.' Jake's voice was affectionate.

'He made me come. Then I sucked his cock. And then he licked me.'

'Making you come, again?'

'Yes.'

'And did he slide his cock into you?'

'Yes.'

'I see.' He paused, and to Debra's surprise, changed the subject completely. 'And you're heading for the British Library, tomorrow?'

'Once I've gone home to change, yes.'

'Don't do that. Borrow something from Jude, instead. I'll meet you for lunch, after I've checked the house out – just in case he's managed to get our address from somewhere, and is skulking around, waiting for you.'

Debra shivered. 'That's creepy. Surely he wouldn't do that.'

'Let's face it, you thought he was harmless when you went to his flat.' His voice deepened. 'And quite what you were doing, going to a strange man's flat and drinking champagne with him, then fucking him . . .'

'The same as you were doing when you were with Lissa Sykes,' she said sharply. 'For very similar reasons. And at least I saw the papers.'

'I asked for that, didn't I?'

'Yes, you did. Before you ask, no, he wasn't as good as you. And I don't want to talk about it any more, okay?'

There was a pause. 'Deb.'

'Mm?'

'I miss you.'

'Oh?' She recognised the timbre of his voice: he was aroused, thinking of her. Thinking of her, with Henry, perhaps, and wondering if she'd acted any differently? Whether she'd made the same noises as she came? She wondered if he was stroking his cock; for some reason, she felt too shy to ask him. They'd never actually had an erotic telephone conversation. He rarely rang her at work, and they hadn't spent a night apart since they'd first met.

'What are you wearing?' he asked softly.

'A very unsexy, ancient and voluminous T-shirt I borrowed from Jude.' She paused. 'What about you?'

'I'm in bed, too.' He chuckled. 'Let's just say I'm wearing the male equivalent of Chanel No 5.'

'Aramis?' She adored Jake's aftershave. The scent of it, caught unawares when she was walking through a department store, was enough to make her wet.

'Aramis,' he confirmed, 'and nothing else.' He paused. 'If you were next to me, right now . . .'

'What would you do?'

'I'd lick every inch of your skin, like a cat.' His voice grew huskier. 'I'd start from your fingers, sucking them one by one. Then I'd lick your palm, and the soft skin on the inside of your wrists. I'd kiss my way up to the crook of your elbow, tasting you there, and move up to your shoulders. I'd lick the hollows of your collar-bones, and you'd tip your head back, offering me your throat.'

'And then,' Debra took up the tale, 'you'd kiss your way down over my breasts, cupping them and lifting them up and together, and drawing your tongue down the length of my cleavage. Then you'd suckle one nipple while you stroked the other, nipping gently at it until I was writhing beneath you, parting my thighs and pushing at you, wanting to feel your mouth on my quim.'

'Though I'd make you wait, first,' Jake said. 'I'd kiss my

way over your abdomen, licking your belly. You'd whimper, tipping your head back against the pillows, and I'd nuzzle your thighs, then lick the soft skin behind your knees. I'd move down to your ankles, licking the hollows there, before working my way up the other leg.'

As he spoke to her, Debra couldn't help sliding one hand between her thighs, stroking her quim. 'What then?' she asked, her voice growing deeper and slightly ragged.

'Then I'd bury my head between your thighs, breathing in your aroma. When you're aroused, you smell like honey and seashore and musk. That's how you taste, too, sweet and salt and spicy. I could drown in your honey-box, and I'd die happy.'

'Jake . . .'

'I know, sweetheart, I'm driving you mad, just feeling me breathe against your quim. I can feel you growing wetter against my mouth. So I know I've teased you enough; then, I draw my tongue very slowly down your sex, parting your labia. Your clitoris is hot and engorged; I take it between my lips, pulling gently at it, and you can't help a small murmur of pleasure. You twine your fingers in my hair, urging me on, the pads of your fingers digging into my scalp as you get more and more impatient.'

Debra made exactly the noise he was thinking of, as she stroked her clitoris; Jake smiled to himself. She was in the same sort of state as he was, he thought, rubbing gently at his penis.

'I make my tongue into a hard point, and slide it along to your entrance. You feel warm and wet and spongy, and I love the way you taste. Spicy and musky and honey. I push my tongue in, as far as it will go, and you groan and push your body up to me, wanting me deeper, deeper.'

By this time, Debra's middle finger was deep inside her, acting out Jake's words. 'Oh, yes,' she said, spreading her legs wider and lying back against the pillow, the mobile phone cradled between her ear and her shoulder.

'My cock's hard, so hard; it feels like it's on fire, I want you so much. I want to bury it deep inside you, feel your flesh clinging round me like warm wet velvet, fuck you until your quim shudders round me, rippling as you come. Though I won't stop: I'll keep thrusting, pushing into you until you come again and again and again . . .'

'Ohhh.' Debra couldn't help moaning as she rubbed at her clitoris; her sex-flesh spasmed wildly as she came.

'Debra.'

'Mm?' Her voice was languid, now, lazy.

'Did you just make yourself come?'

'Mm.' She smiled. 'And I bet you've got your cock in your hand, too.'

'Yes.' He paused. 'I wish it was your mouth. I love the way you work me, licking and sucking and concentrating on the sensitive bit at the bottom of my glans.'

'Mm.'

He grinned. 'You're not going to play, are you?'

Debra smiled ruefully. 'I know, I'm a selfish bitch.'

'No. A simple case of post-orgasmic indolence, I'd say.'

'I'll make it up to you, tomorrow night.'

'I should hope so, too.' He smiled. 'Goodnight, sweetheart. Sleep well.'

'You, too.' Debra switched off the phone, put it back in

her handbag, and settled against the pillows again. Tomorrow, she really would make it up to him. A nice dinner, a good bottle of wine, and then a lengthy bout of sex.

Thirteen

Debra saw Jake sitting in the café, and she was immediately wet with desire for him, remembering how he felt when he was lying between her legs, his long thick cock filling her to the hilt. Or when he was crouched between her thighs, lifting her buttocks to give him a better angle while he licked her quim and sucked her clitoris.

He hadn't seen her in the doorway. With a smile, she picked her way through the tables so that she approached him from behind, and slid her hands aver his eyes. 'Hello, lover,' she said huskily, licking his earlobe. A glance at his groin made her smile; he had an immediate erection.

'Hi.' He leaned over to kiss her as she sat down. 'How are you?'

'Fine.' She nodded at the rust-coloured T-shirt she was wearing. 'I've discovered that Jude's taste in clothes doesn't quite suit me, though.'

He grinned. 'I prefer you not wearing any clothes, in any case!'

Her face flamed. 'Jake! Don't say things like that, so loudly!'

'You deserve it,' he said in a quieter voice, 'after what you just did to me.'

'Well.' Debra paused. 'Good journey?'

'Mm. Though I have a small bone of contention to pick with you.'

She frowned. 'What?'

'Burglar alarms,' Jake told her, 'are only effective if you remember to turn them on, first.'

She closed her eyes. 'Oh, hell. I *knew* I'd forgotten something.' A sudden thought struck her. 'Jake. We weren't burgled, were we?'

He paused. 'Yes and no.'

'Either we were, or we weren't. Don't equivocate.'

'Only *you* could use a word like that.'

'Jake!'

'Someone broke in, yes – but they didn't find what they were looking for.' Jake's face was grim. 'So they made a nice little mess for us. And they redecorated, to show their appreciation.'

She frowned. 'How do you mean?'

'Let's just say that some of the walls are a nice shade of brown.'

'Brown?' She still didn't follow.

'Human excrement.' His mouth tightened. 'And they smashed the frame of *The Hyacinth Girl*.'

'Oh, no.' Debra bit her lip. 'I'm so sorry, Jake.'

'It can be fixed. And if the print's damaged, I can always get another copy.' He took her hand. 'I'm just glad that you weren't there when they decided to pay us a visit.'

'Do you think it was the same people as before?'

He shrugged. 'Who knows? But your common-or-garden tea-leaves don't usually spread shit over your walls. And they usually go for things they can sell, like videos and computers and CD players. Whereas our thieves . . .' He sighed. 'Whoever's behind it knows about the prints.'

'But who? I mean, the only people who know are Jude and David and the valuer. Oh, and the bank.'

'Maybe it was the valuer – or one of his friends.'

'That's a bit *Lovejoy*, isn't it?'

He smiled. 'Yes, I suppose so. How about the bank? A poor clerk, who desperately wants to escape from the rat-race . . .'

'Then surely he'd take them from the bank vaults, not smash up our house?'

'Good point.' Jake spread his hands. 'But we're no closer to guessing who's behind it.'

She swallowed hard. 'It might be Henry Buchan. Though he doesn't know our address.'

'It wouldn't take him long to find that out.'

Debra shook her head. 'Not overnight. He'd need either the university – who wouldn't give out my address or phone number without my permission, in any case – or the electoral roll.'

'And who says that he didn't find all that out before he wrote to you, asking you to meet him?'

Debra chose to ignore the question, not wanting to think about what it meant: that Henry Buchan had been checking up on her and following her for weeks. 'What about Lissa Sykes? She knows our address.'

'But she doesn't know about the paintings,' Jake pointed

out. 'As far as she's concerned, you're just writing a book about Buchan, and we were merely checking up a possible lead.'

'Which takes us back to Henry Buchan, or whoever he really is.' She tipped her head to one side. 'So, what now?'

Jake thought for a moment. 'I think we'd better go public about the find, and either give them to the Tate or sell them. The sooner, the better.'

'But, Jake . . .'

'You said yourself that we can't keep them,' he reminded her. 'And after what's happened to the house, I'd rather that the whole world knew that we don't have them.'

Debra sighed. 'That's the sensible option. But can't we wait until we've found out the truth about Richard and Mary? I mean, those papers I saw, yesterday . . .'

Jake took her hand. 'You don't have a hope in hell of getting your hands on them, now.'

'No.' She bit her lip. 'Okay, we'll do it your way. Go public.'

'Tomorrow,' he promised. 'Once we've cleaned the house up.'

'Look, come back to the library with me. I'll get my stuff, then we can go home and clean the place up.'

'Okay.'

When they reached home and went through the front door, Debra sucked in her breath. 'Christ, what a mess.'

'I *did* warn you.'

'I know.' She swallowed hard, fighting back the tears. 'We worked for this, Jake. We worked so hard. And now look!'

'It's surface, sweetheart. Nothing that a bit of disinfectant, soap and water won't shift.' Jake stood behind her, his arms folded protectively round her and his lips against her ear. 'It'll be fine again, by the end of today.'

'The bastards, though. What a *horrible* thing to do.'

'Criminals aren't usually nice. They don't leave you a bunch of flowers, finish off your ironing and water the plants for you,' Jake said drily.

'No.' She tipped her head back, smiling wryly at him. 'Well, better get cracking. I'll change, first.' She paused. 'Have you reported this to the police?'

Jake nodded. 'They've already been round, taken a statement, and dusted for fingerprints. And I bought a load of cleaning stuff before I met you.'

'So let's get cracking and sort this mess out.'

They worked hard for the next four hours, both amazed at how much mess someone could create in so little time. Eventually, Jake flexed the muscles in his shoulders, looked round, and said, 'Well, back to normal.'

'Yeah.' Debra's face tightened. 'Though it's going to take me a long while to forget this.'

'I know.'

She came over to stand next to him, taking his hand. 'Jake.'

'Mm?'

'I know you'll probably think I'm being foolish, but—'

'What?'

'I don't want to stay here. Not tonight.'

He nodded. 'I was going to suggest that we go somewhere else. A nice little hotel somewhere, just outside London,

243

with a leisure centre and a good restaurant. After this, we deserve a break.'

She smiled at him. 'Thanks.'

'Go and get your glad rags, then, Mrs Smith,' he quipped.

She grinned. 'And what would you do, exactly, if I came down to dinner dressed in rags?'

'If we were here I'd have great fun ripping them off you, and fucking you senseless.' The timbre of his voice deepened. 'Considering that I haven't actually had my cock in you since yesterday morning . . .'

She cupped his face in her hands. 'Then let's go and find ourselves a nice four-poster, hm?'

Jake smiled. 'You're on, Batwoman. Let's go and pack.'

It hadn't been quite what Debra had had in mind, the previous night; she had intended to seduce her lover, but the setting had been their own home. Though in the circumstances, a four-poster bed in an old coaching inn somewhere would be even better. And it would help to dull the Henry Buchan incident in her mind.

She still felt slightly ashamed about what she'd done: and she could understand, now, how Jake had felt in Blakeney, when he'd given in to Lissa Sykes' demands to get the letters. The letters still hadn't turned up; Lissa had simply made a clever bluff, and she and Jake had both fallen for it. Whereas Henry Buchan really did have the letters.

'What are you thinking?' Jake asked, seeing the scowl on her face.

'We've both been duped, you know. You, with Lissa, who probably never had any letters in the first place. She'd probably seen something on the telly which gave her the idea.' Her face tightened. 'And Buchan. He really did have the letters. You know, if he was the one behind all this, I reckon we're perfectly justified in breaking into his posh Docklands flat, stealing the letters, and sowing cress seeds in his carpets.'

Jake grinned. 'Remind me never to cross you. I don't like the idea of my clothes taking an acid bath!'

'I'm serious.'

He took her hand. 'Forget it, Deb. We know the truth, anyway. It doesn't matter that we don't have the papers to prove it, officially: we know, and that's the important thing. Buchan can just moulder with his papers.'

'I suppose so. Though I'd still like to get my hands on them.'

'Sleep on it for a while, and we might come up with a way of doing it,' Jake advised softly. 'And I'd prefer that you slept on it with me.'

She smiled, then. 'Are you in sex-fiend mode, by any chance?'

'If I'm not now, I will be when I find this four-poster . . .'

They ended up in Essex, in an old coaching inn which boasted a four-poster bed. After a leisurely candle-lit dinner, Jake ushered Debra up to their room.

'It's a shame there isn't a jacuzzi as well,' he said, 'but I suppose you can't have everything.'

Debra smiled at him. 'You know, it's the first time that I've ever slept in a four-poster?'

'Who said anything about sleeping?' Jake teased.

She rolled her eyes. 'Oh, honestly!'

He undressed her slowly, taking pleasure from seeing her body being revealed from her semi-formal skirt and top. She was wearing a white lace body beneath her clothes; he sighed contentedly. 'Beautiful.'

'I thought you might like it. And no, it's not Jude's, before you ask!'

He smiled. 'I can't see Jude wearing anything like this. Maybe I'll ask her, next time I see her.'

'She'll tell you she's wearing a peephole bra and crotchless panties, just to be outrageous.'

'I bet she wears plain old M&S white cotton knickers.'

Debra, who knew the contents of her friend's underwear drawer rather better, having been on several shopping sprees with Jude, simply smiled, and changed the subject. 'Do you think Buchan ever did this with Mary?'

'What?'

'Booked into a nice hotel as man and wife. She wore a ring, so it would have looked respectable.' Debra tipped her head on one side. 'If my theory was right, and the child was Buchan's, I can't imagine her making love with him in her own marital bed.'

'Do you really know enough about her to make that sort of assumption?'

'Yes. Let's face it, she spent however many years as a respectable widow in Blakeney, bringing up Dicky.'

Jake nodded. 'I suppose so. But then there are those pictures. If she really modelled for them, and Buchan didn't just paint her face and use another model's body . . .'

'Of course he didn't.' Debra rolled her eyes. 'You said

yourself, the look on her face in *Leda and the Swan* was too realistic to be faked.'

'But he could have painted it from memory.'

'Maybe. The thing is, we know they slept together, at least once.'

'How?'

'It was in that letter I read. Buchan talked about "being as one" with her. And I don't think he meant spiritually.'

'Hm.' Jake traced the curve of her cleavage with one finger. 'Let's just forget about him for now, shall we?'

'Right.'

He led her over to the bed. 'I love you in that thing. Would you mind leaving it on?'

She smiled at him. 'I thought you might say that.'

'And that's why you bought it?' he said hopefully.

'Something like that.' She gave him a sidelong look. 'I bought something else, as well.'

He caught the devilish look in her eyes, and grinned. 'Oh yes?'

'Something very special.' Her voice was soft and honeyed.

'Are you going to show me?'

'Better than that.' She undid his shirt, sliding her hands across his chest and delighting in the feel of the crisp dark hair underneath her fingertips, and the contrast in texture of his soft skin. 'I love the way you feel. Like silk – when I'd expect you to be hard, you're soft and warm.'

'I can assure you that other parts of me are hard,' he informed her, *sotto voce*.

'I thought they might be.' She undid his dark trousers, sliding the material over his hips. He stepped out of them, folding them neatly and hanging them over the back of the chair.

'Prissy,' she teased.

He shook his head. 'Merely avoiding having to iron them again.'

'Hm.' The outline of his cock was clearly visible through the thin stuff of his underpants; Debra couldn't resist stroking it through the cotton, and it swelled slightly in response. She drew her tongue over her lower lip, moistening it, and hooked her fingers into the sides of his underpants, pulling them down so that his cock sprang free. 'Very, very nice,' she purred.

'So what's this special thing you've bought, then?'

'Tut, tut. So impatient. What am I going to do with you?'

He smiled. 'I can think of a few things I'd like you to do with me.'

'Why don't you sit down and tell me about them?' she asked, giving him a sultry look. Her eyes were very blue, and the expression on her face made Jake shiver with anticipation.

He sat down on the bed.

'Just lie back,' she said softly. 'Close your eyes.'

He suspected that she was plotting something; but he also suspected that whatever it was, he was going to enjoy it. He did as she asked, closing his eyes and settling back against the pillows.

Debra took the blue silk scarf from her hair, and smiled. It had been right under Jake's nose, all the time, but he hadn't noticed. Which meant that this was going to be even more fun . . . She shook her hair out, and knelt on the bed next to Jake, keeping the scarf behind her back in case he decided to peep.

It was a wise precaution; as soon as Jake felt the mattress dip, he opened his eyes, and smiled at her.

'I thought I asked you to close your eyes?' she asked.

He grinned. 'You're the bossy schoolmarm type at heart, aren't you?'

'Yup,' she confirmed. 'So close your eyes.'

'Yes, ma'am,' he teased.

'Now stretch out for me.'

He frowned. 'Why?'

'Because I love seeing you stretch, like a cat, all your muscles rippling under your skin.'

'Weird woman,' he said, laughing, but did as she said, lacing his fingers together and stretching his hands above his head, his palms touching the wall.

Gotcha, Debra thought, and deftly wrapped the silk scarf round his joined hands, binding them to one corner of the four-poster.

Jake opened his eyes in shock. 'What the hell?'

'Relax, darling. I just fancied having you at my mercy.'

He smiled then. 'So that was your something special.' He glanced up at the scarf. 'Weren't you wearing that in your hair?'

'Oh, so you did notice, then?'

'Perhaps I should have told you how ravishing you look.'

She grinned. 'There's one particular word in that sentence which is very, very appropriate . . .' She reached over to the fruit bowl, taking a handful of white seedless grapes from the bunch in the middle, and halving them neatly. Then she laid a trail of grapes across Jake's abdomen, and along his thighs.

He groaned. 'This is torture! How come you get to eat all the grapes?'

'Because this,' she told him, blowing him a kiss, 'is my idea.'

'Hm.' His eyes narrowed. 'Don't I get even one?'

'If you're good, yes.'

'Meaning what, precisely?'

'Don't cheek the teacher,' she said, laughing. 'Or I might be forced to spank you.'

He looked at her in amazement. 'What?'

She rolled her eyes. 'Joke. Now shut up, you're putting me off.'

'Putting you off what?'

'My grapes.' She pulled the neck of her lace teddy so that her breasts were bared, and knelt next to Jake on the bed. Making sure that he could see her perfectly, she slowly ate her way down the trail of grapes.

As she bypassed his cock and started on the grapes by his thighs, Jake gave a small moan of disappointment. Because his hands were tied, he could do nothing about it – he couldn't tangle his fingers in Debra's hair and urge her gently towards where he wanted her to lick him. All he could do was to tilt his pelvis and push up towards her, hoping that she'd take the hint.

She finished the grapes, and looked up at him. This big man was completely at her mercy, she thought. And she was going to enjoy every bit of it. She traced the outline of his cock with the tip of her nose, dropped a kiss on its tip, and reached over to the fruit bowl again. Apples, oranges – and a fresh nectarine. She grinned. Absolutely perfect.

'What are you up to?' Jake asked suspiciously.

'Wait and see. You'll *love* this,' she promised.

Jake wasn't so sure, but there was nothing he could do about it.

Debra climbed off the bed, and took the fruit knife, quickly removing the stone from the nectarine. She cut one half into thin slivers, and fed one of them to Jake.

'Perfectly ripe, do you think?'

'Yes.'

'Good.' She picked up the other half of the nectarine, and wrapped it round his erect penis. Jake gasped at the sudden coolness against the heat of his cock. Debra smiled and began massaging the fruit into him, rubbing the nectarine up and down his shaft.

'This is going to make a hell of a mess on the sheets,' Jake told her.

'Not necessarily.' She bent to lick the drops of nectarine juice off his abdomen. 'You'll just have to make sure you lie still, won't you?'

'With what you're doing to me,' Jake said, with difficulty, 'I'm not sure if I can.'

She pursed her lips. 'Oh, dear. Do I have to tie your ankles up, as well?'

He groaned. 'Oh, no. I should have guessed you'd think of that.'

She shook her head. 'Actually, I only brought one scarf. So you'll have to make an effort, won't you?'

'One day,' Jake told her, 'I'm going to turn you into a proper fruit salad, for this.'

'Oh, yes? Like how?'

'Raspberries on your nipples, fresh peach slices on your breasts, a kiwi fruit or one of those little berries like Chinese lanterns decorating your navel, and a banana in your cunt. And then I'm going to eat it out of you, very very slowly.'

'Is that a threat, or a promise?'

Jake considered it for a moment. 'Both.'

'I'll look forward to it. And in the meantime . . .' She continued massaging the nectarine into his cock; when the fruit was reduced to a pulpy mash, she ate it off him. By the time she'd finished, Jake was at the point of coming; as soon as her lips fitted round his glans, he couldn't help ejaculating.

'Mm,' Debra said, swallowing the last drop of creamy fluid and eating another slice of nectarine; she fed another piece to Jake.

'Well, it's the first time a nectarine's made love to me,' he said, when he recovered his breath.

'I thought you might like to try something different.'

'And how.' He tugged at his bonds. 'Do you mind untying me, now? This is starting to get uncomfortable.'

'Okay.' Debra loosened the knot, and removed the scarf from his wrists, rubbing them. 'Better?'

'Mm. Though after what you've just done to me, I think I need a shower.' He sat up, kissing her. 'Care to join me?'

'Why, thank you, Mr Smith. I believe I will.'

He peeled the lace teddy from her, scooped her into his arms, and headed for the bathroom.

Debra walked down the street, smiling to herself. It was funny to think how much life had changed in the past few months. Six months ago, she'd been bored and restless, stuck in a tiny studio flat in Holland Park, and having just split up with Marcus. She'd vowed at the time not to bother with relationships again, and throw herself into her work – that, at least, was reliable. And then Jake had exploded into her life.

Jake the chameleon, who could switch between being Jake the Lad – she smiled to herself at the pun – and Jake the academic with the sharp brain. In Jake, she had the best of both worlds. In fact, the best of all worlds, as Judith had said: Debra had an intelligent man who could make her laugh; he looked like a model, shagged like a donkey and could cook. Sometimes, Debra thought, it was better not to think that you couldn't believe your luck, but just to celebrate it.

And then the house, the perfect house, and Jake had been the perfect person to help her do it up. As if that wasn't enough, there had also been the paintings under the floorboards. It was a little too good to be—

The world suddenly went dark as something was pushed over her head. She tried to scream, but whatever had covered her head muffled every sound she made. Unable to see, unable to find her bearings, she would have fallen, had her assailant not been half-pushing, half-dragging her along the street.

As she found herself being shoved into something – a car, a van, whatever – she began kicking hard, her foot finally connecting with flesh. Her assailant swore roughly at her. 'You bitch! You'll pay for that.'

Debra ignored the menace in his tone and continued kicking. Then she felt the sack being loosened. 'Well, if you won't come quietly, I've got no choice,' her captor muttered. A hand appeared inside the sack. She tried to bite it, but she wasn't fast enough. It clamped over her face, holding a handkerchief or something like it, covered in something that smelled of . . .

The world went black again.

The burglar alarm began beeping as Jake walked through the front door so he punched in the code to turn it off. He was surprised that Debra wasn't home, but assumed that she'd been working in the British Library on her book, and had simply forgotten the time.

He grinned. When she came home, and saw what he had in his arms . . . He set the puppy gently onto the ground. 'Well, Sykes, we're home,' he told the boxer, letting him sniff his way along the hall.

Then he noticed the envelope on the doormat.

Frowning, he picked it up. There was no name on it, and no address – and it wasn't the right sort of envelope to be junk mail. There was only one way to find out what it was. He ripped open the envelope, to find a piece of paper covered in letters which had been cut out from a newspaper or magazine.

We know you've got them. Hand them over, and we'll set her free. Don't call the police, if you know what's good for her.

It didn't quite sink in. Who knew that they had what? Were they referring to the Buchan paintings, or the books, or the poetry? And what did they mean, 'set her free', and 'don't call the police'? Had someone actually kidnapped

Debra? He wasn't sure if it was serious, or just some sort of very sick joke. It seemed too much the stuff of fiction or film to see a ransom letter made out of newspaper print.

On the other hand, there had been that episode with Buchan's so-called great-great nephew. Could he be the man behind all this? And if so, would he really harm Debra? He suddenly remembered what Debra had told him. Henry Buchan hadn't actually hit her, but that had been only because she'd stood up to him. And that was when she had lost her temper, and told him about the paintings.

He stared at the note again. *Hand them over.* 'I would,' he said quietly, 'if I knew who you were and where you wanted them. Just as long as you don't hurt her.' He turned it over, hoping that there might be more instructions on the back – but nothing.

He shivered. His first reaction would have been to phone the police – but how did he know that the house wasn't being watched? Or that the phone wasn't being tapped? He couldn't take the risk. On the other hand, he couldn't just sit there and do nothing. And right then, he didn't want to be on his own. He headed for the phone, Sykes pattering along at his heels, and dialled Judith's number. She was Debra's best friend – maybe she'd have some ideas.

She might know if Debra had gone somewhere for the day, on a whim or on a lead for her book, and maybe then, he could prove that this was all some sick joke, that Debra was all right and would be home soon.

It seemed like hours before Judith answered. 'Hello?'

'Jude? It's Jake.'

'Oh, hi. How are you?'

'Fine. Look, um, have you seen Debra today?'

'No.' Judith's voice was puzzled. 'Why?'

'Can you come over?'

'Now?'

'Yes. Now.' He sighed. 'I can't explain on the phone, but I wouldn't ask you unless it was important.'

'Is it anything to do with that bloke who had the Buchan papers?'

'I'm not sure.' He swallowed. 'But it might be.'

'I'm on my way,' she said. 'I'll leave a message on David's answerphone so he knows where I am, and I'll be there.'

She was as good as her word; half an hour later, she rang the front doorbell. Sykes bounded to the door, barking.

Judith bent down, making a fuss of him. 'Well, hello! And who are you then?'

'His name's Sykes. I got him for Debra.' Jake sighed. 'Except I'm not too sure if she's ever going to meet him.'

Judith's frown deepened as she saw his haunted face. 'What's going on, Jake?'

He handed her the note in silence; she read it rapidly, and then twice more, letting the words sink in. 'Christ. Is this for real?'

'That's what I thought, at first. But yes, I think it's for real. I've phoned the British Library, and she's not there. She's not at the university, either – I've already checked. So if she's not with you . . .' He dug his nails into his palm, hard. 'Is there anyone else you can think of that she might have gone to see?'

'Not in London. And she would have left you a note, if

she'd decided to go off somewhere for the day, and wouldn't be back until late.'

'I've tried her mobile phone, but that's switched off.' He swallowed. 'We'll just have to ring the police.'

'If you do that,' Judith said quietly, waving the note at him, 'they might do something to Debra.'

'That's what worries me.' He bit his lip. 'They want me to hand "them" over. I assume they mean the paintings, or maybe the books.'

'What else could it be?'

Jake shook his head, his face colouring with anger. 'I don't see why the bastards should get their hands on those paintings. But if that's the only way to keep Debra safe, then I'll hand them over.' His eyes were bleak. 'All I need to know is where and when. But they haven't told me. They've just said that they've got her, and they want the paintings. That's all.'

'Maybe they'll call you, soon.'

'I bloody well hope so. I've left the answerphone on, so I can tape anything they say. Or maybe they'll send me another letter. God knows where she is. They could have taken her anywhere. And if they've laid a finger on her, just once, I'll—'

Judith put her hand on his arm. 'Jake. Calm down. I'm sure everything will be all right.'

'I'm not. Did Debra tell you how much those paintings are worth? A lot of people would do anything for that sort of money. If anything happens to her, Jude . . .'

'It won't.' Judith thought for a moment. 'Though there is a way where you could get Debra back *and* keep the paintings.'

'Such as?'

She whispered in his ear; as Jake took in what she was saying, his face relaxed. 'Jude, have I ever told you that you're a genius?'

She gave him an over the top wink. 'I try. Though, to be on the safe side, I'll make the call from my place.'

'Good idea.'

'You ring the bank, to get the paintings out, and I'll be back as soon as I can.'

'Right.' To Judith's surprise, he kissed her.

'What was that for?'

'Just to say thanks – and I appreciate what you're doing.'

'I'll always be there for my friends,' Judith said softly. 'And that includes you as well as Debra. Now, stop worrying. She'll be all right. She did a self-defence course, you know.'

'Which only works if you're not caught by surprise. If they came up behind her and grabbed her, and she was on another planet, as usual, thinking about her book or—'

'Jake, stop thinking about it. All you're going to do is upset yourself even more. Deb'll be all right. Honestly.'

'I just hope you're right.'

'And in the meantime, you've got Sykes to look after you.'

'Yeah.' Jake smiled wryly, and made a fuss of the pup. 'Though I think it's supposed to be the other way round, at the moment.'

Fourteen

Groggily, Debra tried to open her eyes, and discovered that either she was blindfolded, or she was in the dark. Her hands were tied behind her back, so she couldn't work out which. She wanted to yell and curse, and tell them to let her go, but they were talking to each other. As soon as she heard one of the men say, 'Paintings, she said. Definitely paintings,' her ears pricked up. They were talking about her, and the Buchan drawings. Maybe if she pretended that she was still unconscious, she could find out exactly who had brought her here, and what they were planning. She kept very still, and listened.

'What sort of paintings?'

'Obscene ones. That's all she said.' There was a harsh laugh. 'And I bet she's brought herself off in front of them, before now. She goes like a train.'

Debra suddenly recognised the voice. Henry Buchan. You bastard, she thought angrily. So *you're* behind this.

'She's a hot bitch,' Henry continued. 'You ought to try her. She's got nice tits. Like melons.'

'I noticed.' There was a laugh. 'Yeah, I wouldn't mind having her, John.'

John? Who the hell was *John*? Wasn't his name supposed
to be Henry? So he'd lied to her about that, too. He wasn't
Henry Walter Buchan's great-great nephew at all. He was
some spiteful common thief called John.

'But,' the second voice continued, 'if Madam finds out,
my life will be hell. She's jealous enough of her, as it is.'

John laughed. 'I'll cover for you. I reckon I know a good
way of keeping her mind off it.'

The other man laughed back. 'If anyone else had said that,
John, I'd have knocked their teeth down their throat.'

'But as it's me?' There was another sound; Debra imagined
that John had punched his friend on the arm, a real man-to-
man gesture. 'I've always wanted to give her one, actually.
But as you're my best mate, I wouldn't do it without asking
you first.'

'Right. Well, now you've asked me.' There was a pause.
'So these paintings . . . what do you know about them?'

'Just that they're obscene. I bet they're worth a fortune.'
There was a pause. 'For someone who's meant to be so
clever, a doctor and all that, she's not very bright. She fell
straight into it. Hook, line and bloody sinker. I mean,
who's called *Henry*, nowadays? After their great-whatever
uncle?'

'Yeah. I know.' There was another pause. 'Did you have a
look through those letters and what have you?'

'I did, yeah. They didn't tell me much, though. I thought
the letters were going to be the things that were worth a lot —
or the poems. Lissa said that's why she wanted them so
much.'

Lissa? Debra was shocked. Lissa Sykes was behind the

260

kidnappers, and the fake Henry Buchan? She could hardly believe it. She certainly wouldn't have credited Lissa with that much intelligence.

'But we've struck even luckier. Pictures are always worth more than letters and what have you. Some of them go for a bomb at auction.'

'And these ones, if they're by a famous artist – which Lissa says they are – could be worth a fortune.'

'Do you reckon he'll give us the paintings?'

'Course he will. He'll want her back, won't he?' There was a pause. 'Let's face it, she sucks cock very well. She'd give Mary a run for her money, I'm telling you.'

Mary. Lissa's mother. Maybe Mary was the brains behind it all, Debra thought. But who was John, and where did he fit in? The other man had talked about Lissa – maybe he was George, Lissa's dodgy boyfriend. Or was John really George?

She bit back a groan. It was too much for her to think about, right then. And her head ached.

'When she comes round, I'll see how friendly she can be, then.' He paused for a moment. 'You didn't give her too much of that stuff, did you?'

'Oh, for God's sake. What do you take me for, an idiot?'

'No, of course not.'

'Susie told me exactly how much to give her. I measured the stuff out, for Christ's sake. She's not dead.'

'She'd better not be. I don't want anything to do with murder.'

'George, what the hell's got into you? Stop fussing, man. She'll be fine.'

'Yeah, I suppose.' There was another pause. 'Wait till she's come round. Then if you want to take Lissa over to my place . . .'

'It's a deal.'

Oh, is it? Debra thought angrily. Not if I've got anything to do with it. Lay one finger on me, sunshine, and you'll get a kick in the balls. I'm not just a piece of meat for you to pass between each other.

'I'll just check her pulse,' George said. 'Just make sure you haven't killed her, or anything.'

'I told you, I only gave her what Susie said. She's just knocked out, that's all.'

Debra couldn't help flinching when a hand descended on her wrist.

'Oh, so you're awake, then?'

She nodded, and wished that she hadn't as a wave of giddiness shot through her.

'Here, she's awake. You'd better get her some water or something.'

'Right.'

'Sit up.' He pulled her to a sitting position, and she felt the rim of a cup at her mouth. 'Drink this.'

She refused to open her mouth.

'It's water. It'll make you feel better.' He pushed the cup against her mouth so that her lips opened; a trickle of water forced its way into her mouth, and Debra swallowed.

'That's better. Hungry?'

She remained silent.

A finger traced the neckline of her shirt. 'I hope you'll be feeling a bit friendlier, later.'

Debra was tempted to spit at him, but thought better of it. She simply remained silent.

'We'll have to see what Loverboy says then, won't we? When we ring him and tell him we've got you. Or maybe he thinks more of the paintings than he does of you.' There was a pause. 'Then we're really going to have to think about what happens next.'

A trickle of fear ran down Debra's spine. Was he threatening to kill her? And would he really do it, if it came down to it?

The telephone shrieked; Jake answered it immediately. 'Hello?'

'Jake Matthews?' A flat voice, with the trace of an accent – but not one he recognised.

'Speaking,' Jake said shortly.

'I take it you've read our note.'

'Yes.' Jake pressed the record button.

'What's that noise?'

'I had the phone on answerphone. I just switched it off before it kicked in,' Jake said, wincing at his stupidity. He had to keep them calm.

'Right.'

'Where's Debra?'

'Don't worry, she's safe, with us.'

'I want to talk to her.'

'No.'

'How can I be sure that she's all right?'

'You'll just have to take our word for it.'

Jake swallowed. 'So what do you want?'

'You know what we want. The paintings. The obscene drawings.'

'Right.'

'So what's it to be? The girl or the paintings?'

Jake sighed. 'I'll get them for you. They're in a safe deposit box at the bank, so it'll take three days before I can have them.'

'Three days? No way. We want them quicker than that. We want them tomorrow.'

'Bank security has to be cleared, first. They won't let me have them any earlier. If I insist, they'll know that something's up, and they'll call the police. So it has to be three days,' Jake said urgently.

There was a pause. 'All right. You've got three days.'

'Where do you want me to meet you?'

There was a short laugh. 'What do you think I am, stupid? If we meet you, you'll know who we are. No, leave them in a black plastic bag in the phone box at the end of your road, at midnight.'

'I need proof, first, that Debra's all right. Otherwise I'm not going to the bank.'

The line went silent; Jake thought for a moment that the kidnappers had hung up, but then there was a crackle. 'Jake?'

'Debra. Thank God,' he said as he recognised the voice. 'Are you all right?'

'Don't worry about me. And don't give in to these bastards. Don't give them the—' She was cut off, and one of the kidnappers came back on.

'As you can tell, she's all right.'

'What have you done to her?'

'Just a hand over her mouth. She's not very friendly – she just bit my friend.' There was a short laugh. 'But no doubt she'll be a lot friendlier, by three days' time.'

'You lay one finger on her,' Jake shouted, then realised that he was yelling into a dead line.

He banged the receiver down. 'Bastards! If I get my hands on them . . .'

'Jake, you're not going to solve anything like that. Is Debra all right?' Judith asked.

He nodded. 'I spoke to her – she was fine. She told me not to worry about her.'

'Did they force her to say it?'

Jake smiled wryly. 'I don't think so. The next thing, she told me not to give into the bastards, and not to give them – I think she was going to say "the paintings", but one of them put a hand over her mouth. She bit him.'

Judith winced. 'That wasn't very clever of her.'

'Mm. The one talking to me said that she'd be a lot friendlier, in three days' time – when I give them the paintings.'

'In that case, I'll call Ray, and ask him to work a bit faster,' Judith said.

'If they hurt her—'

'They won't,' Judith said practically.

'But she knows who they are. She can identify them.'

'Not if they've blindfolded her. Which they probably have.'

Jake hadn't thought of that. 'Oh.'

'Have you eaten, yet?'

Jake shook his head.

'Neither have I. I'll make us something. And before you start saying that you couldn't possibly eat anything, let me remind you that you'll be no good to Debra if you pass out from fasting, will you?'

'You're a bully, Jude.'

'I'm just being sensible.' She squeezed his hand. 'Stay by the phone, in case they ring back.'

'That wasn't very clever, was it? Biting my friend. You've upset him.'

'So?' Debra lifted her chin, defiance written all over her face.

'So, you ought to be more careful. In your position.'

Her laugh was completely without mirth. 'I couldn't give a fuck about your friend.' John the liar. John the bully-boy. He could go to hell, as far as she was concerned. Together with Melissa bloody Sykes.

'That isn't what he says. He says you're a good lay.'

Her face tightened. 'That's none of your business.'

'Isn't it, now?'

'No.'

'You've as good as told your boyfriend not to rescue you, telling him not to give us the paintings.'

Debra made a scornful noise. 'I don't see why you should have the paintings, for that trollop.'

'Trollop? And which trollop might we be talking about?'

'Lissa Sykes.'

There was a short pause. 'I've never heard of her.'

Debra lost her temper. 'Come on, George. I know who you are. I know who all of you are. And I know now who's been breaking into our house and smashing it up – and smearing the walls with shit. That wasn't very clever either, was it?'

'I don't know what you're talking about.'

'Oh yes, you do.' Debra scowled at him. She was still blindfolded, and her hands were still tied behind her back. 'Those paintings belong to me and Jake. They came with the property. And just because Lissa's great-great grandmother slept with the painter, it doesn't give her the right to have them. Or any of you the right to treat me like this!'

'It doesn't have to be this way, you know.' Again, a finger traced the neckline of her shirt. 'I can be nice.'

'Oh, really?'

'Very nice.'

'I don't think your Lissa would be very happy, if she could see you right now.'

'But she can't.' At least he'd admitted who he was, Debra thought with relief. His next words chilled her again. 'And she's not very likely to.'

She swallowed. 'So there's just us, here? Alone?'

'Just you and me, alone,' he confirmed.

'Where's "here"?'

He laughed. 'That'd be telling, wouldn't it?'

A sudden thought struck her. 'Would you answer my questions, if I was friendlier to you?'

He laughed again. 'It sounds like you're coming round to my way of thinking.'

Had her hands not been tied, she would have slapped his face for mocking her. As it was . . . She just had to play this one by ear, and hope that there was some way out. 'There's just one thing.'

'What?'

'Your friend. John – or Henry, as he called himself, to me.'

'What about him?'

'I don't want him touching me.'

There was a pause while he digested this. 'And if I make sure that John keeps away from you?'

Debra smiled at him. 'Well, in that case . . .' She drew her tongue along her lower lip. 'Then I might be more friendly.'

'I see.'

'It's not very comfortable, having my hands tied.' She paused for effect. 'And if you can't use your hands, you can't be very friendly, can you?'

'You're very quick to catch on.'

'Didn't Lissa tell you that I'm a doctor?'

'Not a medical one, though.'

Debra shook her head. 'No.' She swallowed. 'Just an academic. A scholar who thought she might be able to find out the truth about something that happened a hundred years ago.' She sighed. 'That's why I fell for your friend's line. I so wanted to believe that the letters existed, I went along with him.'

'The letters do exist.' The words were out before he could stop them.

'George. Haven't you ever wanted something badly, so badly that you'll do almost anything?'

He thought about it. 'I suppose so.' His voice suddenly grew wistful. 'Lissa. And a big Ducati bike.'

'So you see why . . . I wasn't going to cheat Lissa out of any money, believe me. If she'd let me have those letters, I could have got her some money for them. The university could have bought them outright, so the papers could be stored in the university library. Those letters could be important – both for studies of Buchan and for studies of Victorian life.'

'What about the paintings?'

Debra was careful not to challenge him. 'The paintings?'

'She thinks they should be hers, by rights.'

'What about Dicky?'

'Oh, *him*. Like bloody Percy Sugden in *Coronation Street*, always poking his nose in.' George paused. 'I think that's what really upset Lissa. He said to her that she ought to be more like you, a proper lady.'

'I'm no lady,' Debra said. If she could only win George over to her side, maybe she had a chance to do something – and to stop Lissa getting her hands on the paintings.

'How do you mean, no lady?'

'How do you think?'

'John said you were a hot bitch.'

'There's only one way you'll find out, isn't there? Untie me.'

He laughed. 'Not yet. Besides, if what John said is true . . .'

To Debra's horror, he ripped her shirt open, pushing it back over her arms. 'I've always wanted to do that,' he said.

Debra coughed. 'So what are you going to tell Lissa, when she asks what's happened to my shirt?'

'Not a lot.' He traced the edge of her lace bra; Debra had a nasty feeling that he was going to ruin her bra, too, ripping it off her, but instead he simply slid his fingers underneath the lace cups, pushing them down so that her breasts were bared and uplifted by the material. 'You're beautiful,' he breathed.

Half of Debra wanted to spit at him, push him away: but she knew that she couldn't afford to get on his bad side. If she did, he might start being rough with her. The other half of her was calculating; if she did what he wanted, let him screw her, then maybe she could bond with him in some way, and he'd let her go – or at least stand up to Lissa Sykes and his friend John.

He urged her to her feet, and removed her skirt and half-slip so that she was wearing just her knickers and the lewdly arranged bra. 'Very, very nice,' he said. 'Your tits are bigger than Lissa's.' He stroked them, cupping them and lifting them up. Her nipples were beginning to stiffen; he smiled, and bent his head, taking one into his mouth and rolling his tongue round it.

Debra gasped, aroused despite herself. Whatever George's bad points, he certainly knew how to make love. His fingers had burrowed down the front of her knickers, and he was massaging her mound of Venus with the heel of his palm, while his middle finger was sliding back and forth between her labia. She had to force herself not to spread her legs wider and push against him.

'So, what's the verdict?' he asked.

'What verdict?'

He smiled, noting the catch in her voice, and knowing that it was arousal and not fear which had affected her. 'Are you going to be friendly?'

She swallowed. 'That depends. It works two ways.'

'Do you really think you're in a position to bargain?'

Something he'd said had given her a bargaining tool. She smiled. 'It depends how friendly you want me to be. I heard what your friend John said about me.' She paused. 'And about Lissa's mother, Mary. Where does she fit in?'

George laughed shortly. 'I'll give you this, you're persistent. What if I decide not to tell you?'

'Then—' she closed her thighs hard round his hand '—I might stop being friendly. Just as we were getting on so well.'

His eyes narrowed. 'I ought to spank you for that.'

'Go ahead. Hit me.' She lifted her chin. 'But you might be in for a very nasty surprise if you make me give you Mary's speciality.'

He looked at her for a moment, torn between annoyance and admiration. 'What are you saying, exactly?'

Debra gave him a cynical smile, opened her mouth, and shut it again very quickly in an exaggerated biting motion.

'I see.'

'But if you're friendly to me – then you'll get the chance to see if John was telling you the truth.'

'I answer the questions, you give me a blow job?'

'Or whatever else you want.'

His hand was still in her knickers; the feel of her warm moist sex-flesh against his fingertips was his undoing. 'Okay. Three questions.'

She thought for a moment. 'Where does John fit in?'

'How do you mean?'

'I can see where you fit in – you're Lissa's boyfriend. And Mary, because she's Lissa's mother.'

'Mary isn't in on it.'

'John talked about Mary, earlier.'

'That's because he fucks her, occasionally. Between girlfriends, or when he's bored.'

'But I don't understand how come he's in on it, when Mary's not.'

George rubbed thoughtfully at her clitoris. 'He's my cousin. My best mate.'

'I still don't see how he fits in.'

'Lissa thought the letters might be worth something – and that you'd be able to tell how much, straight off. She couldn't show them to you herself, because you know who she is. Mary looks too much like her, so she couldn't do it. So we thought about it, and reckoned that the only person who could let you see those letters was someone to do with the painter. So we asked John.'

'I still don't see why.' Debra was careful not to phrase it as a question.

'Because he did a bit of acting, when he left school. He can put on a posh voice.'

'Right. That's why he pretended to be Buchan's great-great nephew.' Debra paused. 'So—'

George coughed. 'Your turn to be friendly.'

'But you've only answered one question!'

'I didn't say I'd answer them all at once.'

She swallowed. 'What do you want?'

'You know.'

She shook her head. 'After the third question.'

'Right.'

He was still rubbing her clitoris; Debra could feel her orgasm building, but she tried to keep it at bay. Focus, she told herself. Focus on the questions. You know why Lissa's involved, and George – and now John. Ignore what he's doing to you. Just focus on what you want to know.

She swallowed hard, hoping that her arousal wouldn't be too obvious in her voice. 'How did you know where to find me?'

'When?'

'Where I work, where I live, what I was doing in the long vacation.'

'That's easy. Loverboy gave Lissa your address.'

Debra detected a note of jealousy in George's voice; obviously Lissa had played on it, taunting him with what she'd done with Jake. The bitch. 'I don't see how you got my work address.'

'We rang round a few universities. It didn't take long – the third one said you didn't work there, but gave us the number of your office. It was easy to get a letter to you, then.'

'And I told Henry – John, that is – that I was working in the British Library.' She swallowed. 'So you were following me.'

'What do you expect?' George recognised the hectic flush on her cheeks, the tell-tale mottling over her breasts, and smiled. Just a little bit more, and—

'Oh,' Debra said, unable to hold back her orgasm any longer. George stroked her as her quim spasmed madly, and held her arm with one hand so that she didn't fall.

'So now we're a bit friendlier, you and me,' he said, when her breathing had slowed down again.

Debra nodded. 'But I've still got one more question. Why did you kidnap me?'

'Because we want the paintings.'

'But what do you get out of it?'

'That's a fourth question.'

'No, it isn't. I can see why Lissa and John were in this – they're greedy. I haven't met Mary, but I imagine she's the same, from what Dicky told me about her. If she knew about this, she'd want her share. But you're not like them.'

He laughed shortly. 'Don't try to soft-soap me.'

'I'm not. You *are* different, George. John wouldn't have been like you. He'd have just bullied me.' She paused. 'I don't think he likes women very much.'

'Not clever women,' George admitted. 'One turned him down, once – she told him that he looked as though he was a closet gay.'

'I can see what she meant. He does look a bit like a public schoolboy.' Debra paused. 'What do you look like?'

'Why? Does it make any difference?'

'I just wondered, that was all.' She sighed. 'Considering I can't see you, and I can't touch you . . .' She drew her tongue along her lower lip.

'That can be arranged.' The words were out before he could stop them.

'Untie me, George. If you don't want me to see you – at least let me touch you.'

He was slightly wary, wandering if she was going to try to trick him: then decided to trust her. Even if she managed to get him off balance, she wouldn't get very far with a blindfold on. And the way she was dressed – there was no way she'd go into the street, dressed like that. It wouldn't hurt, he decided, spinning her round and untying the rope round her wrists.

She rubbed the skin. 'That's better,' she said softly. 'They were beginning to hurt.'

'I didn't tie them *that* tight.'

'Tightly enough.'

To her surprise, he took her wrists, rubbing them gently and dropping a kiss on the pulse points before releasing them again. 'Better?'

She nodded, not trusting herself to speak. She couldn't work him out. One minute, he was playing the tough kidnapper; the next, he was gentle, unexpectedly kind. On the one hand, Dicky couldn't stand him; on the other, Dicky thought that Lissa was Little Miss Innocent, being led astray by George. Dicky was completely wrong about Lissa – could he be wrong about George, too, and the truth was that it was Lissa who was leading George astray?

'Your hands are free. What now?'

'Where are you?'

'Here.' He put his hand on her arm.

She smiled at him, and gently walked her fingers up his arm, across his shoulders, until she reached his throat. She stroked upwards, cupping his chin, then brought her other hand to join it, trying to read his face like a blind person would.

'Strong jaw. Nice cheekbones,' she said. 'Nice hair, too.' Wavy, by the feel of it, and slightly longer than Jake's. Clean, too, to her relief. 'Dark?' she guessed.

'Yes.'

'What colour are your eyes?'

'Is it important?' His voice was half-nervous, half-impatient.

'Yes.'

'They're blue.'

'And you shaved today.' His skin was slightly rough with the beginnings of stubble. 'No moustache. That's good.'

'Why are you doing this?'

'Because I want to picture you.'

He said nothing, and Debra continued her exploration. He was wearing a T-shirt, and she could feel the muscles of his chest through them: George was well-developed, like Jake. Maybe he even looked like Jake, and that was why Lissa had taken such a fancy to Jake. Lissa. Debra smiled to herself. Lissa had had her man; now she was going to have Lissa's man. And she was going to do more for him than Lissa ever had . . .

'You're smiling,' George accused.

'Laughing at myself.'

'Why?'

'How am I going to take your T-shirt off, if I can't see you? So either I ask you to do it, or I make a hell of a mess of it.'

'I'll do it.' He tugged at the bottom of his T-shirt, ripping it off, and placed Debra's hands against his chest. 'Better?'

'Mm.' A light covering of hair – nowhere near gorilla proportions, but not boyishly smooth, either. If George looked anything as good as he felt, Debra thought, Lissa Sykes simply didn't deserve him.

She let her hands drift down over his abdomen. Flat, nicely toned; if he drank a lot of beer, it certainly didn't show, yet. She reached the waistband of his jeans, and undid the button. She felt him tremble slightly in anticipation, and smiled to herself. George was about to have the best blow-job of his entire life. And then, perhaps, he'd be on her side . . .

Slowly, she undid the remaining buttons of his fly. His cock was a nice size, long and thick and hard; again, she had the thought that he felt very much like Jake. She'd have to be very, very careful not to call George 'Jake'.

She pushed the denim down over his hips. 'Are you going to take them off?' she asked quietly.

George shook his head, then remembered that she couldn't see him. 'No.'

'Pity.' She ran her nails along his thighs. 'You might lose balance.' She stroked lightly upwards again, until she found the waistband of his underpants, hooked her fingers into them, and drew them down. 'Sure about that?'

George thought about it for a moment, then stripped swiftly. 'Okay. We'll do it your way.'

'Good.' She ran her tongue along her lower lip. 'Help me down.'

'Down?'

'I don't want to spend the next half-hour bent double. It's easier if I kneel.'

She felt the shudder run through his whole body, and smiled to herself. By the time she'd finished with him, George would definitely be on her side.

He helped her kneel before him; Debra could picture the scene. A man, standing naked in the middle of the room; a blindfolded woman kneeling before him, her knickers covering her modesty but the crotch soaking, and her bra pushed down lewdly to reveal her breasts. It was like something that Buchan would have painted, in this day and age, and she found the idea arousing.

She reached out to George, running her palm over his thighs; then she rubbed her cheeks against them. At George's sharp intake of breath, she urged his thighs apart slightly, and bent her mouth to his groin. He smelled clean; the musky tang of his arousal filled her nostrils. This, she thought, could be very good indeed. In different circumstances . . .

She pushed the thought from her mind, and drew the tip of her tongue along his shaft. George gave a soft murmur, tangling his fingers in her hair and urging her on. She brought her hands up to cup his balls, massaging them gently while she took the tip of his penis into her mouth. George couldn't help pushing his hips towards her, wanting more; Debra imagined that his head was tipped back slightly, his mouth already open in pleasure.

You just wait, she told him silently. I've hardly started.

She swirled her tongue over his glans, pressing her tongue hard into the eye; then she lapped at the sensitive spot beneath the head, making her tongue into a sharp point to give him more pleasure.

He moaned, his breath coming in juddering gasps as Debra continued to lick and suck her way along his shaft, taking him more deeply into her mouth. She made a ring of her finger and thumb, squeezing the base of his shaft gently, and then pushing the ring up and down his shaft in exact opposition to her mouth.

With her other hand, she continued to massage his balls. As they began to lift and tighten, she stroked his perineum, running just the tip of her finger along the sensitive part of his skin. George's breathing was ragged, and he made soft moans as Debra's mouth stimulated him more and more. He was on the point of coming when the door suddenly burst open.

'What the *fuck* is going on here?'

Debra recognised the voice as Lissa's, and smiled to herself. Who was it who said that revenge was a dish best served cold? She continued to suck George's cock, knowing how much it would annoy Lissa to see her boyfriend being pleasured so well; when she felt her mouth fill with warm salty fluid, she swallowed every last drop, kissed the tip of George's cock, and sat back on her haunches, licking her lips.

'What the fuck is going on?' Lissa demanded again.

'What does it look like?' George asked.

Lissa's fury was evident in her voice. 'We need to talk. Now. Without *her*.'

'Next door, then.'

George dressed swiftly, and touched Debra's cheek gently as he left; Debra guessed that Lissa must have turned away, and couldn't see what he did. She simply smiled, and pulled the cups of her bra back up. She tried tugging off the blindfold, but she couldn't undo the fastening; in the end she gave up and started crawling round on the floor to locate the rest of her clothes.

Fifteen

Debra could hear every word of the row going on in the next room: wherever they were, the walls were very thin, she thought.

'What the fuck were you doing with her?'

'Enjoying myself. What did it look like?'

'You bastard. I should have known you couldn't keep your sticky hands off her. You sent John round to me on purpose, didn't you? Just so you could be on your own with her.'

'If it was all right for you to fuck her boyfriend, then it's all right for me to have her. Or are you saying you can do what you like, and I can't?'

There was a pause. 'I don't know why you bothered. She's a frigid bitch, anyway. Tight-arsed. You can see it in her face.'

Debra's lips twitched. Says who? she thought, amused. She had a feeling that she could probably teach Lissa a trick or two. George's reaction to her hadn't been that of a man who'd sampled all the pleasures of sex, and was jaded with them.

His next words made Debra want to laugh out loud. 'Actually, she's very responsive. She certainly uses her mouth better than you do – and at least she isn't a trollop.'

Debra heard something smash: it sounded like Lissa had thrown a plate or something at George, and he'd ducked it.

'I'll make her less attractive!' Lissa screamed. 'You just watch!'

Debra swallowed hard. Lissa could have a lot of things in mind – none of them very pleasant. If Jake didn't get her out of this place soon, or if Lissa swayed George against her, things could turn nasty.

George's voice was calm, and very cold. 'Lay one finger on her, and you'll answer to me.'

'And whose army?' Lissa taunted.

'Just me. Now, we're going to get the pictures; you'll have what you want in a couple of days, so just leave her alone.'

There was a short pause, and then Debra heard a door slam. Lissa had left – for the moment, at least. Now what? she wondered.

'You look tired, Jake. Go to bed.'

He shook his head. 'I can't. They might ring. Anyway, I won't be able to sleep, thinking about what they're doing to her.'

'It's gone midnight, Jake – they're probably asleep. Like little Sykes here.' She nodded at the puppy, who was curled up asleep on Jake's lap.

'Maybe.'

Judith squeezed his hand. 'Look, if it makes you feel any better, I'll stay over, and we can take turns in sitting by the phone.'

He smiled. 'Thanks, Jude. I have to admit, it'd be nice to have company.'

'Being alone with your thoughts is the worst thing. Just tell me where the sheets are, and I'll make up the spare bed.'

'Debra's horrible futon, you mean?'

Judith winced. 'Oh, no. I've never been able to work it out. It's worse than the deck chairs you used to get at the beach when you were a kid – I could never work them out, either. They always used to collapse on me.'

'Look, you have our bed. I'll sleep on the sofa.'

'And end up with a crick in your neck? Come on, be sensible. I'm shorter than you. I'll take the sofa.'

He shook his head. 'You're not sleeping on the sofa, Jude.'

'Let's compromise. We'll both sleep in the bed.' At Jake's widened eyes, she added, 'We can manage to sleep together in the platonic sense, can't we?'

He thought for a moment. 'Mm. And there's a phone by the bed, so if it rings . . .'

'Exactly. Come and count some sheep. You'll be much more use to Debra in the morning if you've had some rest, than if you've spent the whole night sitting in a chair and letting your imagination run riot about what's happening to her.'

'I suppose so.'

He lifted Sykes gently, placing the still sleeping boxer in his bed in the kitchen, put some newspaper down, and followed Judith upstairs. It felt strange, having her lying in bed next to him rather than Debra; but she was right, Jake thought. They could manage to keep it platonic – especially as she was wearing a T-shirt and her knickers, and he was wearing his underpants. Judith had remarked that they didn't quite need the proverbial sword or the bolster between them, making him smile.

But he missed Debra. He missed the way she curled into him when she was asleep: her buttocks pressed against him, his arm round her waist, and her arm on top of his. He missed the scent of her hair, the feel of her skin against his. He shut his eyes, trying not to think about it, and gradually fell asleep.

Some time later, he half-woke; Debra was lying in his arms as usual, but she was wearing a T-shirt. His mind was groggy with sleep, and he couldn't quite work out why she was wearing a T-shirt and knickers. It wasn't the wrong time of the month, he knew that for a fact. He couldn't remember having a row with her, either. Why else would she come to bed half-dressed?

What the hell, he thought, burrowing one hand under the T-shirt. Her breasts were soft and warm, and he cupped one in his hand, loving its fullness. She gave a small murmur, and pushed back against him; he nuzzled her neck, and began to play with her nipple, arousing it with his forefinger and thumb.

She murmured again, arching her back; Jake let his hand slide down over her abdomen, and burrowed under the top of her knickers. She parted her thighs as he worked his fingers down towards her sex; as he probed her quim, he smiled against her shoulder. She felt warm, and very wet.

He couldn't work out why he, too, was wearing underpants, but quickly wriggled out of them. He pushed his cock between her parted thighs, pulling the gusset of her knickers aside, and guiding his erect penis into her sex. She felt like warm silk wrapped round him, and the extra friction of her knickers rubbing against him only added to his excitement as he began to thrust into her.

She wriggled forward slightly, changing the angles between their bodies to give them the most pleasure, and he moaned in bliss. As he came, he felt her quim rippling round him, lengthening and deepening his own orgasm; with a sigh of contentment, he folded his arm round her, pulling her back against his body, and drifted back into sleep.

Debra had wrapped her shirt round her, but as half of the buttons had come off when George had ripped it from her, she hadn't bothered trying to do it up. When George came back into the room, she was sitting on the floor, cross-legged, looking very wary.

'All right?' he asked softly.

'Mm.' She swallowed. 'What happens now?'

'Lissa, you mean?' At Debra's nod, he continued. 'She's gone out.'

'I could hear what you were saying, in the next room.'

George nodded. 'Don't worry. I won't let her touch you.' He sighed. 'She can be a real bitch, at times. Sometimes I wonder why I go along with some of her stupid ideas.'

'Maybe you love her,' Debra suggested.

'Maybe I just need my head examining.'

'I shouldn't think so. Everyone goes through bad patches.'

'Even you and Loverboy?'

Debra nodded. 'When I realised what had happened, in Blakeney . . .'

'Lissa guessed it would annoy you, if she had him. She's got a real downer on you, for some reason.'

'I'd never met her before, though.'

'Well. Sometimes you just don't take to someone. No particular reason. Or maybe she's just jealous that you've got everything she wanted – your own place, a good job, the man you love living with you. And there she is, stuck behind the bar at the Red Lion, living with her grandfather, and not much chance of life changing.'

Debra decided not to ask him why he wasn't living with Lissa himself. She had a feeling that the nerve was too raw, and she didn't want to risk upsetting him.

George looked at her. 'Are you hungry?'

'Not really.' She indicated her shirt. 'I could do with something to replace this, though.'

He pulled off his T-shirt, putting it into her hands. 'Here. Use my T-shirt.'

'Thanks.'

'And I'm sorry about your shirt. I'm not usually rough.'

'No.' Debra pushed her shirt off again. She was about to put George's T-shirt on, when he stopped her. 'What?' she asked.

'Your boobs really are beautiful, you know. You're all curves, and I like that in a woman.'

'Lissa's thin,' Debra said, before she could stop herself.

'Yeah. Lissa's – well, Lissa.' He drew his finger down her cleavage, unable to help himself. 'Loverboy must be going insane without you.'

'He'll survive,' Debra said drily. 'You are intending to let me go, then?'

'Why do you think we wouldn't?'

'Because I know who you all are.'

'Lissa and John don't know that,' he pointed out, sliding his finger under the cup of her bra to caress her nipple. 'So if you don't tell, either, we're all right, aren't we?'

'I could go to the police, as soon as you let me go,' Debra reminded him. 'They know that.'

'Is that what you're going to do?' His thumb grazed the hardening nub of flesh.

'George?'

'You haven't answered my question.'

'I know.' She licked her suddenly dry lips as he started working on her other nipple. 'When do you think Lissa will be back? Or John?'

'Not for a while.'

'So what happens now?'

'That depends on you. If I can persuade you not to go to the police . . .'

She smiled, guessing exactly the form that George's persuasion was going to take. 'Take my blindfold off, and I'll think about it.'

'I can't risk it in case the others come back early.'

'It feels like you were planning on taking a different sort of risk,' Debra said as his hand slipped under the hem of her skirt and started caressing her calves.

'I'm just being friendly.' There was a smile in his voice. 'Carrying on where we left off after being so rudely interrupted.'

'Supposing John comes back?'

'He won't touch you. I'll knock his teeth down his throat

287

if he so much as tries it on with you.'

'You just told me that you're not usually rough.'

'I'm not. And you talk too much.' He suddenly bent forward and kissed her; Debra was taken by surprise, and didn't resist when his tongue slid between her lips, exploring her mouth.

When he lifted his head again, she was flushed, her lips swollen and reddened with arousal. 'Debra,' he said softly.

'Yes?'

'The floor's not very comfortable. It's not very clean, either – not what you're used to.'

'I don't know about that.' She touched his face. 'We've been renovating our place – as you know. And just recently, it hasn't been clean at all.'

He winced. 'That wasn't my idea. Breaking in, yes, to find where you'd hidden the pictures, but I told him not to touch or take anything else.'

'Amazing that someone who acts so fastidious should like smearing shit over the walls.' Her voice was dry.

'Sometimes he gets a bit carried away. And not on the right sort of things.' He leaned forward to kiss her. 'Whereas I . . .' He pulled her to her feet, and led her to a bed at the far side of the room. 'I want to do this properly,' he said softly, taking her skirt off again. He undid the clasp of her bra with little difficulty, then hooked his thumbs in her knickers and drew them down. He lifted her up, placing her on the bed, and stripped swiftly.

Debra felt the mattress give slightly as George lay down beside her. Then she felt the flat of his palm sweeping down over her body as he familiarised himself with the way her body curved. 'Beautiful,' he said softly, cupping her breasts and pushing them together; he rubbed his cheeks against them, breathing in her scent, then opened his mouth over one nipple.

He drew fiercely on the hard nub of flesh, so that Debra gasped and arched her back. She felt him laugh against her skin, and then he was kissing down over her abdomen, rubbing his face against the curly triangle of hair at the base of her belly. She gave a sigh of pleasure as his tongue moved along her labia; he licked and lapped and sucked until Debra was writhing beneath him, making small soft moans of pleasure.

Then he knelt between her thighs, positioning the head of his cock at the entrance of her sex; as he drove into her, Debra's legs came up to grip his waist, her ankles crossing behind his back. He moved back until his cock was almost out of her, then let himself sink back into her, repeating the action again and again until the long slow strokes were almost driving her insane.

She pushed up to meet him, wanting to feel him inside her to the hilt; everything else was overcome by this sudden lust, this sudden need. He felt it too: he held her close while he thrust into her, nuzzling her shoulders and face and neck, murmuring soft endearments.

At last, she felt her orgasm bubble through her veins, rolling up through her body and suddenly exploding in her solar plexus. She gasped, and at that same instant, George's body stilled over hers, and she felt him hold her tightly as his seed pumped into her.

When he finally slipped from her, he lay on his back, pulling her into his arms so that her head was pillowed on his shoulder. 'That's better,' he said softly.

'Mm.'

'So are you going to tell the police all about us?'

She sighed. 'No. Not about you, anyway.'

'I'm in it as much as John and Lissa.'

She shook her head. 'They're the ones who've caused me all the grief. You've been nice to me, at least.'

'Even so.' He rubbed his cheek against hers. 'Just don't tell the police. I don't think I could stand being inside.'

'It's not very nice, being a prisoner,' Debra agreed.

The irony wasn't lost on George. 'We're calling Loverboy, tomorrow morning. If he tells us the deal's on, you'll be free in a day or so.'

'Right.' She paused. 'And in the meantime?'

'When the others aren't here, I'll keep the ropes off you. When they're here . . . I think it'd be safest to keep you tied up.'

'I'm not going to try anything. Let's face it, I'm blindfolded. So even if I did manage to break free, I wouldn't get very far before you caught me again.'

'I wasn't thinking that, so much.'

'You mean, keeping me safe from John and Lissa?'

'Mm.' He stroked her face. 'It wouldn't surprise me if she's gone down the pub. A few brandy and cokes down her neck, and she'll either cheer herself up, or be in a worse mood than ever. So when she gets back, she'll either want to kill you, or she'll want to use you for her pleasure.'

'What sort of pleasure?'

'Lissa swings both ways,' George said drily. 'Work it out for yourself.'

'She can't force me to do anything.'

'I wouldn't bet on it. You're tied and blindfolded, right? What if she decided to tie you to the bed, and squat over your face? You'd have no choice but to lick her.'

Debra shifted uncomfortably. 'I don't get off on the idea of doing it with another woman. Or being tied up.'

'Lissa does. Well, as long as she's the dominant one. She did it with a girlfriend of John's, once, and it kept her going for weeks. She went on and on and on about how good it was, asking me if I'd enjoy watching her do it again.'

Again, Debra wanted to ask him why he put up with Lissa's behaviour; but she kept silent.

'She's done it with her boss, too.'

'Susan Wetherby?' Debra was shocked.

'The old cow at the Red Lion, yes.'

'She didn't look the sort.'

'Just goes to show. You never know what's going to turn someone on.' George began stroking her breasts again.

Debra smiled. 'Jake told her we were engaged, to make it seem more respectable.'

'She wouldn't have turned a hair if you'd booked a room for three, believe me.'

'You mean you and Lissa have both had sex with her, at the same time?'

'No, that's not my scene. It's just village gossip, anyway.' George shifted her so that she was on her side. 'Do you mind if I . . . ?'

'What?'

'This.' She felt his cock slide between her breasts, and his hands squeezing her breasts together, putting greater pressure on his cock. 'Oh, that's good.'

And something that Lissa couldn't do for him, Debra thought. Keep George sweet, and he could help her a lot. She stroked his buttocks as he continued to thrust between her breasts; he shuddered, and she wondered if he was about to come, but then he seemed to control himself again.

'Not fair on you,' he muttered; to Debra's surprise, he burrowed down the bed, spreading her thighs and rubbing his cheeks against her skin before drawing his tongue along the length of her quim.

She couldn't help a soft moan of pleasure; encouraged, he began to lick her, making his tongue into a hard point as it travelled up to her clitoris, teasing it, and then lapping back down her vulva.

'George,' she said, pushing her quim up to meet his mouth, 'what about you?'

'There's one way round it,' he said laconically.

'Oh?'

He turned round so that his knees were parted by her shoulders, and his heavy penis hung by her face.

Debra reached for him, taking the tip of his cock into her mouth; George sighed with pleasure, and stretched out over her body, lifting her buttocks and reapplying his mouth to her quim. She quivered beneath him, prevented from crying out loud by the fact that his cock was filling her mouth. And then she felt the blissful rolling sensation of her orgasm flowing through her, coiling tightly in her stomach, and then exploding . . .

When Jake woke, the next morning, Debra was still asleep in

his arms, her bottom pressed into his lap and her fingers laced through his. 'Mm, Deb,' he murmured,' nuzzling her shoulder; then he suddenly realised that the woman in his arms didn't have the jaw-length unruly mop he was used to. This woman had short hair – red hair. Not Debra: Judith.

Everything slammed back into focus: Debra kidnapped, the Buchan drawings, the fact that he'd made love to Judith in the night, persuading himself that she was Debra . . . He closed his eyes tightly, hoping that when he opened them, the world would be back to normal again.

It wasn't.

Very gently, he removed his arms from Judith, hoping that she wouldn't wake, but he was too late. She was already stretching and yawning.

'Um. Judith.' He flushed. 'Er – would you like some coffee?'

She smiled at him. 'Thank you. Did you sleep well?'

'Sort of,' he muttered, his colour deepening. Did this mean that Judith didn't know what had happened during the night?

'Jake.' She touched his face. 'Loosen up.'

He swallowed, hard. 'Judith, I think we need to talk.'

'No, we don't.' She smiled at him. 'It's okay. Think about it.'

'You're Debra's best friend.'

'I know. We both missed her, we were both worried sick, and we needed comfort. That's all we did, comfort each other. There's nothing more to it than that, and no one else needs to know. It's just between you and me – and I'm certainly not telling. Now, why don't you sort out that coffee, while I have a shower and get dressed? I'm sure your dog could do with going out, too.'

He smiled back at her. 'Right. I'll see you downstairs, then.'

Sykes was pleased to see him, and even more pleased to go out into the garden. Jake smiled, watching the puppy gambolling around; Debra would love him, he was sure of it. Debra. His face tightened again, and he went back into the kitchen to make the coffee. Just when the kettle had boiled, the telephone rang; Jake dashed towards it.

'Hello, Loverboy.'

Jake gritted his teeth, and managed to stop himself making a rude comment. If he upset the kidnappers, they'd take it out on Debra. 'Who is this?'

'I think you know. So what did the bank say?'

'Where's Debra?'

'She's here. And she's very comfortable.' He rolled his r's lasciviously.

Jake's eyes widened with shock. Was the kidnapper hinting that he'd raped Debra? 'I want to talk to her. Now.'

'I want doesn't get.'

'Have you hurt her?'

There was a pause. 'No.'

'Then why can't I talk to her?'

There was a crackle, and then Debra spoke. 'Jake?'

'Hi. Are you okay?'

'Yes. They're treating me well.'

'And they haven't touched you?'

'They haven't hurt me.'

'Or raped you, or anything like that?'

294

'No.' George had been as good as his word, and had kept John away from her. 'Look, they want the two drawings.'

Jake grinned. So they didn't know how many prints there were. That would make his job easier, at least. 'The two drawings.'

'Yes. You know, the one of the woman and the swan, and the one of Echo and Narcissus.'

'Right.' Jake was torn between admiration and amazement. She'd kept a far cooler head than he had over this business – even cool enough to tell him which two prints she wanted him to keep.

'They want to talk to you again, Jake. But I'm all right, so don't worry. They won't hurt me.'

'As long as we get the prints,' the man added, taking the phone back again. 'The day after tomorrow.'

'You said to leave them in the phone box. How do I have any guarantee that you'll release Debra, then?'

'You'll just have to take our word for it.' The line went dead again, and Jake slowly replaced the receiver.

'Was that them?' Judith asked, walking into the kitchen.

He nodded. 'Deb told me that they wanted the two drawings.'

'So they don't know you've got four?'

'Nope.'

'That makes it a bit easier, then.' She narrowed her eyes. 'You look as if you're about to explode. What is it?'

'I'm sure one of them's been pawing her. I asked her if they'd touched her, and she said that they hadn't hurt her.'

'Same difference.'

'No, it isn't. You know how Debra always says exactly

295

what she means.' Jake frowned. 'If only I knew where she was.'

'Well, we don't. All we can do is deliver two drawings, and hope they keep their word and give her back.' Judith paused. 'Did she say which ones?'

Jake nodded. 'Even if she hadn't, I know which two she'd want to keep.'

Sixteen

Lissa didn't bother coming back at all, that night, much to Debra's relief. The last thing she wanted was to have her face forced into Lissa's crotch, licking and sucking the woman to give her pleasure – particularly as it would have been a floor show to amuse John, too. George could have done nothing about it – any protests, and they would have guessed that he was trying to protect her. That would make everything much worse.

She imagined that Lissa would have involved John in it, too. Maybe she'd have sucked his cock while she forced Debra to lick her quim. Or maybe she'd let Debra be John's plaything, for her amusement, watching everything that went on between them. John would no doubt have wanted her to fellate him – naked, blindfolded and still tied, a slave for her master's amusement. And then he'd have put his cock into her, not caring whether she had any pleasure. Just using her. And all the while, Lissa would have been grinning away, pleased to see Debra being humiliated.

Debra's face tightened at the thought. She simply counted herself lucky that it hadn't happened – yet. But until Jake gave them the pictures, there was still a risk that she'd fall foul of Lissa.

When Lissa finally returned, the next morning, she was with John; the tightness in George's voice and the triumph in hers led Debra to guess that Lissa had spent the night with John, mainly to taunt George. Why does he stay with her? Debra wondered. Why doesn't he just dump her, and find himself a decent woman, one who won't flaunt her lovers in his face?

The day passed without event, and Debra found herself thinking more and more of Jake, wondering what he was doing, if he was missing her, and whether he'd taken her hints about the pictures. She still didn't see why Lissa Sykes should have them at all, but if they had to give up the pictures, Debra was determined that they should only give up *some* of them.

The evening was equally boring; Lissa had obviously decided that she wasn't going to leave George on his own with Debra, and George kept his promise about not leaving Debra on her own with John. Debra spent all her time curled up in a corner, saying nothing; Lissa tried to provoke her once or twice, but Debra didn't bother rising to the bait. Eventually, Lissa gave up – after making veiled threats that if George left the room, John would keep him outside so that Lissa could have a bit of fun with Debra. The fun wasn't specified, but it was obvious that Lissa didn't intend Debra to enjoy it.

Debra simply turned her face away, and kept her mouth shut. It would be too easy to end up in a slanging match and, being blindfolded and tied, she'd come off worst. Somehow, she managed to sleep; the next morning, she was stiff and sore and aching, but at least she was alive. And Lissa Sykes hadn't laid a finger on her.

'D-day,' George said to her, feeding her some dry toast and some water. 'We're taking you back, and picking up the paintings.'

'You're not going to chloroform me again, are you?'

'No. But it looks too obvious, putting you in the car with a blindfold on.'

'You're taking it off?' She was surprised.

'No, just disguising it,' George said, producing a large pair of dark glasses and putting them on her nose. 'Yeah, that looks realistic enough. I looks like you've got some sort of headband on, and it's slipped a bit.' He touched her face briefly. 'Chin up, sweetheart,' he whispered. 'Nearly there.'

Lissa must have seen something – or suspected it – because she insisted that George should drive, and Debra should sit in the back with John. Debra wasn't happy with the arrangement, and vowed that if John so much as thought of touching her, she'd kick him, hard. Luckily, John's mind was more on the paintings and the money they'd make, so he left her alone on the way back to London.

Eventually, they stopped; Debra heard the car door slam, as George or Lissa got out to check something. They drove a little further – round a couple of streets, she guessed – then the car door was opened next to her, she was hauled out unceremoniously, and left sitting on the pavement.

'See you later, bitch,' Lissa spat, and the car drove away.

'When hell freezes over,' Debra muttered.

A few minutes later, by which time Debra had discovered

that she was too firmly tied to undo herself, and the blindfold would have to stay where it was until someone came past to give her a hand, she heard a screech of tyres.

'Debra! Thank God! So they weren't lying when they rang me to say you were here.' Jake lifted her up, setting her on her feet, and swiftly removed the ropes at her wrists and the blindfold. 'Thank God,' he repeated, hugging her tightly.

For the first time since she'd been kidnapped, Debra burst into tears.

Jake held her close. 'It's all right. They can't harm you now. You're safe, with me.'

'It's not that,' Debra said, sniffing, her eyes hurting at the unaccustomed light. 'I'm just so bloody glad to be home.'

'And I'm bloody glad to have you back.' He kissed her gently. 'Come on. Let's go home.'

'I need a bath,' Debra said as she walked in the door. 'And I'm starving.'

'Bath, first; then food.'

'I could do with a massage, as well.' She flexed the muscles in her shoulders. 'I ache.'

'Just before I sort everything out for you . . .' Jake opened the kitchen door, and the puppy bounded out. 'Meet Sykes.'

'Sykes?'

'Yes. Remember when we were in Blakeney, and we talked about having a little boxer called Sykes? I brought him home, the day they kidnapped you. He's been dying to meet you.'

'Well.' Debra squatted down to make a fuss of the puppy. 'He's beautiful, Jake. Though I wish you hadn't called him Sykes. It just makes me think of that bitch Lissa.'

'Let's call him Bill, then,' Jake suggested.

'Bill the boxer. Yes, I like that. Now, are you going to answer to your new name, Bill?' The puppy licked her face, and she laughed. 'What a beautiful boy you are.'

'Jude fell in love with him, too.'

'Jude?'

'Mm. She came over, when I got the ransom note and started panicking. She calmed me down a bit.'

'The departmental whirlwind making someone calm — now that, I'd like to have seen,' Debra said, laughing.

'It involved force-feeding me with pasta. Well, Bill helped me out a bit, there.'

'I bet he did.' Debra fondled the pup's ears. 'Do you like bacon sarnies, Bill?'

The puppy barked.

'I'll take that as a yes.'

'And I'll take it as a hint. When you've had a bath, I'll do you some food,' Jake said. 'In the meantime, Bill — back in your bed, for a while, so I can sort Debra out with her bath.' He smiled at her. 'And a massage. Your wish is my command.'

'New lamps for old?' she teased.

He laughed. 'That's very appropriate, in the circumstances.'

Debra didn't catch his reference, and simply stroked his face. 'I know how much those paintings meant to you. I really appreciate the fact that you gave them up, to make them release me.'

He smiled at her. 'I don't know about that. In your shoes, I'd want to kill me for the delay.'

'Well, you had to get them out of the bank. That takes time, doesn't it?'

'Sort of.' Jake coughed. 'I didn't want to give the drawings to them, but I couldn't see any way out of it. Anyway, Jude's got this friend, Ray.'

'The graphic artist?' Debra asked.

'Yes. I didn't know you knew him.'

'Not well, but he seems a nice bloke. Anyway, what's he got to do with our paintings?'

'He copied two of them for us – the two you specified – in the three days. So the kidnappers have the copies, not the originals.' Jake shrugged. 'As you said, new lamps for old.'

'*What*?' Debra was shocked.

'I did it for the best of reasons, Deb. The kidnappers didn't know any different.'

'As soon as they try selling them, they'll find out. Ray's good, but any valuer would spot the fake a mile off.' Debra's face was grim. 'What then?'

Jake stroked her hair. 'Considering that I delivered the originals to the Tate, this morning, and the story's going to break in the press tomorrow . . . you've got nothing to worry about, Deb. I told the police all about it. They've got the house under surveillance, and then tomorrow morning, you can go down to the station and tell them everything.'

'Right.' Debra swallowed. 'Though they weren't all bad. I don't want them all treated the same.'

'How do you mean?'

'John – he's the one who pretended he was Buchan's great-great nephew – and Lissa were the main two.'

Jake's eyes narrowed. 'Lissa Sykes?'

Debra nodded. 'John's her boyfriend's cousin. They were in it together.'

'What about Lissa's boyfriend – George the Thug?'

'He wasn't like that. He was good to me, Jake.'

'I gathered that.' Jealousy sharpened Jake's voice. George hadn't had to say explicitly that he'd enjoyed Debra: it had been all too obvious in his voice.

'What would *you* have done in the circumstances? Tried to keep them sweet, so they didn't hurt you – or be stroppy and uncooperative, giving them an excuse to beat you up?'

Jake's eyes glittered. 'If they laid a hand on you . . .'

'They didn't, Jake. George made sure they didn't touch me.'

'And what about George?'

Debra smiled. 'He reminded me of you, in a way.'

'I'm not sure,' Jake said drily, 'whether that's a compliment or not.'

She grinned. 'It was meant as one. Anyway, I don't see why he should get the same treatment as John and Lissa. He's not like them.'

'He still helped them kidnap you.'

Debra sighed. 'I don't want to fight with you, Jake. Not on my first night back. And I want that bath. I'm filthy.'

'Okay.' He walked upstairs with her. 'I'll wash your back for you.'

He ran the bath, adding liberal quantities of scented bath oil, then began to undress Debra. 'I didn't know you had a T-shirt like this.'

She coughed. 'I don't. It's George's.'

'Might I ask why you're wearing his T-shirt?'

She sighed. 'My shirt got damaged, okay?'

'No, it's not okay. I'd like to rip those bastards apart with my bare hands.'

'Leave it to the police, Jake,' Debra said, her voice cracking with tiredness.

He nodded, but his face was still grim. He removed the rest of her clothes, and lifted her into the bath, washing her gently. Debra relaxed as he removed all the grime and sweat from her skin, and massaged her tired muscles; she flopped forward, letting him work on the muscles in her neck and shoulders. He washed her hair, too, wrapping it in a towel, turban-style when he'd finished rinsing out the suds, Debra relaxed back against the bath as he concentrated on her front, tenderly washing her breasts.

'Mm. This feels nice, being pampered,' she said.

'You deserve it, after what you've just been through.' He rubbed his thumb against her hardening nipple. 'I'm almost tempted to get in the bath with you.'

'You have such good ideas, Jake.' Her gaze slid down to his groin, where a large bulge was already evident. 'Do I take it that a certain part of your anatomy wants a reunion with a certain part of mine?'

'Something like that.'

'Then stop wittering, and do something about it.'

He grinned, knowing for sure now that Debra was all right: she hadn't lost her bossy streak. 'Okay,' he said, stripping swiftly.

Debra appraised his body. Although she hadn't actually seen George naked, she could remember the way he felt; he definitely reminded her of Jake, albeit a slightly smaller version. Not that she could tell Jake that. He wouldn't appreciate it.

'So what now?' he asked.

Debra leaned forward, and pulled the plug out of the bath. 'Now,' she said, a sensual smile curving her lips, 'for something we both need.' She stood up, taking the towel from her hair and shaking her hair free. Then she beckoned Jake to come and stand next to her in the bath.

As soon as he was beside her, she closed the shower curtain, and switched the shower on. The water was cold; Jake gasped. 'Are you intending to warm this up a bit?'

She gave him a wicked grin. 'Yes – but not the water.' She reached up to pull his head down to hers, pressing her lips against his. His mouth tasted warm and sweet, and she realised with a sharp pang just how much she'd missed him, the past few days. She'd blanked him out of her mind, most of the time, knowing that if she thought about him too much, she'd crack and do whatever Lissa and John wanted; now, she was with him again, and her need for him was almost painful.

His hands slid down to span her waist, holding her for a moment; then one hand stroked the slope of her buttocks, while his other hand cupped one breast, teasing the nipple between thumb and forefinger.

'Mm. I've missed you,' he said softly.

'So I see.' Her hand curled round his erect cock. He felt good, the shaft long and thick, and she badly wanted to feel him inside her. 'Jake . . .'

'Shh, it's all right.' He lifted her, holding her against the wall; she put her arms round his neck, and her legs came up to grip him. She was already wet with anticipation, and he slid easily into her. 'God, Debra, you feel so good,' he said, closing his eyes and resting his forehead on her shoulder.

'So do you.' She flexed her internal muscles, gripping him hard.

'Mm.' He lifted his head again to kiss her, and began to thrust, pushing his powerful body as far into her as he could. All the time, the freezing water of the shower beat down onto them; neither of them even noticed. It wasn't important: the only thing that mattered was the way their bodies joined, the sheer rush of pleasure they felt as his body surged into her.

At last, Jake cried out her name, and she felt his cock twitch inside her, his seed pumping into her; it was enough to trigger her own release, and she moaned with pleasure as her quim contracted round the hard rod of flesh.

'Welcome home,' he said softly, lowering her back to the floor and turning off the shower.

'And what a welcome.' She kissed him lightly. 'It's good to be back.'

'Yeah.' He lifted her out of the bath, drying her before he dried himself; then wrapped a clean towel round her, sarong-style, and combed her hair. 'So what do you fancy for dinner, then?'

'Apart from you? Anything.' She grimaced. 'Except a cheese sandwich. I never want to eat another cheese sandwich again.'

Jake was surprised. 'Is that all they fed you on?'

'That, and toast. I think I was offered beans, once.' She grimaced. 'I thought about refusing all food and water, but hunger and thirst got the better of me, in the end.'

'I thought you said that George the Thug looked after you?'

'He did. Not all men can cook like you do, you know. And wherever we were, there might not have been any cooking facilities.'

'Where did they actually take you, then?'

'I've no idea. I was knocked out, at first.'

'You mean, they hit you?' Jake clenched his fists, his knuckles whitening.

'No, no. They used chloroform,' Debra told him hastily. 'One of John's girlfriends was a nurse, so she got it for him. No questions asked.'

'Right.'

'The rest of the time, I was blindfolded. All I know is that there were at least two rooms – George and Lissa had a screaming row in the one next door.'

'Why?'

Debra's lips twitched. 'Because George and I were being – how shall I put it? – a little friendly. And before you get annoyed, just remember that Lissa deserved it, for what she did with you.'

'I don't think I want to know.' Jake's voice was harsh with jealousy.

'Which is just as well, because I'm not going to tell you.'

'Did he force you?' Jake's fists were clenched again.

'No, he didn't. Stop worrying. I told you, he didn't hurt me, and he didn't force me to do anything. I could have said no.'

'And if you had?'

Debra winced. 'I don't know,' she admitted. 'Just trust

me. I did what I thought was for the best, at the time.'

'At least you're all right. That's the main thing.'

She put her arms round him, hugging him. 'I've thought about your offer, by the way.'

'What offer?'

'The one where I was going to take a week to think about it?'

His face cleared. ' Oh. *That* offer.'

'The answer's yes. Provided that Jude's our best man.'

Jake grinned. 'If you wanted to do it in the middle of Stonehenge, that's fine by me.'

'Now there's an idea . . .' She smiled. 'Come on. I'm starving.'

'Go and ring Jude, and tell her you're still in the land of the living, while I cook you something nice. And no cheese, I promise.'

'Right.' Debra walked downstairs, and picked up the phone, dialling Judith's number.

'Hello?'

'Hi, Jude. I'm back.'

'Deb! Are you all right?'

'Relatively. Jake's going to feed me in a minute, then I'll be okay.'

'Jake was worried sick. We both were.'

'Well, I'm okay.' Debra paused. 'It was a brilliant idea of yours about the pictures, getting Ray to copy them.'

'I didn't see why they should get away with it, that's all. And Ray—' her voice bubbled with laughter '—says he hasn't had so much fun in years, copying them.'

'Hm.'

'Look, you could probably do with a bath or something, and you said you were starving. I'll come over tomorrow, and you can tell me all about it,' Judith said.

'Okay. Actually, something smells *very* nice, in the kitchen, so I'd better go before Bill eats my share.'

'Bill?'

'Sykes. I just renamed him.'

'Right.' Judith's voice was rich in understanding.

Debra smiled. 'See you tomorrow, then.'

She replaced the receiver, and went into the kitchen to discover that Jake had made her a rich creamy omelette, filled with mushrooms and bacon. She ate ravenously, demanding a second helping and demolishing that, too, with a little help from Bill; eventually, she pushed her plate away, sated. 'Mm.'

'Better?'

'Much.'

'Right.' Jake took the plate away, putting it in the sink. 'I'll wash this up, tomorrow. And I think you could do with a decent night's sleep.'

She grinned. 'Or even an indecent one, with you next to me.'

'I'll be there,' he promised. 'Just try and stop me.'

She coughed.

'What?'

'So where's Bill sleeping, then?'

'In his basket, in the kitchen.' Jake pointed to the wicker basket next to the radiator. 'I was very tempted to have him sleeping up with me, while you weren't here, but I didn't want to start that without checking with you.'

'Right.' She coaxed Bill onto his basket. 'But if your master has to go out on business, you're coming up with me,' she promised.

Jake grinned. 'You'll spoil him rotten.'

'And what makes you think I'll be the only one?'

'Mm.' He put his arm round her. 'Come to bed, then.'

As soon as Debra walked into their bedroom, she noticed the picture hanging on their bedroom wall. A small picture, modestly framed: her eyes narrowed. Unless she was hallucinating, the picture looked very much like the erotic version of *The Hyacinth Girl* . . .

'Jake?'

He followed her gaze. 'What?'

'Just tell me that it isn't the original.'

He coughed. 'Hasn't the weather been nice, lately?'

'Jake! Is that the original, or Ray's copy?'

He spread his hands. 'Well. You know how I feel about Buchan. It's the only way we'd ever be able to afford an original – keeping one of the paintings we found.'

'And the ones you gave to the Tate?'

'I was thinking about giving them one of Ray's copies, instead of this one.'

'You didn't!'

'No. I just gave them three pictures, not four.' He stroked her face. 'After all the hassle you've been through, I thought you deserved to keep one.'

Debra rolled her eyes. 'You're completely out of your tree, but . . .' She grinned. 'At least you kept the right one.'

'Our very own Hyacinth Girl.'

'Mary Sykes.' Debra looked thoughtful. 'You never know,

if we talk to Dicky again, he might just let us borrow those letters . . .'

'Absolutely not,' Jake said. 'I don't want to risk you being kidnapped again. Besides, Mary kept her secret for so long. Wouldn't it be a bit mean if we told the world about it, now?'

'I suppose you're right.'

'I know I'm right.' Jake stroked her face. 'So let's just forget it, let the letters moulder away in Dicky's loft or wherever he's put them, and think of something else.'

She grinned as she noticed a familiar bulge in his jeans. 'I think I've got just the subject . . .'

A Message from the Publisher

Headline Liaison is a new concept in erotic fiction: a list of books designed for the reading pleasure of both men and women, to be read alone – or together with your lover. As such, we would be most interested to hear from our readers.

Did you read the book with your partner? Did it fire your imagination? Did it turn you on – or off? Did you like the story, the characters, the setting? What did you think of the cover presentation? In short, what's your opinion? If you care to offer it, please write to:

The Editor
Headline Liaison
338 Euston Road
London NW1 3BH

Or maybe you think you could do better if you wrote an erotic novel yourself. We are always on the look-out for new authors. If you'd like to try your hand at writing a book for possible inclusion in the Liaison list, here are our basic guidelines: We are looking for novels of approximately 80,000 words in which the erotic content should aim to please both men and women and should not describe illegal sexual activity (pedophilia, for example). The novel should contain sympathetic and interesting characters, pace, atmosphere and an intriguing plotline.

If you'd like to have a go, please submit to the Editor a sample of at least 10,000 words, clearly typed on one side of the paper only, together with a short resumé of the storyline. Should you wish your material returned to you please include a stamped addressed envelope. If we like it sufficiently, we will offer you a contract for publication.

Adult Fiction for Lovers from Headline LIAISON